GUARDING BRISTOL
CRIMSON POINT SECURITY SERIES

NEW YORK TIMES AND *USA TODAY* BESTSELLING AUTHOR
KAYLEA CROSS

GUARDING BRISTOL

Copyright © 2025 Kaylea Cross

∾

Cover Art: Sweet 'N Spicy Designs
Developmental edits: Pamela White
Line Edits: Pamela White
Copyedits: JRT Editing
Digital Formatting: LK Campbell

∾

This book is a work of fiction. The names, characters, places, and incidents are products of the writer's imagination or have been used fictitiously and are not to be construed as real. Any resemblance to persons, living or dead, actual events, locales or organizations is entirely coincidental.

All rights reserved. With the exception of quotes used in reviews, this book may not be reproduced or used in whole or in part by any means existing without written permission from the author.

ISBN: 9798282892819

She was just trying to help him get back on his feet.

Once upon a time, Bristol Moreau managed to drag her late brother back from the brink of the abyss. So when she finds out that one of his former brothers-in-arms is living on the streets, she makes it her mission to do the same for him. But he makes it clear from the start that he doesn't want her help —or anything to do with her. When she persists, it unleashes a chain of events that lands them square in the crosshairs of a deadly cartel. And now her only hope is the man who wants nothing to do with her.

Instead, she accidentally blew up his world.

It feels like every time former Ranger TJ Barros turns around, she's there. The exasperating, stubborn, and gorgeous woman who refuses to take no for an answer. He shouldn't want her —because he knows the scorching attraction between them could destroy them both. She deserves better than him, a broken man who's spent the past year living on the streets. But now they've both got targets on their backs and armed gunmen hunting them down. And just when he finally breaks away from her, things go sideways. Now she's facing certain death because of him, and TJ will do anything to save her— even if it means trading his life for hers.

AUTHOR'S NOTE

I love a tortured hero, and even better if they're all dark and brooding. TJ's about to meet his match, and no amount of resistance will help. Hope you enjoy the twists and turns in this one.

Kaylea

ONE

Bristol finished wiping the gel off her pregnant patient's rounded belly with a flourish and a smile. "*Voilà.* You'll no doubt be happy to know this concludes our session, and you can finally empty your bladder. Not here, though," she added.

OB scans were her favorite part of the job.

The woman laughed in the middle of sitting up, then put a hand on her stomach and grimaced. "That's cruel, making me laugh when I'm literally about to burst. Do you know how hard it is to hold it in right now? I've got half a gallon of liquid in my bladder, which is currently a quarter of the size it normally is. Well, you saw it," she said, waving one hand at the ultrasound screen and accepting Bristol's help with the other to get her upright on the edge of the table.

"You're right. That was mean. I'm a terrible person."

"I'll try to find it in my heart to forgive you." She slanted Bristol a conspiratorial look. "By the way, was that what I thought it was?"

"Was *what* what you thought it was?"

"You know. That...shadow down there." She gestured to the area between her legs.

"Shadow?" Bristol asked, all innocence. The patient had specifically told her she didn't want to know the baby's sex, and Bristol wasn't allowed to tell her anyway.

"It was! I knew it!"

Bristol shook her head and held up a hand. "Whoa, I didn't say anything."

"You didn't have to. I can read your face."

"You can read my face?"

"Yep. You have a very readable face."

Shoot. She really did. She sucked at poker and was a terrible liar. "I can neither confirm nor deny that there was a shadow...down there." She adjusted her glasses, kept her face straight.

"It's okay. I was pretty sure on my own." The woman patted her belly. "This is my fourth, so I've had some practice reading ultrasounds. Now help me off this thing and point me to the bathroom before I embarrass myself and pee on the floor."

Bristol got her up, pointed her to the bathroom, then wiped down the table and equipment before exiting the ultrasound room and making her way to the lockers inside the staffroom with a spring in her step. It had been a good day. She loved her job, but sometimes it was hard when she discovered something bad on the ultrasound. Thankfully today, she hadn't needed to pass on a single piece of bad or worrying news to the radiologist for confirmation.

"There she is," Travis said, looking up at her as he laced up a shoe. He was an incredibly popular Physician Assistant here at the hospital, as well as a PJ with the Air National Guard. "All done for the day?"

"Yep." Since his hands were busy, she bent to pick up his

discarded boots and set them in the bottom of his locker for him. "Guess you're just starting?"

"Thanks. You know what they say. No rest for the wicked."

"Please, you're the furthest thing from wicked." There was something in the water here in Crimson Point. All the men were ridiculously hot. Most of them were either former military or law enforcement. And pretty much all of them were taken.

He stood, shrugging into his lab coat, his arm muscles straining the sleeves. His wife, Kerrigan, was a lucky lady. "Got any plans for tonight?"

"Cassie's coming over soon. We're having wine and lady tapas."

"Lady what?"

"You know, picky plates." She mimicked picking something off a plate and popping it in her mouth, then chewed, rolling her eyes in ecstasy.

Travis laughed. "Well, you enjoy."

"I sure will. Later."

"Later," he said, heading for the door to start his shift.

Outside the hospital, Bristol paused to raise her arms over her head and stretch, closed her eyes, and pulled in a deep breath of the warm August evening. Even up here on the top of the hill overlooking Crimson Point, the air held the faint salty tang of the ocean.

The drive home was extra gorgeous at this time of year. The sun hung low on the horizon, spilling its deep golden rays across the sea that stretched out as far as the eye could see as she headed south to her quiet little neighborhood nestled on a rise facing the water. The three-story townhouse was the first place she'd ever owned, and she loved every square inch of it, but especially the view of the water from her bedroom on the second floor.

Everleigh was bent over pruning the hydrangeas bordering the walkway when Bristol got out of her car. "Hey, neighbor."

"Hi. Got big plans tonight?" Everleigh answered. The petite physiotherapist looked like an angel sent to earth with the deep golden sunlight shining on her silvery-blond hair.

Bristol stopped to pick up a few cut branches lying on the grass and toss them in the pile on the tarp. "Lady tapas with Cassie. You wanna come over?"

"Love to, but I'm taking Grady on a long overdue date when he gets off. They're on exercise this coming weekend, so we're getting quality time in before he leaves."

Her husband Grady was an L&D nurse at the hospital and also a PJ in Travis's unit. Seriously, Crimson Point was a hotbed of hot military men. She wouldn't mind finding one for herself, as long as he didn't try to change her. She didn't do well with controlling men. "Awesome, enjoy."

"Oh, I will," Everleigh replied with a sly wink that made Bristol grin.

Cool, citrus-scented air greeted her when she opened her front door and walked in. She rushed upstairs to change into yoga pants and a long tunic top, then hurried back down to the kitchen to put together dinner. Crackers with hunks and slices of various cheeses she'd bought from a shop in town, fresh berries and other fruit, toasted nuts, sliced veggies, ranch dip, hummus, rotisserie chicken, a few roasted pepper slices, marinated artichokes. All the good stuff, and the best part was, she hadn't had to make any of it.

"Knock-knock," a familiar voice called from the front entry.

"Come on in. I'm in the kitchen putting the finishing touches on this masterpiece."

Cassie appeared around the corner a few moments later, tall and slender in snug cropped jeans and a form-fitting top that hugged her trim figure to perfection. Her short cap of black hair was wispy around her face, the dark color a sharp contrast to her pale skin and startling, silvery eyes. "Hi, honey. How was your day?"

"Great, you? Oooh, yeah, you brought the good stuff." Bristol took the bottle of her favorite red from her and fished in the drawer for the corkscrew to open it.

Cassie perused the board she'd built. "Lady tapas? Nice."

"Right? I love not cooking." She handed over two wineglasses. "Pour us a glass and make yourself comfy on the couch. I'll be right there."

Cassie took the glasses to the attached living room and stretched out on the couch with a deep sigh. "Oh, yeah. Been looking forward to this all week."

"Same." It was so nice to have Cass around. It hadn't been easy to convince her to make the move out here from Vegas, but Bristol knew her stepsister was way happier here. Now they got to hang out whenever they felt like it.

She finished arranging the board to her satisfaction and carried it to the coffee table, accepting a glass of wine as she settled into the opposite corner of the couch. "Cheers, babe."

"Cheers." Cassie clinked glasses with her and grinned. "Look at us, hanging out by choice all on our own as if we actually like each other."

"I know, right? We've come a long way."

"I'll say. You hated my guts when we first met," Cassie said with a smirk. "Stone-cold Elsa-freeze treatment."

Yeah, because her dad had decided the best way to introduce her and Cassie was to bring Cassie over to dinner one night and announce over roast chicken that they were going to be sisters when he eloped with Cassie's mom in a few weeks.

Bristol had been singularly unimpressed. "I know. Sorry I was such a moody bitch."

Cassie snorted a laugh in the middle of taking a sip of wine, wound up choking. Bristol leaned forward to pound on her back.

"It always cracks me up when you swear," Cassie wheezed when she finished coughing. "You're so damned adorable, you look like sugar wouldn't melt in your mouth."

She frowned. "Whatever, I swear."

"Hardly ever. And I don't think I've ever heard you say the word 'fuck.'"

Bristol brushed at a crumb on her pants. "Be grateful. Because that would mean I've gone nuclear."

Cassie's eyes danced with silent laughter. "I think I'd pay good money to see that."

"You say that only because you haven't witnessed it first-hand." She gestured to the mostly demolished food remaining on the board. "Want more? I've got lots more."

Cassie groaned. "No, I couldn't. Maybe another glass of wine for dessert though."

"It's made of fruit. It counts." Bristol topped up Cassie's glass and took the mostly empty board to the kitchen. "So, tell me about work. What's the latest at CPS, the best security company in the entire Pacific Northwest that you love working for and will be eternally thankful I made you apply to earlier this year?"

Being a cop in Vegas had burned Cassie out, and a bad breakup she was annoyingly secretive about had made her miserable. Private security work—and the higher pay—suited her way better.

"Yeah, all right, I'll give you that one." Cassie took another sip. "Got a gig coming up later this week, not sure of the details yet. And after that, there's a security detail for a celebrity coming into town. Good friends with Ryder, apparently."

"Who?"

"Dunno. I don't have the details yet." Cassie got up and took her wine across the living room to examine the framed photos lined up on the shelves along the wall.

"Is this week's upcoming gig a solo thing, or will you be working with a partner?"

"Partner."

Bristol watched her. Cassie's back was to her. That plus the nonchalant tone was a giveaway. "Who? Tristan?"

"Maybe." Cass swirled her wine, kept her back to her.

Bristol chuckled softly. "Man, you are so twitterpated."

Cassie shot her a look over her shoulder. "Twitterpated? Who the hell uses that word?"

"Me. And I'm right," she added smugly.

Cassie huffed and went back to looking at the photos. "You're not always right."

"Mostly. What's he like? Other than his sweet Kentucky twang." She'd seen him and his twin Gavin around town but never met them.

"He doesn't have a twang, it's more subtle than that. And he's...fine," she said with a shrug.

"Girl, that goes without saying. As in, fiiiine." And like most of the former military men around here, they were hot. "But I meant his personality. I'm seriously curious about what kind of guy would have you all tied up in knots."

"He doesn't have me tied up in anything, he—wait." Cassie grabbed a framed photo from the shelf, stared at it a second before looking over at her. "Who's this?" She marched over, holding it out for Bristol to see.

The one of Eric and four guys in their utilities on a deployment overseas a few years ago. "Some guys in my brother's unit on deployment."

Seeing Eric didn't hurt as much anymore. Time had softened it to an ache instead of the jagged grief she'd felt for those first few months after losing him.

"When was it taken?"

"I dunno, a year or two before we pulled out of Afghanistan. Why?"

"This guy." Cassie tapped the guy on the far left. "Who is he?"

"Buddy of Eric's. Why, you recognize him or something?"

"Remember the good Samaritan I told you about from the Portland riots?"

"The guy who rescued Gavin's daughter from the idiot who grabbed her to use as a shield?"

"Yes. I swear this is him. God, I knew I'd seen him somewhere before. Didn't put it together until just now."

Bristol looked at the photo again. "You sure?"

"Almost positive. We still don't have much information on him. Even Ivy didn't dig up anything when she looked."

Ivy, the legendary female badass goddess living right here in Crimson Point. Engaged to one of the heads of Crimson Point Security, it was rumored she used to be some kind of government assassin or something. "Huh."

"Do you know his name?"

"Tomás, I think." Eric had been pretty tight with him while they were deployed. "I can't remember his surname." It would be such a weird coincidence that he had wound up here, just a few hours away from her.

"Yeah, that fits. He told us his name is TJ. I swear this is him, minus the beard and longer hair."

A disturbing thought occurred to her. "Wait. Didn't you say this TJ guy is homeless?"

"Yep. On the streets in Portland, working odd jobs when he can get them."

"Oh, no..." Bristol took the photo from her, staring at Tomás's smiling face.

He looked so young, so cocky and full of life. To think that he'd earned a Ranger tab, served his country honorably, and survived the war only to come home and wind up hitting rock bottom just like Eric had...

Her stomach tightened in distress. It hurt to think about, dredged up all sorts of painful memories she didn't want to confront anymore.

"He seems to be doing okay, all things considered," Cassie added softly. "I mean, relatively speaking. He was clean when I saw him."

That didn't mean anything. His situation filled her with sadness and anger. What if TJ *was* Tomás? She couldn't stand the thought that a buddy of her brother's was on the streets. Discarded. Alone, like Eric had been.

"Do you think you could find him again?"

Cassie's gaze shot to hers. Then she shook her head. "Oh, no. No, come on. Don't do this to yourself. He's not Eric, you—"

"I can at least find out if it's him, can't I?"

"And then what?" Cassie folded her arms, looking every inch the protective big sister Bristol hadn't had until their lives had intertwined seven years ago. "Save him from himself?"

She lifted a shoulder, feeling suddenly defensive as dark, ghostly memories swirled in her mind.

Of walking the darkened streets and alleys in search of her brother. The awful fear and uncertainty that she was too late. The endless, painful weeks that followed once she had finally found him.

"Maybe." She'd helped pull him from the abyss, if only for a short while before tragedy had taken him from her forever.

Tomás deserved at least a chance to turn his life around.

"If it's him, then he was Eric's friend, and I can't turn away." Eric would want her to do what she could for him. "Maybe he just needs to know someone still gives a crap about him."

Cassie sighed and rubbed her forehead. "Shit, now I wish I hadn't said anything."

"I don't." Bristol would never have known about his situation otherwise. "Just help me find him. That's it. It might not even be him."

Cassie eyed her a long moment, exasperation clear on her face. "If I say no, you'll just try to find him on your own, won't you."

Bristol didn't deny it. "I need to see if it's him. For Eric."

"For Eric, or for you?"

Okay, point taken. "For both of us."

Ultimately, she hadn't been able to save her brother. But maybe she could help save Tomás.

TWO

"Just want to restate one more time for the record that I still hate this idea," Cassie said from behind the wheel as their exit to downtown Portland appeared up ahead on the highway.

"Duly noted," Bristol answered. She'd been well aware of Cassie's feelings on the matter since Bristol had first mentioned it yesterday. "But hey, at least I brought you for backup instead of coming on my own."

"Lucky me." Cassie sighed. "Your dad's gonna kill me when he finds out."

"So don't tell him."

Her stepsister slanted her a look. "Are *you* gonna tell him?"

"Hell no. Are you insane? It would just dredge up everything with Eric all over again. I wouldn't do that to him." He had barely survived it.

"Okay, then, we're agreed."

Bristol nodded, slightly amused that her highly trained and confident stepsister was intimidated by him, a retired public accountant. "What he doesn't know won't hurt us."

"Preach."

She glanced at the GPS on the dash display. It was just before noon, and they only had a little under ten minutes left until they reached their destination. They were starting at the construction site Cassie had met TJ at in May, in the hope that he was still working there and had picked up a shift today.

"So we just go ask the foreman if he's working today?"

"Yep."

"And if he's not there, then what? Where should we start looking after that?"

Finding someone on the streets was never easy. Even with her past experience and the hard-won knowledge she'd gained while searching for Eric, finding Tomás would be a challenge. And if it turned out that he didn't want to be found, then it just might prove impossible.

"Hell if I know. Maybe someone on site will know where he hangs out. Or better yet, we leave word for him to contact you and just head back home."

"Not happening." There was no way he would reach out to a total stranger. She wanted to talk to him in person, verify whether he was Eric's friend, and wasn't leaving until she'd given finding him a real shot.

Cassie exited the freeway and drove them toward the city center. Downtown Portland looked calm and normal now, except for the blackened end of the large hotel that was still in the process of being demolished almost three months later. "Hard to believe the riots reached all the way down here from the conference center."

Cassie had witnessed them firsthand while providing personal security for a Canadian billionaire at a global summit here back in May. The resulting protests had spun out of control fast. People had died in the chaos.

"The entire city center was affected. Couldn't move along

this street with the number of protesters, cops, and then all the people evacuating the hotel."

The latter had included Gavin's young daughter, whom TJ had rescued from a deranged protestor trying to use her as a human shield to avoid arrest. Thankfully the idiot was behind bars.

Bristol imagined what it would have been like here, adding to everything she'd seen on TV and online. "And TJ was in the middle of it."

"He says he wasn't a protester, but he showed up near the front line wearing a gas mask, so regardless of what he did for Gavin's daughter, my money says he's full of shit."

"He can't be all bad if he risked his life to protect Carly." That spoke to the core of his character as far as Bristol was concerned.

Most traces of the riots were long gone from the streets, but there had been a definite change in vibe over the past few months. A surprising number of shops and businesses were still boarded up and covered in graffiti. Homeless people and their belongings littered the sidewalks everywhere in this area.

"It's a lot rougher here than I remember."

Cassie grunted as she waited for a pedestrian to cross the street before making a right turn. "Drug epidemic, housing crisis, and high cost of living. Reminds me of working the beat in Vegas. Day after day dealing with the same people and the same shit, rinse and repeat through a revolving door."

"I'm so glad you got out of that."

"Same." Cassie gave her a pointed look. "Well, most days I am."

"What, not today? Look at this adventure we're going on together, both of us working for a good cause, trying to do something positive in this weary world."

"Don't try to make me feel good about this. It won't work."

Bristol was just glad Cassie had agreed to come. "That's fair." She eyed the tops of the construction cranes sticking out above the tops of the buildings near the river. "What are they building down here—any idea?"

"Industrial complex." Cassie made a final turn, and the job site was directly ahead of them. She parked near the chain link fence and shifted in her seat to face Bristol. "You sure about this? He wasn't exactly warm and fuzzy with Gavin and me last time. He's not gonna like us showing up now."

Bristol undid her seatbelt, mind made up. "I'm sure."

They were stopped by a security guard at the gate briefly before entering the site. A row of prefabricated buildings stood inside the entrance. Bristol followed Cassie up the wooden steps of the first one and walked through the door where a heavyset man sat behind a computer, a hardhat placed on the corner of his desk.

"Hi. Can I help you ladies?" he asked, fingers poised on the keyboard.

Bristol stood back and let Cassie do the talking. Her stepsister was far more imposing than she was, and radiated authority. "Yes. I'm with Crimson Point Security." Cassie pulled out her company ID to show him.

"Oh, yeah, you called earlier."

"I did. Is TJ Barros on site today?"

"What's this in regard to?"

"A security matter relating to the Portland riots. Can you check if he's here, please?"

The man frowned slightly, no doubt at Cassie's tone, which made it more of a command than a request. Bristol hid a smile. "Hang on a minute," he muttered, and pulled a radio from his belt. "Hey. Is Barros on site?" He released the key button.

"Yeah, he's pouring concrete at the main site," another man answered.

"Find him and send him to the main office, will you?" He set the radio on the desk and looked at them. "Not sure how long he'll be."

"That's fine, we'll just wait over there." Cassie walked over to the plastic chairs set around the wooden cable spool serving as a table, and sat.

Bristol did the same, trying not to feel awkward as the man muttered something under his breath and went back to work on his computer. As the minutes ticked past, a sort of nervousness began to take hold. She wasn't going to tell her dad about this to spare him all the painful memories about Eric—and also to spare her the lecture she knew she would get—but this was dredging up all kinds of memories and emotions for her. What if TJ wasn't Tomás after all? Or what if he was, and he didn't want her help?

Or, worst of all... What if he wanted her help and she failed him?

Her gaze shot to the door at the sound of footsteps coming up the wooden stairs. The door opened, and a man walked in wearing a hard hat, a neon yellow vest over a blue flannel plaid shirt and worn jeans. He was tall and broad-shouldered, with a dark beard and hair that needed a trim. He looked over at them, stilled for a second as he stared at Cassie.

Bristol stood, drawing his gaze. And the moment those dark eyes met hers, a current of warmth surged through her body. It was him. Had to be. She felt it in her bones.

Hiding her nerves, she put on a friendly smile. "Hi. Are you...Tomás?"

THREE

TJ didn't move. He couldn't, somehow frozen in place by the shorter woman standing before him, and her use of his name. No one had called him that in more than a year. It felt like it belonged to a stranger now.

Immediately on the heels of that shock, suspicion took hold. He tore his gaze from her to the other one still sitting in a chair. He'd recognized her immediately. She had come here the day after the riots to talk to him and worked for Crimson Point Security out on the coast. What the hell did she want this time? He'd answered all her questions last time.

He kept his expression impassive as he looked between them. "Can I help you with something?"

His tone was guarded. He didn't like this. Didn't like the feel of it at all, especially that the new woman knew his name. And he didn't like the weird flash of attraction he felt toward her either, to her sweet curves and pretty face.

Whoever she was, whatever she wanted from him, she needed to leave. He had work to do. He got paid by the hour and had another eight to go before he would have enough to afford a couple more nights in a cheap hotel. The overcrowded shelters around the city rarely had beds available these days, and he hated sleeping outside even though the weather was warm.

The standing woman's smile slipped a notch. "Could we talk outside, maybe?"

He shot a glance at the office manager, who was watching them with interest, then focused back on her. "What about?"

"It's private." She adjusted the narrow, dark-framed glasses that emphasized the stormy blue eyes still locked on him.

He didn't want to talk. Not to her or the CPS woman, or anyone else for that matter. He just wanted to be left alone. "I gotta get back to work."

"It won't take long."

He bit back a retort. Life on the streets had hardened him. He had no problem being rude anymore, didn't give a fuck what anyone else thought of him. But for some reason, locking stares with her, he couldn't find it in him to walk off or tell her to go back to wherever she'd come from. She looked so…earnest. Hopeful, almost.

For reasons he couldn't fathom, he gave a curt nod and a gruff, "Fine. But make it quick."

He stepped outside onto the small bit of decking that led to the steps and stopped to wait for her, leaning back against the wooden railing with his arms folded across his chest.

She came out a moment later, alone. "Just you?" he asked.

She nodded and reached a hand up to adjust the right side of her glasses again, her shiny brown hair loose in subtle waves around her shoulders. The fabric of her red summer dress clung to her curves in all the right places, leaving her shapely calves bare. "Cassie's just here for moral support."

She'd needed moral support to come here? "What do you want?"

"Well." She took a breath, released it. "Your name is Tomás, right?"

"No. It's TJ." Tomás was dead, had been for a long damned time.

A slight frown appeared over the bridge of her nose. "Okay, but…I think you might know my brother." She reached into her hip pocket, pulled out a photograph and held it out for him to see. "Eric Moreau."

Shock hit so hard and fast, his pulse thudded in his ears. He stared at the image of him, Moreau, and two other guys during their first deployment in Afghanistan. It sucked him back in time to a different life. A span of six months that had been some of the best and worst moments of his time on earth.

"That's you, isn't it?" she asked quietly.

Dragging his eyes up from the photo, he met her gaze. Now that he understood the connection, he could see a bit of resemblance in their coloring and eyes. "Where is he?" he asked instead of confirming it.

How the hell had Eric's sister found him? And why?

She hesitated a moment, and he knew what she was going to say before she spoke. "He died a couple years ago."

Damn. "I'm sorry to hear that." Moreau had been a great soldier and an even better person.

She lowered her gaze, nodded. "He…struggled a lot. It started when he came home from that first deployment and got progressively worse. But the toughest part was when he left the military. He couldn't adjust back to regular life, didn't feel like he fit in anywhere, and couldn't relate to anything anymore."

Yeah, TJ knew the feeling.

"His drinking got out of control. He wound up on the streets for a while."

Hell. A guy like Moreau had wound up homeless? Fucking broken system.

"But he made it out," she said with a proud smile that belied the slight wobble in her voice. "For a while. Unfortunately, not long after that he was killed by a drunk driver. I know he would appreciate the irony."

Fuck. "I'm sorry," he said again, her pain clear in her face and voice. "He was a good guy."

"Yes, he was." She blew out a breath. "Anyway, Cassie—my stepsister," she clarified, aiming a thumb over her shoulder to indicate the woman inside, "was over the other night and saw this picture. She thought this might be you and had told me you've been living down here, so I thought…"

"Thought what?"

She opened her mouth, closed it. "I thought I would come and see if it was you and find out if you needed help with anything."

"I don't need your help." The answer was immediate and instinctive, the sudden spike in anxiety catching him off guard as much as her offer. It was almost a crawling sensation along his skin, a mounting need to get away from her. Or get her away from him.

"Okay, but please at least just take this," she blurted before he could turn away, holding out a business card.

"What is it?" He wasn't going to contact her.

"A potential job with good benefits. They're a specialized residential reno company based in Crimson Point that work mostly on heritage homes, and they exclusively hire veterans. I was told you only work part-time here, so if you're up for a change of scenery and a move to the coast, they're looking to hire more people on full-time. They also provide their full-time employees with housing. The owner is an Army vet too. He said to call him if you're at all interested." She offered the card again.

TJ reluctantly took it, staring at her as he tried to figure her out. Or at least her angle. Was she for real? She'd driven up here from the coast to find him, not even knowing for sure it was him, just to check in on him and offer him potential work? Who did that shit?

She licked her lips. "I know all this must seem pretty presumptuous of me, but I just wanted to meet you and see if you're okay. Eric would have wanted me to."

He couldn't remember the last time anyone had checked in to see if he was okay. Or given enough of a shit about him to care how he was. He was so used to being unwanted and invisible to the rest of society, he didn't know what the hell to make of her standing in front of him now.

"My number's on the back," she added when he didn't say anything, and clasped her hands behind her. The motion pushed rounded breasts that he definitely should not be noticing against the fabric of her dress. "In case you need anything, or...want to talk or whatever."

It was too much. That crawling, panicky sensation was unbearable now, a constant alarm clanging at the back of his head. "I don't need anything," he said gruffly and turned away, the thud of his boots sounding hollow on the wooden steps.

As hollow as the emptiness inside him.

It wasn't until he was on the other side of the site that he realized he still had the card in his fist. He started to crumple it up. Then stopped, thinking about Eric.

Cursing under his breath, he tucked the fucking thing into

his jeans pocket, tugged on his work gloves and got back to pouring concrete, hoping that the day's hard labor ahead of him would make him stop thinking about Eric Moreau's sister and her pretty, storm-blue eyes.

FOUR

Jordan kept his eyes on the lines of musical notes in front of him, letting them guide his hands as his fingers floated over the glossy keys of his cherished Fazioli. It was his pride and joy, the first significant purchase he'd made when he'd earned enough money early on in the business.

Ironically, he'd hated piano lessons as a kid. Hated his parents for making him take them at his far better-off pastor's house across town on Saturdays, for forcing him to take that opportunity because they'd never had it. And for making him take the bus over there after school to practice an hour every day.

Now, he understood. Playing the piano was his joy. His escape. And these days, he needed that escape more than ever.

The music flowed through him. Around him. He was so deep in the zone that he wasn't even aware of his fingers moving over the keys or his feet working the pedals. They were merely a conduit for the gorgeous swell of the crescendo building as the concerto came to a climax.

The rest of the world ceased to exist. There was only this. Only now. Him alone with the hauntingly beautiful notes as they filled the room.

His hands moved faster over the keys as the tempo continued to build. Faster. Faster, his eyes straining to keep up with reading the music in front of him, his feet simultaneously working the pedals until he played the final, dramatic chords and held them. The blended notes echoed off the vaulted ceiling above him, their reverberations throbbing in the air until they gradually faded away into silence.

He sat up straighter on the padded bench, removed his hands from the keyboard and stiffened when the door opened and his right-hand man walked in. "What?" he snapped in a hard voice.

They knew never to bother him in here. This was his private sanctuary, where no one was to disturb him. Ever. Between never-ending business and security threats, he got precious few hours to himself.

Jon stopped, cleared his throat, and folded his hands in front of him. "Sorry to interrupt. But we just got news you need to hear."

Jordan grunted and waved a hand at a servant hovering nervously behind Jon by the doorway. The man quickly hurried forward with the usual gin and tonic on a tray. Jordan took it, then dismissed him with another wave and focused on Jon. "Well?" He took a sip, savored the cool bite of the gin and the twist of lime as it slid down his throat.

"Another shipment was intercepted."

His hand tightened around the tall glass. "When and where?"

"Three hours ago, in Seattle."

That was the second one in the past three months. "How much was seized?"

Jon hesitated before answering. "All of it."

Jordan shot to his feet and hurled the mostly full glass at the opposite wall where it exploded and fell to the shiny black marble floor in a pile of glittering shards. "Who the fuck is doing this?" he demanded.

Jon hadn't moved. "We aren't sure, but...it seems someone has been leaking intel to the cops."

Jordan whirled back around, a murderous rage taking hold. He shook his head, fighting to regain his control. "Not possible."

He ran a small, tight organization for a reason. He vetted everyone who worked for him personally, from his housekeeper, his driver, his bodyguard, accountant...all the way up the chain to Jon. And he made sure he had leverage over every single one of them.

Leverage ensured absolute loyalty. And those few motherfuckers who had dared step out of line since he'd taken charge of the Pacific Northwest territory had paid with their lives. Most of them begging for death after creative torture or watching their loved ones die in front of them.

So no, he couldn't believe anyone else within his circle would have risked talking to the cops or Feds.

When Jon didn't say anything more, Jordan tugged on the cuffs of his dress shirt to straighten them, angered by the loss of control he'd just displayed. But losing that much product in such a short time frame meant catastrophic financial losses for him.

The boss wouldn't be happy, would hold him responsible for the leak. There would be repercussions.

"Tell the falcons I want a detailed intel report by midnight. And get Angel in here."

Jon left immediately and the servant scurried in with a fresh gin and tonic. Jordan took it and walked through the glass doors out onto the adjoining balcony for some air. He paused at the railing, resting his forearms along the top of it as he gazed out at the unobstructed view of the vineyard and the water beyond it, his mind racing. Who would have the balls to leak intel? Who would have a death wish?

He stood there in the balmy summer evening air enjoying his drink until a discrete clearing of a throat behind him drew his attention.

Jon stood in the open doorway. "Angel's here."

"Have him wait in the library." Jordan took his time finishing his cocktail before walking back inside and making his way down to the library he used as his office on the ground floor. Angel rose from the leather sofa when he entered.

Jordan motioned at him to sit down, shut the wood-paneled, reinforced steel door behind him and got straight to the point. The room was soundproof and swept for bugs twice a day, and so was anyone prior to entering. "Someone's leaking intel to the Feds. One of ours. We don't have any leads yet, but we will soon, and when we find out who it is, I want you to handle it."

Angel answered with a single nod, his expression neutral.

He was a fairly recent addition. Unassuming, with an average appearance that made him able to blend in without being noticed. He was quiet. Well-trained.

And, most importantly, a deadly professional.

Angel served a very specific purpose: to eliminate enemies and threats to Jordan's part of the organization. Torture wasn't his job. He tracked, confirmed, and killed. Quickly and efficiently, without leaving any trace behind except the bullet in his victims. That made him Jordan's most valuable weapon.

Unlike some others who had managed to rise to the rank of lieutenant within the cartel, Jordan didn't fuck around with gangbangers, or guys looking to stroke their egos by putting rounds through skulls and chests when it came to hiring killers. His enforcers were all pros. Disciplined, with a variety of useful skill sets. And they also all came from poor backgrounds, just like he had.

Money was the most powerful motivator in the business. Along with fear.

Angel met all those qualifications, and based on the reports Jordan had received from his falcons, Angel also had the most interesting motivation of anyone Jordan had hired. One that gave him all the leverage he needed to keep Angel from turning on him.

He decided who was worthy to keep on the payroll and who was a liability that needed to be eliminated. *He* held the lives of enemies and employees alike in his hands. That was the nature of the world he ran.

Angel still hadn't said anything, just sat watching him. Meeting that dark stare, Jordan appreciated that this guy was all business. "You eaten yet?'

"No."

"Come up to the kitchen, we'll have some dinner together."

"That's generous of you, but—"

"I wasn't asking." No one refused his hospitality when he extended it. He expected good manners in addition to unwavering loyalty.

Angel shut his mouth, his jaw flexing slightly in annoyance. "All right."

That was better. "Come on." He motioned for him to follow. "We'll talk more business over steaks." He'd had some wagyu beef shipped in the other day. Only the best for him now, in both his professional and personal lives.

He wouldn't let anyone jeopardize or take away the lifestyle he'd scratched and clawed for his entire adult life.

As soon as Jordan found the source of the leak, Angel would plug it with a bullet.

FIVE

Bristol parked across the street from the house she'd found using her GPS, an adorable late-period Victorian, by the looks of it. The basic bones of the place were good, but judging from the sagging roof and the sad state of the wooden shakes and columns on the exterior, it was in serious need of love and attention.

It was Saturday, but the place was a hive of activity. Two full-size pickups marked with the construction company logo were parked out front. A huge Dumpster sat in the driveway, already half full of debris from the demo they were doing.

The whine of a saw and loud bangs from inside greeted her as she went around into the backyard. Beckett Hollister stood in the center of the large lawn with his phone to his ear. He raised his chin at her when he saw her and kept talking.

She didn't know him personally. By all accounts he was a bit gruff, but she didn't mind that. He'd been born and raised here in Crimson Point and gave back to the community with every project his company took on, saving heritage homes that would otherwise be lost to a bulldozer. He also gave military veterans steady work with good pay and benefits. That told her everything she needed to know about his character.

"Hi," he said once he'd finished his call, walking over to offer his hand. "Thanks for coming by."

She shook with him. "Thanks for meeting with me."

"No problem. Watch your step." He took her hand in his larger one, helped her step over a pile of debris until she was safely on the grass on the other side.

"Thanks." She glanced around the space, took in the various piles of lumber and other materials stacked neatly along the fence line, awaiting completion of the demo phase. "How long until you can start building?"

"Another few days. Hoped we might be able to work with most of what was inside, but it turned out to be a complete gut job. The wiring was a ticking time bomb. Honestly, can't believe this place didn't go up in flames years ago."

She winced in sympathy. "I'm looking forward to seeing the transformation." They did impeccable work.

Glancing left, she noticed an elderly dog sprawled out on a comfy-looking oval doggy bed in a patch of shade made by a pile of bricks. "Oh my gosh, is this the famous Walter I've heard so much about?"

A slight smile softened Beckett's hard features and warmed his eyes. *Aww.*

Everyone knew the story of how he had adopted the senior pup from a local shelter after someone had left him at the dump. And his wife was the town vet. No wonder she'd fallen for him. "The one and only. You can go pet him. He's an old guy, so you'll have to go to him. Not much pep in his step these days, unless he's in the truck or a dune buggy."

"Dune buggy? That I'd like to see." Bristol grinned and went over to crouch next to the dog, some kind of spaniel-basset mix if she had to guess. Walter thumped his tail softly but didn't move, gazing up at her with droopy brown eyes. "Well, aren't you a gorgeous, distinguished gentleman, huh, Walter? Yes." She stroked a hand over his silky head and down his back, earning another tail thump. "You look pretty comfy, my friend."

"Sierra's got him all dosed up on arthritis meds and doggy weed. He's not in any pain."

Doggy weed. Ha. "That's good. Oh, you are a sweet little guy." Bristol rose and faced Beckett again. "Well, I don't want to take up too much of your time. I just wanted to come by and tell you that I managed to find Tomás."

His dark eyebrows rose, a scar running through the middle of the left one. "Did you?"

"Yes. He goes by TJ now though. I told him about your company and that you offered to meet with him. I'm not sure if he'll contact you, but I wanted to let you know just in case he does. I hope he will."

It was all she'd thought about since meeting him yesterday. Well, not all. He'd certainly made an impression. Physically, he'd fit right in with the rest of the men around here.

"You said he served with your brother?"

"Yes, Rangers. They were deployed together a couple times. Eric always spoke highly of him. And for what it's worth, the foreman Cassie and Gavin talked to in May said he was a good worker. No problems with him." She felt the need to add that, because too many people saw homeless people as useless and disposable.

"Good to know."

"I don't know why he changed his name, but Cassie mentioned that Ivy had done some digging to find out more about him. I'm told there's not much background information on him."

Beckett frowned slightly. "Yeah, that's kind of a red flag, Ivy not finding anything."

"I'm sure he—"

"I'm not saying it's a deal-breaker. I'll meet with him if he's interested."

She breathed a sigh of relief. "Thank you."

"Sure." He eyed her for a moment. "This is really important to you. Helping him."

"Yes. He was my brother's friend. Eric was in a similar situation once, so if I can help TJ get back on his feet, I will."

"I respect that."

They both turned at the sound of uneven treads coming down the wooden steps behind them. A tall, built, good-looking man with a short auburn beard and hair came toward them with a noticeable limp. "The lads are about to knock off for some scran," he said in a lovely Scottish accent, and gave her a smile. "Who's this, then? I'm Mac." He held out a hand.

"Bristol. Hi." She shook with him.

"She's trying to recruit a former Ranger for us," Beckett said.

"Ah, that's grand." He shifted his attention to Beckett. "You want the lads to pick up anything for you in town?"

"Nah, we're meeting Sierra soon. Come on, Walter." He bent and scooped the dog up in his arms. Bristol's insides went all squishy at the way he cradled the little guy to his broad chest and carried him across the yard.

She walked with them, unable to resist scratching behind Walter's long, floppy ears. His swishy tail thumped against Beckett's ribs. "I'll let you know if I hear anything from TJ," she said as they reached the driveway.

"Good." Beckett strode for one of the pickups. "I'll text you if he contacts me."

"Thanks." Bristol hurried over to his truck. "Which door?"

"Right rear. He can still see me from there, and he's safe from getting hit with an air bag."

She opened the door for him. Beckett leaned in, set Walter on another comfy-looking bed, and strapped him into a special doggy seatbelt. He straightened and ruffled the dog's ears, a crooked grin on his face. And oh, yeah, she could totally see why Sierra had fallen for this hard-edged warrior.

"Thanks again. Enjoy your weekend," she said. Or what was left of it. "Bye, Walter."

"See you," Beckett answered.

She got into her car and headed toward home, calling Cassie on the way.

"Just heading into a meeting," Cass said. "What's up?"

"I met with Beckett. He's still open to meeting with Tomás. TJ," she corrected.

"That's great, hon, but I wouldn't get my hopes up. He wasn't exactly thrilled to see either of us."

"We took him off guard, and my offer stung his pride." Damned, stubborn male pride made everything so much harder in her experience. "He's had more than a day to process everything. I hope he's at least thought about the offer."

She'd sure thought a lot about him. Those dark, intense eyes, and all those hard muscles under his flannel shirt. Thinking about him sleeping on the street without anywhere to go weighed like a rock in the pit of her stomach.

"You know what they say. You can lead a horse to water, but you can't make it drink."

"I know." But she had also managed to help drag her brother out of the black hole he'd fallen into. She wasn't giving up on TJ. "You free later? I was thinking of heading over to the parents' place for dinner later. That work? Dad's golfing until then."

"I've got training after the meetings. No idea when I'll be done, but I'll text you."

"Okay, sounds good. Talk to you later."

"Bye. And hey, don't let it get you down if he doesn't take you up on the offer. You tried. That was good of you, and way more than most people would do."

"No promises."

"Yeah, I know. Just felt the need to say it anyway."

Good of her.

Those words rolled around in Bristol's head as she drove home. Was it good of her just because she didn't want to see a veteran who had served honorably with her brother live out the rest of a bleak existence and then die forgotten on the street?

She'd planned to go home and enjoy a glass of wine in the sunshine on her back patio, but now she felt restless and bored, the idea of going back to her empty place suddenly unappealing. If Eric was still here and he'd known about TJ, he wouldn't sit back and wait for his friend to make a move.

She knew her brother. Knew he would have done everything in his power to help his buddy, to get him off the streets. TJ didn't seem violent. She hadn't seen any needle tracks on his forearms. He'd been sober at the site. If he had any addiction issues, he was high-functioning. That gave her hope. Made her believe it wasn't too late for him.

A plan formed in her mind. It was impulsive. A bit invasive. A lot invasive, actually.

She considered it for another few minutes. Dismissed it. But after driving another mile, the feeling of rightness in her gut wouldn't go away.

It was early afternoon. She had hours of daylight left yet.

It wouldn't be that risky as long as she left by the time it got dark. Besides, Cassie was busy. And Bristol was strong. She had done this before and could do it again now. For Eric. She could almost hear his voice in her head.

Help him. He's got no one else.

She turned the car north and headed up the hill toward the freeway, determination taking hold now that she'd made her mind up to do this. She would start at the construction site and go from there.

The rest of the world might have given up on TJ. But not her.

SIX

TJ was in the midst of unrolling his sleeping bag when he heard someone approach his tent where he'd set up camp for the night.

"Hey, man. Apparently, some chick's here looking for you."

What? He pushed the flap aside and ducked his head out of the tent to follow the guy's gaze.

At first, he didn't see anything out of the ordinary. Just a small group of tents and some mattresses set up under one of the quieter overpasses near the city center, with seven or eight other guys sitting around the makeshift campsite.

Then he caught a flash of bright pink out of the corner of his eye and stood there gaping as Eric's sister appeared.

She made her way down into the culvert, wearing flip-flops, jeans, and a snug fuchsia-pink top that hugged the sexy curves of her breasts and waist. Her brown hair was loose around her shoulders, a thin shaft of light from a streetlamp above them highlighting it with shades of gold and caramel.

What the hell was she doing? She stuck out more than a clown at a funeral here.

She stopped picking her way down the side of the steep incline to scan the area. When she saw him, her face lit up with a relieved smile. "Hi," she called out, seeming oblivious of the stares she was getting. Some curious. Others hostile. All suspicious. "Boy, you were not easy to find."

Fuck. Me.

He strode forward, making a beeline to intercept her before she came any closer. She stopped at the hard look on his face, her smile slipping a notch.

"What the hell are you doing here?" he demanded.

She faltered, took a step back. "I—"

He took hold of her upper arm, spun her around and started marching her back up the incline toward the road. Flip-flops, for fuck's sake. She could get jabbed with a needle. "You can't be here."

"Why not?"

"Because it's not safe," he muttered, exasperated. She could have been assaulted out here while out searching for him. "How the hell did you even find me?"

She scrambled to keep up with him as he practically towed her up the incline. "I went to the jobsite, but they told me you weren't scheduled today. So I asked around, and someone said to try the shelter on MLK Junior."

He shot her a disbelieving look. "You went to the shelter to find me?"

"Yes, and then three others before one of the volunteers said you sometimes camp down here if the shelters are full."

Jesus God. He shook his head, kept going. "Please tell me you're not alone."

The guilty look on her face gave him his answer.

Sweet baby Jesus. "Shit. Seriously?"

"Cassie knows where I am."

"Yeah? That doesn't do much to keep you safe though,

does it?" He ran a hand through his hair. Why was she so damned insistent on finding him? "All right, where did you park?"

"A few blocks up that way." She pointed up the hill toward the streets located in the roughest part of the city.

The thought of her wandering through it alone almost made him break out in a sweat. "What were you *thinking*, coming down here by yourself to look for me?" The sun had disappeared. It was getting dark out, for Chrissake. "And what if I hadn't been here?"

"Then I would have asked if anyone at the campsite had seen you or knew where else you might be and tried there."

"At night?" Because yeah, that was a great idea for a hot woman alone in this neighborhood.

"It wasn't dark when I started. And I have pepper spray."

Given what he'd seen of her to this point, he had his doubts about her knowing how to use it.

She lifted her chin and faced him, blue-gray eyes full of indignation. "I know you think I'm naïve and maybe even stupid for coming here, but I assure you I'm not. I've done this many times before, alone, in rougher areas than this to find Eric. I've been mugged and forced to run for it a few times, but I'm still here. And guess what? Zero regrets."

He stared at her, at a loss for words. She'd been lucky she'd walked away from any of it without serious injury or trauma. "And how do you know I'm not dangerous?"

She didn't answer. The top of her head barely reached his chin. He easily outweighed her by sixty pounds or more, even though he was the thinnest he'd been since bootcamp. If he'd wanted to hurt her, she would have zero chance against him, even without his training. He had twice her strength.

The risks she'd just taken to find him made him incredulous—and furious.

"Hm? You think you're safe with me just because I served with your brother?" he pressed when a shadow of doubt clouded her eyes. Dammit, she smelled good too. Something light and clean and irresistibly female he was struggling to ignore. He was struggling to ignore a lot of things about her that he shouldn't be noticing or thinking about. "You don't know me. What makes you so sure I'm not a threat to you?"

She stared right back at him, unflinching as she searched his eyes. "Are you?"

No, but that wasn't the point. Because he could have been.

In his gut, he knew he should do or say something right now to drive the point home and scare her off for good. But he just couldn't do it. Staring into those eyes, reading the determination and sincerity there, scaring her away like that was impossible. It would be like kicking a sweet, friendly puppy.

"You have no idea what I'm capable of," he said instead. Zero idea of who he was, or what he'd done to wind up here.

She held her ground and didn't back down, didn't look the slightest bit uncertain or contrite. That surprised him even more. "I think that when it comes down to it, you would do whatever was necessary to survive. But no. I don't think you're a threat to me. Am I wrong?"

No. But goddamn it, she shouldn't trust him so blindly just because he'd served with Eric. "Come on," he muttered in irritation, taking hold of her elbow. Albeit gentler this time.

"How've you been, anyway?" she asked as they started up the sidewalk. It was past twilight, the top of the sky already turning different shades of purple and the edge of the moon appearing between some tall buildings ahead.

He shot her a dark look. "Living the dream."

She winced a little. "Have you thought at all about the potential job I mentioned? I spoke to the owner today. He—"

"Jesus, you are relentless." He shook his head and looked up at the heavens. *Eric, you seeing this? Your sister's insane. What the hell do I do with her?*

"Yep. I had to be, to get Eric off the streets."

"He was your brother. I'm nothing to you." It made no sense that she would risk her personal safety to try to "help" him.

"You were his friend. His good friend and brother-in-arms. He cared about you a lot, and so, believe it or not, that means you mean something to me too."

She didn't know what the hell she was saying. "Are you religious? Come to lead me to the light and save my soul or something?"

"No. Why, would that help?"

He clamped his teeth together, prayed for patience and kept his mouth shut, suspecting she would shoot down any argument he made. "Which way now?" he asked impatiently when they reached the next intersection.

"Straight."

Of all the dangers out here, of all ways his night could have gone sideways, this hadn't even occurred to him as a possibility. The sooner he got rid of her, the better, for both of them. He had an upcoming appointment he couldn't miss, and she needed to be in her car driving her sweet, curvy little ass back to the coast long before then. "Now where?"

"Across this way."

He waited for the traffic to pass, then hustled her across the street. The seedier bars, strip clubs, and massage parlors along the street were all coming to life. Music pumped from the doorways they passed. Bouncers and patrons standing outside stared at them as they walked by.

TJ tugged her closer and stared them all down. Warning them all to keep their distance and their fucking mouths shut.

In darkened doorways and corners, dealers and sex workers plied their trades. A few people were shooting up on the sidewalk. Others were passed out down alleys that reeked of garbage and urine and stale beer.

Just a regular Saturday night in this part of town. He should have hated it, but it felt normal to him now.

"Right at the next light," she murmured, giving no indication that she was scared or alarmed by what she was seeing. Though she'd probably seen it all before and worse when she'd been looking for her brother. TJ didn't like thinking about that one bit.

He stayed vigilant as they turned the corner and continued down the next street, still disturbed that she'd come here to find him. "Now where?"

"Left at the next street." They turned the corner. "I'm parked just up there on the right." She dug in her pocket for her keys and amber lights flashed on a vehicle parked twenty feet from another strip club.

He walked her right up to the driver's side and opened her door for her. She stopped to face him. Opened her mouth to say something, but he held up a hand. "Don't. Just get in." He didn't want to talk. He just wanted her to go.

And not come back.

"Will you please at least give serious consideration to contacting the owner of the company I mentioned?" Framed by those glasses that somehow made her even sexier, her eyes pleaded with him. "For Eric's sake."

That look in her eyes was killing him. Awakening parts of him that should have died long ago. He would have looked away, but he couldn't. She had a strange sort of power over him, and it made him twice as anxious to see her gone. "And if I don't?"

She shrugged. "Then I'll keep trying to change your mind."

"By coming back here to stalk me around the city some more?"

"If that's what it takes."

He flexed his jaw, frustrated by her misdirected stubbornness. The deadline for his appointment was coming up fast. He'd been trying to set it up for a long time. She had to leave. Now.

"Fine, I'll think about it. But don't get your hopes up." He nudged her into the car.

She slid into the seat but threw out a hand to catch the edge of the door before he could close it. "Crimson Point is gorgeous, and the job and the people who run the construction company are legit. I wouldn't have put it out there to you if they weren't."

Her expression was so damned earnest and open, her hope and distress at leaving him here almost palpable. Like she wanted to drag him in the car and take him home with her to get him off the street. It might have been endearing if it wasn't so exasperating.

"Come on," she prompted. "What's there to think about?"

Things she couldn't imagine. "Go home."

She kept a hand on the door so he couldn't close it, still staring up at him. "My name's Bristol, by the way."

"I don't care." A flash of hurt crossed her face before she masked it. He refused to feel bad. He needed to make a point here.

"You deserve better than this, TJ. I hope you believe that."

The steel encasing his heart hardened more. "You don't know what I deserve."

"I don't think you do either," she countered.

They stared at each other for a long, tense moment. Then her expression softened with a slight smile. "Well. Thank you for escorting me to my car."

He held back a sigh, reprimanded himself for getting trapped in her gaze. "Lock your doors and drive back to Crimson Point. And Bristol?"

Hope flared in her eyes. "Yes?"

He paused a moment for effect. "Don't ever come looking for me again."

He pushed her door shut before she could say anything, closing it with a solid *thunk*. Then he stood at the rear bumper of the car in front of hers with his arms folded across his chest and watched while she pulled out of the parallel spot and slowly drove away.

And she fucking stuck her arm out the window to wave goodbye.

He shook his head, testing the sound of her name in his mind.

Bristol.

Staring after the red glow of her taillights, the buried fragments of his conscience pricked at him like knives. Had he considered the job in Crimson Point since she'd given him the business card yesterday? Of course he had. The location was convenient. The drug scene was just as active there as it was everywhere else, the constant flow of product arriving from offshore and flooding inland all up and down the coast.

He thought of the crumpled business card still in his pocket. Maybe it wouldn't hurt to meet with the owner. Check out the area. See how things went.

It would at least get Eric's sister off his back. And they would both be safer for it.

BRISTOL BLEW OUT a hard breath of disappointment as she made the turn toward the freeway entrance, her heart heavy and her stomach still in knots.

That had not gone well at all. Maybe not as disastrous as her first couple of attempts to reach Eric had been, but still. Pretty bad.

TJ was harder than Eric. Hard enough to let the job opportunity in Crimson Point pass him by just to prove he didn't want anyone's help. It made her feel frustrated and powerless.

A call came in, and she wasn't surprised to see Cassie's name pop up on the display. She had left a string of increasingly worried texts over the past hour. So if Bristol ignored this call, Cassie might literally send out a search party.

"Hi. Yes, I'm alive," she answered, "and driving back to the coast right now."

"Thank God for that. Where the hell have you been, and why haven't you been answering me?"

"I was busy." Her tone was borderline irritable, but the last thing she wanted right now was a lecture.

Cassie released a frustrated sigh. "You are infuriating sometimes, you know that?"

"So I'm told." Twice in the past twenty minutes by two different people, and all just because she'd been trying to do the right thing.

"At least you're okay. I take it you didn't find him?"

"I found him."

"You did? Where?"

"In a little homeless camp under an overpass."

"Bristol, seriously? While you were alone?"

"It's nothing I haven't done before," she said before Cassie could launch into a tirade, feeling a little defensive. Somehow the three-year age difference made Cassie feel entitled to do the whole big sister thing. Which, okay, sometimes Bristol thought was sweet, but this wasn't one of those times. "I was perfectly safe." Not really, but she wasn't going to tell Cassie that either. She'd been a bit scared wandering through the unsavory parts of the city on her own, but her mission had been important enough to justify the risk.

"Uh huh. And what did he say?"

"He told me to leave him alone and never go looking for him again."

"Well, good. At least *he's* thinking straight."

Bristol sighed, deflated. She felt like a failure. She'd pushed her luck too far by tracking him down tonight, and ruined any chance of making inroads with him. Now he'd probably refuse to contact Beckett about the job out of pure stubbornness and pride. "Don't lecture me right now, okay? I feel bad enough as it is."

"It was reckless, doing that alone, and you know it."

"I had to try. He was Eric's friend."

It was more than that, though. There was something about TJ. She'd felt that same surge of awareness again when their eyes had locked across the campsite, and every time he'd looked at her after that.

Along with something stronger she didn't want to think about right now.

"I'm aware," Cassie said.

Bristol's throat tightened at the thought of TJ going back to his little tent in that miserable camp. "I messed up, Cass."

She'd gone with her gut, and wound up ruining everything. Maybe if she'd given him more time and space, things would have gone differently. Maybe he would have contacted Beckett on his own if she hadn't pushed the issue.

Cassie groaned. "Honey, I know your heart's in the right place. But whether you want to admit it or not, some people can't be helped. Some people don't *want* to be helped, and this guy doesn't even know you. So, of course, he's not gonna trust you."

Okay, now she felt completely dejected. She was stopping for a piece of chocolate cream pie at the diner at the side of the highway on the way back to the coast. "I thought he might listen to me if I came back a second time. I thought it might prove that I actually care." She'd hoped, anyway.

"Well, you tried, which is way more than most people would've done. No, you went way above and beyond, at huge risk to your personal safety. If he doesn't make the most of the opportunity you handed him, it's his loss."

It felt like her loss though. And it also felt like she'd let Eric down too.

She swallowed the lump in her throat. "Cass, do me a favor?"

"What."

"Don't tell my dad." Not that she was afraid of him. Far from it. She just didn't want to worry or disappoint him. Or hear this same talk from him.

Cassie chuckled. "Fine. But call me when you get home so I know you're back safe. You stopping for pie?"

"Yes." Her voice sounded as sad and pathetic as she felt.

"Figured. Bring me home a slice of lemon sour cream. That's the price of my silence."

"That's extortion."

"Whatever you want to call it. You owe me."

SEVEN

Tristan stopped cleaning his weapon as Cassie came through the door of the indoor shooting range. Her short black hair was wispy around her face, a long-sleeved black shirt and cargo pants molded to her long, lean build.

His day was made already, and it was barely eight a.m. "Morning. What'd you get up to last night?"

She set her bag down next to him and unzipped it. "Watched a true crime documentary while eating the most awesome piece of pie Bristol brought me. You?"

He was ridiculously pleased that she'd been home watching TV instead of out with someone. "I went back-to-school shopping with Carly and Gavin." His only niece started at her new school tomorrow.

"How'd that go?"

"It was incredibly expensive. For Gavin."

She laughed. "I'll bet. But eighth grade is a big deal. It's tough enough for girls that age, let alone for someone starting middle school in a new town. She needs all the confidence she can get when she walks into that building."

"I agree. Which is why I convinced Gav to allow a full makeover while we were at it."

She stopped digging out her gear to look at him, interest gleaming in her stunning silver eyes. With her dark hair and pale complexion, they almost seemed to glow. "What's that entail, exactly?"

"New haircut and style, manicure, some light, age-appropriate makeup, perfume, new clothes and shoes. The works."

Cassie gave a low whistle. "And what did your totally chill twin think of that?"

"Funnily enough, it was the perfume that put him over the edge. He was all, 'I don't *want* her to smell good on top of looking like *that*.' He thinks she's growing up too fast and wants her to stay twelve forever. Which is hilarious, since he's only been a dad for three months."

Neither Gavin nor Autumn had known the truth until recently, due to DNA results for Carly's family genealogy project for school of all things. It was wild that no one had ever seen the similarities between her and Gavin before that.

"And what about you?"

He shrugged. "I'm the funcle. I'm for whatever makes her happy. Because I'm fun."

"Gavin's not fun?"

"Come on. I'm *way* funner than he is."

"Nice English. How did Autumn react to the transformation?"

"She saw the smile on Carly's face and thought it was great. We kept things subtle, nothing overboard. But they said I spoil her too much. You believe that?"

"No," she gasped, widening those pretty eyes in fake astonishment for a moment before a smirk took hold. "She has all three of you firmly wound around her little finger, and you know it."

"Yeah, that's fair." He was good with it.

Growing up, he and his siblings had been the opposite of spoiled. After their parents had died, too often they'd gone to school or to bed with empty stomachs, their sister and older brother scrambling to make ends meet and put food on their table. So yeah, he was just happy that Carly would never know that kind of life.

"There are worse things for a teenage girl than being adored and spoiled by her dad and uncle." He didn't miss the almost wistful edge to her tone as she took out her sidearm and began taking it apart.

He picked up his own to finish cleaning it, dying to know more about her background but knowing he had to be careful not to pry. For all her friendliness, Cassie was private. She tended to keep to herself and never talked about anything personal.

It made him want to know about her even more. "Bet you've got your parents wrapped around your finger too."

"Maybe once upon a time. But not anymore." She got busy cleaning the pistol.

And that was it. Nothing else, and her closed reaction told him he'd hit a nerve.

He curbed his impatience. But it seriously bothered him that after months of working together she still didn't seem to trust him. She was professional and a good teammate but continued to hold herself a little aloof from him and the others and didn't socialize with them much outside of work.

He'd realized a while ago that if he wanted to win her trust, he was going to have to earn it. He just wasn't sure how.

It was a new experience for him, and he didn't like it. None of the women he'd been interested in before were like

Cassie. Most of them were the exact opposite with talking about personal stuff, to the point of oversharing.

He racked his brain, searching for something to get her talking again.

Food. She loved food. Ironic, since he had issues with sharing it. "So what's so great about this pie you had?"

Her face brightened as she wiped down the barrel of her pistol. "Best lemon sour cream pie ever. Made from scratch, with a graham crust, then the lemon sour cream layer, and whipped cream with grated zest on top. It's incredible."

"Is it from a place in town?" He would have to find it and bring her a piece.

"No, there's a diner on the highway between here and Portland. Bristol stopped on her way back."

"She went back again already?" She and Cassie had just gone there the other day.

Cassie made a frustrated sound. "She— Never mind."

He set his weapon down to watch her, sensing she'd been on the verge of opening up a bit. He wanted her to. "No, what?" Something was bothering her. It was just the two of them here. If she was ever going to talk to him, *really* talk to him, this was as good a moment as any.

She hesitated, seemed to battle with herself, then sighed. "She decided to go back there yesterday to track down that TJ guy across the worst parts of the city—alone, as it was getting dark."

"Why?"

"She's on another crusade. Won't listen to anything I say." Her tone was loaded with annoyance.

"I got a twin like that."

She gave a grudging chuckle, and it warmed him inside. "This isn't the same thing. But it's all good. Although, apparently, I'm not allowed to be mad, because she had pepper spray with her." She rolled her eyes, sarcasm dripping from every word.

"What did you mean by 'another crusade?'"

She paused, seemed to weigh her words carefully before answering. "She did this once before. Granted, she managed to pull it off that time. This time, not so much."

Sounded to him like she was worried about Bristol and wanted to protect her from being disappointed or hurt. "You guys are pretty close," he said to keep her talking. This was the most she'd ever told him about anything personal, and he didn't want her to stop.

"We are now, yeah."

"You weren't before?"

She shook her head. "Didn't get off on the best foot when we met. She didn't trust my mom and me in the beginning, but then eventually she saw we weren't so bad." She looked at him. "Is this what it's like to have a sibling? Feeling exasperated half the time?"

"Pretty much, yeah."

"Awesome." She straightened, checked the chamber of her weapon, and took a full magazine out of her bag. "Ready to put some rounds downrange? Callum asked me to drop off some weapons at the office after."

One of CPS's owners. "I'll do it."

Cassie stopped and looked at him in surprise, her safety glasses dangling from one hand. "Really?"

He hid a frown. It was like no one had ever offered to do her a favor before. "Sure, it's no big deal. I'm headed that way anyway." He lived just up the hill from the office.

He got up and followed her to the doors that led to the firing lanes, trying not to notice the way her cargo pants hugged her ass. He made it a point not to look at his coworker's asses, male or female. But with her he couldn't help sneak a peek.

"If you're sure, then thanks. By the way, you get an update on the upcoming detail yet?" She handed him a pair of bright yellow earmuffs marked with the CPS logo. The C was a curling blue wave topped with a whitecap.

"Yeah. You?" He slid on his own safety glasses.

"This morning." She had been tapped as personal security and driver for famous actress Becca Sandoza.

He was the same for Becca's husband, Chase Davenport, Hollywood stuntman and CPS founder's best friend from back in North Carolina. They were coming to town to visit Ryder and scout several locations for an upcoming movie. Chase and his crew might also film some stunt scenes in the area. Which meant Tristan would be working closely with Cassie during that week.

He couldn't wait. "No pressure."

She shot him a grin that made his insides tighten. "None whatsoever."

"You must've been on security details for celebs in Vegas from time to time."

"No. I did security for various events when celebs were present, but not personal protection details. They usually came with their own bodyguards." She went quiet as she stepped into her own firing lane, all business. Squaring her body to the target, she raised her weapon before firing six shots, each one hitting center mass.

He'd be lying if he didn't admit that was hot as hell. Even if they were coworkers.

He was always respectful of her and mindful that she was a woman in a male-dominated career and likely felt she had to prove herself to the others constantly to maintain their respect. Currently, she was the only female personal security agent at CPS.

But he was definitely into her. She was already under his skin without even trying, and every time he saw her, she burrowed deeper in there. Even though the attraction might be one-sided. And even though his brain told him that anything between them couldn't go anywhere even if it wasn't.

He stepped into the lane beside hers, adjusted the target, and took aim.

Thirty minutes later, they were both out of ammo.

Cassie lowered her weapon, checked the chamber to ensure it was empty, and set it aside on the small ledge as she tugged off her earmuffs and safety glasses. "You want to keep going? Or are you done?"

"I'm done." He set his safety glasses on his own shelf. "Wanna go grab something to eat on the way back to town? Or we could go check out that diner you mentioned."

It was well out of their way, but he was all for an excuse to spend more time alone with her on the drive there and back. He might even share a bite or two of his, because it was her.

"I'm good, thanks."

The rebuff was polite but firm and took him off guard. Just when he thought he was making progress, she shut down and pulled back again.

"Some other time," he said with a nonchalance that felt a little forced.

"Sounds good." She strode for the doors without looking back.

Tristan stood there for a moment, letting the silence surround him. It was time to be honest with himself.

This was about way more than earning her trust. He didn't

want to break through or pull down the walls she kept around herself.

He wanted her to open the gates for him.

And *only* for him.

EIGHT

Arriving in Crimson Point was like stepping into an alternate universe compared to being on the streets of Portland.

TJ tugged his hood up against the chilly mist in the salty air and shoved his hands in the front pockets as he continued down the sidewalk along the main road that lined the waterfront, the familiar weight of his ruck pressed against his back. "Fogust" was in full effect today in the central Oregon Coast, a thick layer of marine cloud and mist hugging the ground reducing visibility.

The cool weather didn't seem to be hurting the local economy any. Front Street was busy with a mix of locals and tourists visiting the brightly painted shops, restaurants and cafés. Children carried colorful kites or plastic pails and shovels while eating ice cream cones or cookies on the way to the beach.

Everything around him was clean and orderly. Everyone here seemed happy. A few people even offered him polite smiles as they passed by.

The abrupt shift in vibe was more jarring than he'd anticipated. He'd forgotten what it felt like to be seen. To be treated like an actual human being instead of people looking the other way or crossing the street if they noticed him.

Circling seagulls cried overhead, mixing with the rhythmic churning of the surf in the background. He caught the smell of deep-fried food and the tang of malt vinegar as he approached a fish and chips shop, then a waft of something sweet and vanilla-flavored farther up the street. It was coming from an open door of a little café across the road called Whale's Tale, with a lineup that stretched halfway down the block.

He passed a veterinary office, did a double take when he spotted an obviously senior dog with a graying face and long, floppy ears lying flat on the floor just inside the glass door, staring up at him with droopy eyes. For some reason, it reminded him of a deflated air mattress, and one side of his mouth kicked up in amusement.

The sensation startled him. He couldn't remember the last time he'd smiled, let alone laughed. It had been a long time since he'd had anything to smile or laugh about.

At the end of the street, he reached the Sea Hag, the town's popular waterfront pub and the location for his upcoming meeting. When he walked in, the yeasty scent of beer hung in the air along with the mouthwatering smell of grilling burgers.

He glanced around the crowded space, taking in the view as the sound of combined conversations flowed over him. He was about ten minutes early, but even though it wasn't quite noon, the bar was already jammed, and all the tables were occupied.

Two big guys at a booth in the corner turned to look at

him. The dark-haired one raised his arm at him in greeting. Beckett Hollister, owner of the renovation company TJ was here to interview for, and a red-headed guy with a short beard.

He walked over to them, feeling more curious eyes on him as he passed the other tables. The locals knew he was a newcomer.

Both men stood. Beckett offered his hand. "TJ. Thanks for coming out."

"No problem." He shook with him, then with the other man across the table.

"I'm Mac," the second guy told him in a clear Scottish accent.

TJ nodded, set his ruck on the floor, and took the padded bench seat across from them. Even though having his back to the rest of the room made his spine tingle with unease. Combat and needing to stay vigilant on the street left an indelible mark. He liked being able to see what was coming at him.

"You want anything else to drink before we get started?" Beckett said.

"No, the water's good." There were already three glasses of it on the table.

Beckett rested his forearms on the scarred, dark wood table and started the conversation. "So, I hear you served with Bristol's brother. You and her close?"

"No."

Surprise flickered in the other man's deep brown eyes. "Really. She's been so insistent about me meeting you, I thought you guys must be friends."

TJ shook his head. "I met her for the first time when she showed up at the jobsite in Portland on Saturday."

Beckett exchanged a puzzled glance with Mac before looking back at him. "You were a Ranger?"

He nodded.

"I was Army too."

He was being modest. TJ had done some research. Beckett had been Special Forces. And an A-Team leader at that. "I heard."

"Mac served with the Royal Marines. We try to hire veterans exclusively when we can."

He nodded again, not knowing what else to say.

"Honestly, given what Bristol told me about your background, I was surprised you were interested in interviewing for our company. Crimson Point Security might be a better fit for you."

He appreciated Beckett's honesty. "I prefer construction." His background made getting security clearances messy.

"Why's that?"

He lifted a shoulder. "I like physical work, being able to do my shift and then be off the clock." It gave him time for his other…pursuits.

"Fair enough." Beckett paused. "There's just one thing that's bothering me."

He held Beckett's gaze, braced himself for what he already knew was coming. "What's that?"

"We did a standard, preliminary background check on the name listed on your paperwork with the construction firm in Portland. Barros." Beckett's gaze was unwavering. "It didn't turn up any work history."

He'd been ready for this since agreeing to the meeting. "No. I got paid under the table when I worked. And I moved around a lot." They knew he was homeless. He didn't need to spell it out.

"Is TJ a new identity?"

"I needed a fresh start after I left the military. So I officially changed my name to Tiago Joaquin. TJ for short."

Beckett seemed to weigh that for a long moment. TJ glanced between him and Mac before continuing. "I don't have a criminal record. And I received an honorable discharge when I left the service."

"Under what name?"

"Tomás Cordoba."

Mac nodded and jotted it down. "Got it. Though Bristol's already vouched for you, of course." He looked up at him. "We've hired plenty of lads with black marks in their pasts. But we'd rather know ahead of time if there are any surprises we should be aware of."

When TJ didn't answer right away, Beckett folded his arms, looking every inch the team leader he'd once been. "Is there anything else we need to know about you?"

"No," TJ said. Nothing that would affect them or his performance on the job. Information about his name change was available if they wanted to check it. Which he was sure they would.

"I spoke to two of your foremen in Portland. They had nothing but good things to say about you. Good work ethic, you show up on time, and don't cause any problems. But I need to know—are there any substance abuse issues?"

"No."

That dark stare continued to measure him for a long moment. Then Beckett nodded once, and TJ felt like he'd passed muster. "Okay. Good. We're currently looking to hire two more people in the next few weeks, as we're heavy into our busy season. And I'm not sure if Bristol told you, but we can provide housing if you take a full-time position."

TJ raised his eyebrows. "Are you offering me the job?"

Just like that? Even with the potential red flag about assuming a new identity and no work history?

"Bristol's vouched for you. That, your Ranger tab, and your honorable discharge are enough for me."

Wow. He hadn't expected this. And as for Bristol vouching for him, that was crazy. As crazy as her coming to Portland alone the other night and tracking him down in the roughest part of the city. She had no reason to believe in him just because he'd served with her brother. What if he was a shitty person? She'd repeatedly gone above and beyond to help him, and it made no sense.

"Do you want it?" Beckett asked, dragging him out of his thoughts.

He hid his surprise, refused to acknowledge the rush of pride he felt at the offer. Since he'd been on the street, not many people had trusted him enough to give him the benefit of the doubt, or believed him worthy of a chance. Most had assumed that since he was homeless, he was therefore also lazy, useless, as well as being a drunk or an addict, batshit cray, or a combination thereof.

This show of faith by a former A-team leader made him feel more human than he had in almost a year. "Yes, I do."

"Good. Glad to hear it."

"Here's an employment contract for you to look at." Mac slid some papers across the table to him.

Beckett raised an arm to flag down a server. "Let's order first. Lunch's on the company."

Mac ordered fish and chips. TJ and Beckett ordered bacon cheeseburgers with fries, and TJ read over the contract while they waited. The terms were fair and more than generous. Benefits kicked in after just one month of full-time work, and they covered everything from medical to dental, medications, counseling, physical therapy, even a certain dollar amount of massage therapy coverage each year.

He had no idea how long he'd stick around. It depended on how things went.

"You don't have to sign it now," Beckett told him. "Take it with you and read it later if you want. But it's pretty up front. We're not trying to take advantage of anyone."

No, the exact opposite. "I'll sign it now." He took the pen Mac handed him, signed and dated the few places necessary, and slid the contract back.

"Welcome aboard, mate. I'll give you a copy," Mac said, signing the corresponding lines before passing it to Beckett to do the same.

"You start Monday, oh-eight-hundred," Beckett said as he finished the final signature. "It's a two-story Victorian we're starting on up the hill east of here toward the coastal highway. Mac will be your onsite foreman, and you'll meet our business partner Jase too. He handles all the accounting and finances. In the meantime, we'll get you squared away."

"There's a wee, one-bed bungalow we've nearly finished on the north side of town, up on the bluff," Mac said. "The main construction is done. Plumbing, wiring, tiling, fixtures and paint are all sorted, and it's furnished for staging, but some of the finishing work still needs to be done. If you don't mind that and handling some grouting, sealing, cleaning and landscaping in your free time, you can move in as soon as this afternoon. If you want."

TJ stared at him, then glanced at Beckett, too stunned to speak. They were just going to give him a newly finished house to live in? Without even knowing him or having much background on him? That was a hell of a lot of trust to put in a complete stranger who'd been living on the streets for a long time now. How did they know he wouldn't trash it or strip the copper wiring and pipes out of the walls to sell, and take off one night?

"I don't mind doing the finishing," he said.

"Excellent. Do you need to go back to Portland for anything?" Mac asked.

"No." He was done with that place. For now. Everything he had left in this life was in his ruck.

"All right. I'll take you up to the house after we finish up here. But take your time eating. The scran here's amazing. And don't take this the wrong way, but you look like you could use a second serving of chips."

It was true, he didn't have much fat on him now. "I might be open to a second helping of fries."

The food arrived. Maybe it was because it felt like he'd just fallen out of the lucky tree and hit every branch on the way down, but it was the best burger and fries TJ had ever tasted. He still couldn't believe everything that was happening, or how fast.

A niggle of guilt pricked him about his ulterior motive for coming out here to the coast. He smothered it. Things were turning out even better than he could ever have imagined. He wondered what Bristol would think of it all. He had her number programmed into his phone. Not that he would call her. But maybe he'd message her at some point to let her know he'd taken the job. Get her off his back for good.

"Welcome aboard, TJ. See you Monday," Beckett said after they ate. TJ stood with him, shook his hand again. "Message or call if you need anything before then."

"I will." He definitely wouldn't. Beckett had already done more than enough for him. He would do what he could to pay it back. "Thanks."

As Beckett strode through the crowded room, Mac

clapped him on the back. "Ready to go? My truck's in the lot just up the hill. Do you have any gear we need to pick up?"

"No. Just this." He hoisted his ruck from the floor and flipped it over his head onto his shoulders. Besides his beret and service medals, it was the only thing he'd kept from his days in the military.

Mac rounded the table and headed for the door with a noticeable limp in one leg. TJ stayed a step behind him, feeling the curious stares following them. When he stepped outside, a gust of damp wind greeted him, whipping off the rolling waves that washed onto the wide expanse of sandy beach to their right.

"This way," Mac said, and strode for the crosswalk that led to the other side of Front Street.

TJ was halfway across it when he spotted a familiar figure stepping out of Whale's Tale on the opposite side. Bristol stopped on the sidewalk with what looked like a pastry box in her hands, her face lighting up. "Oh my gosh, hi!"

Her dazzling smile was aimed directly at him and full of joy. The power of it momentarily paralyzed him, rooting his feet to the asphalt.

A horn beeped, knocking his brain back into gear. He hurried to the other sidewalk, unable to take his eyes off her.

Mac had paused to speak to her. After a moment, he shot TJ a grin and jerked a thumb up the hill. "I'll bring the truck down. We need to come back down this way anyhow."

As he limped off, TJ stood unmoving on the sidewalk, bracing himself as Bristol approached. Today she wore a frilly white top that left her rounded arms and a thin strip of midriff bare above the waistband of her flowy, calf-length blue skirt with little white polka dots all over it.

"It's so good to see you," she said when she reached the corner, still beaming at him. The breeze tousled her dark brown hair around her shoulders, a blue bow with little white polka dots that matched her skirt holding it back from her face. She looked summery and fresh and so incredibly gorgeous it almost hurt to look at her.

"Hi." It was all he would allow himself to say. The woman was a damned thorn in his side. He couldn't seem to get rid of her no matter where he went. But seeing that genuine smile just for him, some deeply buried part of him was glad he'd made her happy by showing up for the interview today.

"You look…amazing, by the way." She ran an approving gaze over him from head to toe.

He resisted the urge to shift his stance even as his cheeks heated slightly, now exposed by the full goatee he'd shaved that morning. Before leaving Portland, he'd paid for a cheap haircut and an almost new flannel shirt from a second-hand shop, to look more presentable for the interview.

It was embarrassing, to be blushing. But there was also a sense of pride that she clearly liked the way he'd cleaned up. The way Bristol looked at him now made the effort more than worth it. It'd been forever since a woman had looked at him like that, and he couldn't remember ever feeling this level of attraction to anyone.

"What are you doing here?" she asked, still smiling. Her gaze dropped to his mouth for a moment, and a different kind of hunger swept through him.

"I met Mac and Beckett for an interview." He was struggling not to look at her mouth. Or imagine what it would feel like under his.

The leap of hope and excitement in her eyes was anything but fake. Everything about her was so damned real, it sparked his deepest protective instincts. "How'd it go?"

He didn't have it in him to mutter an excuse and walk

away, and he didn't see the point in lying when she was the reason for his sudden good fortune. "I got the job."

"That's fantastic!" She gave him another megawatt smile that shut his brain off and left him staring. "Congratulations. Are you excited? What an amazing fresh start this will be for you. Crimson Point's so great. You'll love it here."

He shrugged. Excited was the wrong word, but her reaction alone was worth accepting the job. Her unwarranted belief in him soothed a raw wound in his soul that had been festering for too long. And he was already addicted to her smile. Already craved it and secretly wanted more of her warmth and care.

That was dangerous. He'd been frozen inside for so long, had gone unnoticed and uncared about since he'd ended up on the streets. He had to be careful not to let Bristol thaw the icy core inside him. In his world, it was all that kept him alive.

"When do you start?" she asked when he didn't respond.

"Monday."

She nodded. "Great. Have you eaten?"

"Yeah. Mac's gonna be here any minute to pick me up."

"Oh." Her smile vanished. "Sure."

He felt like a dick for shutting her down so bluntly, but his lifestyle was hard. He'd known it would be from the outset. And even though things were looking up for him at the moment, he knew all too well that it could all disappear at any time and land him back on the street.

Much as he liked Bristol, as crazy attracted as he was to her, he couldn't afford to let her get mixed up in his life. It wouldn't be right. And he definitely didn't want her hanging around him, seeing what he got up to.

A big silver pickup pulled up to the stop sign to his right, saving him from the awkward silence. Mac waved at him through the windshield. "See you around," TJ said to her, hating being the reason the light in her eyes dimmed as he turned away.

"Yeah. See you."

He headed for the truck, didn't look back. He'd fulfilled his end of the bargain by coming here for the interview. He'd even taken the job. Now he needed to keep his distance from her.

For both their sakes.

NINE

"He's ready. This way."

Angel had been waiting almost forty minutes. He got up and followed Jon out of the reception room and down the marble-tiled hallway. He wasn't sure whether Jon was even the guy's real name, but he was the boss's second-in-command, and Angel knew not to ask questions.

"Stand there." Jon indicated a spot near the wide bank of windows overlooking the vineyard. Until he'd moved here, he'd never realized so much wine was made in Oregon.

He stood where he was told and held his arms out to the side while Jon swept him with a metal-detecting wand and patted him down. He pulled Angel's wallet out of his back pocket to check it. A picture fell out.

Angel instinctively bent to snatch it from the floor, but Jon was faster.

Jon held the photo up to examine it. Angel barely curbed the urge to grab it from him.

Jon looked from the image to Angel and back, then handed it over with the wallet. "How's she doing?"

"Fine." He slid the photo back into the wallet, pushing

down the rush of anger. His wife was off-limits. Period. He didn't want any part of this shit touching her. If necessary, he would die to make sure it didn't.

"That's good. All right, you can go in." Jon walked to the door, rapped on it twice.

A few seconds later the locking mechanism whirred, and the lock clicked open. Jon twisted the knob, opened the door, and stepped aside to admit him.

Inside, the boss stood at the floor-to-ceiling window with his back to Angel, backlit by the setting sun flooding the rows of grapevines stretching as far as the eye could see down the hillside leading away from the main house. Jordan had probably made him wait due to some power trip.

"You wanted to see me, sir?" The sir was mere politeness, nothing more. Angel might despise Jordan and everything he stood for, but he wasn't stupid enough to disrespect him. Much as he disliked it, Angel needed him. His boss was a necessary means to an end, nothing more.

And if Angel wanted to get out of this thing alive at the end, then he needed to be very, very careful.

Jordan turned to face him, the daylight streaming around him like a halo. "The falcons are watching several suspects who might be responsible for the leak. Unfortunately, there's no concrete evidence on any of them. Yet."

Angel said nothing.

Jordan angled his head slightly, watching him. "Aren't you curious as to who's on the list?"

That tone, the flat, measuring stare warned him that he could be a potential suspect. So Angel weighed his response carefully. "No, sir. It doesn't matter to me who the target is."

A slight smile curled the edge of Jordan's mouth. "I'm glad you see it that way."

He wasn't all that worried about winding up a suspect.

He'd been aware from the start that they remotely monitored his personal phone. He made sure there was nothing on it that could be incriminating. Just as he made sure that there was nothing suspicious to see when they watched or followed him. He'd never stepped out of line. Never done anything that might draw scrutiny, at least where they could see it.

"You don't talk much, do you, Angel?"

"No, sir." Talking was a great way to wind up dead in this toxic web he'd entangled himself in. Hard to believe that a little over a year ago he'd had a legitimate job. But it hadn't paid a tenth of what this did, and his skill set enabled him to be silent and lethal. A useful tool for the organization.

Jordan walked over to round the edge of the large, antique mahogany desk and sat in the plush chair behind it, leaning back to regard him thoughtfully. "I like you, Angel. I like the way you work, and I like the way you conduct yourself. Since you started with me, I haven't had a single report on you containing anything that is the least bit worrying. I hope that continues."

Angel didn't answer, repressing the chill starting to creep up from the base of his spine at the thinly veiled threat. Because no answer was required, and the meaning was clear. They were watching him. Always. They would keep watching him, and his continued good conduct wasn't necessarily a guarantee of remaining in the boss's good graces.

All it would take was a single whisper of doubt from one person. A rumor or suggestion from a falcon, or anyone else in the organization for that matter. Any single hint of suspicion against him, and Angel would wind up on the target list himself. Because there were others like him. Contract killers he wasn't even aware of. If his name wound up on that list, they would come for him within hours.

The ticking clock in the back of his mind sped up a little

faster. Time was running out more quickly than he had anticipated.

Realizing he wasn't going to get whatever reaction from him he'd hoped for, Jordan's expression turned bored. "You'll be informed when the target is verified." He flicked his wrist dismissively. "You can go."

Angel did an about-face and left without a word. Jon followed him every step of the way outside to the front entrance where he'd left his car. The armed guard at the gate stared at him for a long moment before letting him out.

Letting out a deep breath of relief, he drove home deep in thought. The little one-bedroom bungalow at the end of the cul-de-sac looked so cheerful with its tidy yard and the rows of red flowers lining either side of the front walkway that matched the red shutters framing the windows.

No one would ever guess that a cartel hitman lived in a place like this.

As far as he could tell, no one had followed him home, and no one was parked along the street. As a precaution he checked for bugs or cameras every few days when he was home, but he was realistic enough to understand that he might not catch everything. He unlocked the back door and stepped into the darkened kitchen.

His heart sank. The only time Liana didn't cook was when she was having a bad day.

"I'm home," he called out, spotting the line of light coming from under the closed door at the end of the hallway.

Pausing in front of it, he put on a smile before opening it. Liana was in bed with the covers pulled up to her chin, the cat curled up beside her. She gave him a tired, apologetic smile. "Hi. Sorry there's no dinner. Again." Her voice was weak. Exhausted.

"Don't worry about that," he said, sitting on the edge of

the mattress to smooth her hair back from her forehead. She was pale, with dark circles under her eyes. "Not a good day, huh."

"Tomorrow will be better."

She always said that. Her bravery and stubbornly positive attitude broke his heart.

Neither of them had known what the strange symptoms had meant when they had begun their honeymoon two years ago, and neither of them could have guessed how dire the final diagnosis would be. Recently, she'd had more bad days than good, yet through everything she'd endured, through all the ups and downs and tests and hospitalizations, she remained the kindest, sweetest soul he'd ever met.

He didn't deserve her, but he was doing everything he could to keep her safe and make enough money to pay for her treatments.

"Get any sleep today?" he asked.

"A little. Never seems like enough these days. I sleep almost as much as Stevie." She nodded at their cat, Stevie Licks, who watched him with one half-closed eye.

The exhaustion worried Angel. As time went on, it seemed like the grains of sand passed faster and faster through the hourglass, and he was helpless to slow them down. But he had to find a way. He would do anything to buy her more time.

Including sell his soul to the devil. Which he'd already done.

"How was your day?" she murmured.

"Not bad." He noticed her laptop sitting on the bedside table. "Find anything interesting today?"

Her face brightened a little. "Yes. The second trial just finished. The initial results look really promising." She started to sit up. He slid an arm around her and pulled her upright, stuffing the pillows behind her back and settling her against the headboard before handing her the laptop. "Thanks." The adoring smile she gave him made his heart squeeze. "Here, look."

She turned it so he could see the screen and read the report released by the medical researchers in Zurich. He didn't understand some of it. She was the scientist, not him, but he got the gist. The latest clinical trial results looked promising. "Seems like good news."

"Yes, and they're going to open up the next trial soon." She brought up another page to show him. "Only twenty-five spots available, though."

When she looked up at him, the hope and anxiety in her big brown eyes hit him hard. She was desperate for a chance to improve her quality of life and outlive the time frame her doctors had given her. Praying for a miracle.

They both were.

He would do whatever it took to make that happen. "And you'll be one of them."

Her smile wobbled. "You really think so?"

"I know so."

"But the money—"

"I'll get the money. We're almost there, not much longer now." The cost of the treatment alone was astronomical, and because it was still experimental, none of it was covered by her insurance. They needed the money for the medication, hospitalization, and treatment, plus travel and living expenses in Europe.

He'd invested every penny he could in the market and done well with the returns. But she didn't know what he'd done beyond that. She thought he'd taken a big promotion with his former government security contractor firm that sent him around the country on various jobs. He didn't intend for her to ever know the truth. It would only hurt and distress her, and stress was the last thing she could handle in her condition. The blood on his hands was something he would answer for on the day he met his maker.

At least it wasn't innocent blood. That made it easier.

"You hungry?" he asked, pushing those thoughts away.

"A little. Mostly, I'm just sick of being in this bed."

"Then come with me, gorgeous." He scooped her up, smiled at her delighted giggle as she looped her arms around his neck.

Stevie followed them into the living room. Angel settled Liana on the couch with pillows and a thick blanket where she could see him in the kitchen, and then set about making them homemade tomato soup and grilled cheese. He chatted to her as he cooked, talking about plans for their life after her treatment.

He brought in a tray for her and set it on her lap, ushering the cat aside to make room for himself beside her. They ate together in comfortable silence, but he watched her closely and saw the moment her energy reserves ran out.

Her hand shook, and she dropped the bit of sandwich she was holding onto her plate. Her face was drawn, her posture sagging.

"I'm sorry," she said. "I can't."

"Don't apologize. Here." He moved closer, cradled the back of her neck in one hand and lifted the sandwich to her mouth with the other.

Her eyes glinted with humor as she took a bite. "This is so romantic," she said around the mouthful of sandwich.

"You know it, baby."

She swallowed, licked her lips. "When I'm better I'm going to spoil you rotten."

"You already do." She showered him with love, even on

her shittiest days. Until her, he'd never known that kind of selfless love existed.

Her situation made him want to howl in rage and agony. He would die for her, trade places with her in a heartbeat to spare her this terrible, unrelenting decline, but he was powerless to stop it or protect her from what was happening inside her own body.

When she had finished half the sandwich and most of the soup, she put a hand on his wrist to push the spoon away. "I'm so full," she said, exhaustion evident in every line on her face.

He set the tray aside, hiding his concern. Her strength faded so fast lately. "Want to stretch out here and watch a movie?"

"No. I need to sleep."

She curled into him like a child as he carried her back to their bedroom. His phone buzzed in his back pocket as he tucked her in.

He straightened, pulled it out and found a message from the organization.

Individual confirmed to be nosing around in the area. People might have talked.

A second later, two names appeared, and then two photos.

The photos were the signal that they had been confirmed as targets.

"What is it?" Liana asked tiredly.

"Work." He leaned over, dropped a kiss on her lips. "I need to head out for a bit. Want me to call someone to come over until I get back?" One of their neighbors was a big help when he couldn't be here.

"No. I'm just gonna sleep," she mumbled.

"Okay. Sleep well. I'll be back before you know it." He kissed her again before straightening.

"Be safe."

"I will." He eased the bedroom door shut. Double checked that all the windows and doors were locked, and the alarm set on his way out.

On the back step, he paused to study the names and pictures again, along with the addresses listed.

He didn't see people when he studied the pictures. He saw features of targets to be eliminated, and how much money each job would transfer into his account. Seventy-five thousand each. The most he'd made yet. The boss wanted this leak fixed bad.

At this rate, he would have the money for a clinical trial spot in a few more months.

He glanced in the rearview mirror at their house as he drove away. Thought of Liana curled up alone in their bed, fighting to put on a brave face in front of him while praying for more time, for the symptoms to recede enough that her quality of life would improve even a little.

She was counting on him to get her a spot in the trial program.

He focused back on the road, mentally switching into hunter mode. Time was running out for them both. He had to get the remaining funds they needed and then get the hell out of this toxic web before the clock hit zero.

TEN

A thick carpet of cedar needles covering the ground cushioned the soles of TJ's boots as he crept through the wooded area, each step releasing their spicy fragrance into the warm night air. Up ahead through the tall trees, the lights surrounding the hospital parking lot came on right on cue.

He stopped just inside the screen of trees at the top of the bank and crouched down in the shadows, balancing his weight on one knee while he used his phone camera to survey this side of the hospital. Every night this past week after work, he'd taken the bus up here to do recon of the property. Watching the comings and goings. Figuring out the security and delivery routine, taking note of the timings, plus all the security camera positions and their approximate areas of coverage.

He checked the time on his phone. It was dusk, the sky above the tops of the tall evergreens shifting to darker blues and purples and the first stars winking to life. The night shift had started more than two hours ago, and by now most of the daytime workers would have gone home. But there was one person in particular who worked odd hours that he had come to see.

The rumble of a delivery truck broke the silence as it approached the service door closest to him. It stopped next to it, and two people hopped out to open the vehicle's back doors. He zoomed in on his phone to watch, and several people emerged from the side exit of the hospital near the far corner of the parking lot.

Unfortunately, the angle the truck was parked at blocked his view of the group unloading it. He rose slowly and moved to the right, picking his way through the underbrush and over fallen logs until he found a hiding place to get a better viewpoint.

He crouched down again and zoomed in, getting a good look at the crew. One of the shorter men turned around, giving TJ a good view of his face.

Bingo. Mark G.

Mark was a big part of the reason TJ had decided to make the move to Crimson Point. He was connected to someone higher up the chain who TJ had been trying to make contact with for months. TJ needed to meet Mark face to face to begin that process but hadn't been able to get close enough to him yet. He needed to do it soon. In the meantime, he would do more homework.

He started recording video, zooming in as close as the camera would allow.

Ten minutes later, the men finished unloading boxes of supplies and transporting them inside. Just as one of them closed and locked the truck's rear doors, TJ saw Mark hand something to the passenger—while standing in a blind spot of the camera mounted on a wall nearby. A small bag or an envelope that the passenger slid into his pocket.

Cash for the product that had just been delivered.

The driver strode for the front of the truck as the passenger did a fist grab and shoulder bump with Mark. As they both climbed into the cab, the door to the hospital opened again and a familiar figure stepped out.

Bristol.

TJ mentally cursed. What was she doing here? She normally only worked until seven, should have gone home hours ago.

She paused to chat with Mark, her pale blue scrubs almost glowing in the lights of the parking lot.

Seeing her warm smile directed at Mark sent an unexpected streak of jealousy through him. He'd bet money she had zero clue that her coworker had just smuggled over a hundred grand worth of street drugs into the hospital along with the regular supplies.

TJ found himself drawn to her against his will, unable to take his eyes off her. Every night he'd come here, he'd made sure he was here in time to see her leave. And every night she took the time to stop and talk with people on her way out.

Her warmth was real. Sincere. People gravitated toward her naturally, unable to resist the natural pull she exerted. Even him, though he was doing his damnedest to ignore it.

What was the deal? Lately it seemed like everything in his life led back to Bristol in some way. This included.

He let out a slow breath, watching her. Life experience had hardened him and made him jaded. He was used to people either ignoring or trying to manipulate him. When she'd first approached him, he'd assumed she wanted something from him. Or that she was a do-gooder out to convert him to whatever religion she subscribed to in the hopes of saving his soul.

She *was* trying to save him in her own way, but watching

her covertly this past week, he was starting to believe she was the real deal. An actual good person. And he could count on a couple of fingers how many of those he'd met in his lifetime.

Maybe it shouldn't have surprised him so much. Eric had always spoken highly of her. The more TJ watched her, the more the empty place inside him craved that genuine warmth and kindness she gave to others so naturally.

She and Mark talked for another minute or so, then both turned and headed off in opposite directions. He'd gotten what he'd come for, but TJ followed Bristol from the shadows as she crossed the parking lot, waited until she was safely in her car driving away before he backtracked up to the road to catch the bus.

It dropped him off several blocks from the house he was staying in. The little white bungalow sat perched between a little Victorian and a craftsman on a quiet street atop a hill on the north side of town. The front porch light was on, casting a warm, welcoming glow against the purple-edged darkness. And the scary part was, it was starting to feel like home.

Inside it was quiet, the hum of the brand-new refrigerator barely audible in the spotless, decked-out kitchen. It still felt surreal that he now lived in a place like this and had it all to himself. That he had a solid roof over his head for the first time in forever, a steady paycheck that paid a good wage, and benefits.

He'd been here a few weeks now and still felt out of place living in Crimson Point. He'd felt like an outsider for so long, he still didn't feel like he fit in here, even though all the guys at work were fellow vets and treated him like one of their own. He hadn't fully made the adjustment yet and wasn't sure he ever would.

The queen-size bed in the corner of his bedroom was

neatly made with fresh sheets he'd put on before leaving for work this morning. He knelt beside the headboard, reached up behind it and took the burner phone from its hiding spot to send a message.

Got an update. He sat on the bed and waited for the reply that came back moments later.

Made contact yet?

Not yet. But I saw the deal happen tonight.

When will you make contact?

Soon, he answered, then shut it off and put it back in its hiding spot.

In the en suite he stripped as he ran the shower, waited until the water was steaming hot before stepping under the spray. It was heaven, standing there with the strong water pressure pounding down on his head and shoulders. And so was knowing that he could stay in here until the hot water tank ran out if he felt like it.

He scrubbed himself with a fresh bar of soap that suffused the humid air with the scent of evergreen, busy formulating a plan. Running drugs through the hospital was common, but risky. To get what he wanted, he needed to approach Mark without raising suspicion. He needed an in.

Once again, the answer led him back to Bristol.

Instantly, he dismissed it out of hand. He wasn't going to stoop to involving her.

But after thinking it through from every angle, he had to admit there was no other way.

He'd been standoffish and brusque with her to protect himself up to this point, but he needed to get closer to her now. It couldn't be helped.

He ruthlessly squashed the shot of guilt about using her that way. He'd kept his end of the bargain. He didn't owe her anything, as long as she didn't get hurt. And this chance... was too important to let it pass him by.

If he had to exploit her to get what he needed, then that's what he'd do.

ELEVEN

"Whoops, hold up there a second." Bristol stopped her patient to adjust the back of her hospital robe and do up the ties more securely to cover the back of her. Then for good measure, she slipped another over top of it, with the front facing the opposite way. "Can't have you giving everyone in the hallway a thrill with a free peepshow. It'd be anarchy."

The elderly woman cackled as Bristol helped her forward and handed her the quad cane she used for stability. "Never know, they might enjoy it."

"Probably some would, yeah, which is exactly why I wanted to protect your modesty."

"You're a gem."

"I try."

"All right," Ethel announced, shuffling for the door Bristol rushed to open. "I'm off. See you next time, dear."

"You bet. I'll be here," Bristol said brightly.

As soon as she closed the door behind Ethel she stood there for a long moment, eyes shut. So far, today's shift had sucked.

Ethel had been coming in for regular scans and ultrasounds since her first irregular mammogram three years ago. She loved to joke around, seemed to enjoy chatting with Bristol during their appointments, and her good humor had been a godsend for not only her, but all the staff who came into contact with her as well.

Yet despite everything modern medicine had done for Ethel—initial detection of the cancer, the mastectomies, chemo and radiation and all the hell that came with them—it had bought her time, but ultimately hadn't been enough to save her.

The cancer was back with a vengeance. Previous ultrasounds showed it had already spread to her lungs and liver. Today, Bristol had found a large metastatic tumor on Ethel's T7 and T8 vertebrae that confirmed the disease had spread to her bones.

It sucked. Sucked so bad.

Ethel had taken the news from the radiologist with a stoicism that had made tears prick the back of Bristol's eyes. Even though she had to already be in terrible pain. And even though she must be terrified of what was coming.

Bristol opened her eyes, swallowed the burning lump in her throat and pulled herself together. This was part of the job. There were more patients waiting. She could cry later if need be. She needed to keep working on coping with the hard parts in a healthy way. It wasn't something she'd mastered yet.

She texted Cassie quickly. *Up for a beach walk later and some wine while we watch the sunset together?*

The response came moments later. *Sounds so romantic, but I'm not into you like that. Sorry.*

Ha. Cute. You don't do it for me either, btw. Well?

I'm tied up at work for a while yet. Text you when I'm free.

She sent back a thumbs-up, pushing back the stab of disappointment. She was a big girl. She could get a glass of wine at the pub by herself and watch the sunset after if Cassie couldn't make it.

After tidying the ultrasound room and clearing her head, she put on her professional demeanor and went out into the hall to get her next patient.

The rest of her shift passed quickly. She finished only a few minutes late, said goodnight to the radiologist, and made her way to the staffroom to get her things. Outside, the summer air was balmy and warm, the sun slanting rays of deep gold through the tall evergreens on the bank above the west side of the parking lot.

She got into her car and drove straight into town instead of going home to change, and parked in the lot beside the Sea Hag. The gorgeous weather had lots of people out enjoying the beach.

The bar was busy inside as usual, but she managed to find a table in the corner by the wall of windows overlooking the beach. In the distance, the sun was a huge orange circle almost touching the water, casting its brilliant rays across the waves. Attempting to put Ethel from her mind, she ordered a large glass of white and the summer salad that came with local organic greens, fresh peach slices, heirloom tomatoes, chilled prawns, and a sprinkling of toasted, chopped pistachios.

She let her mind wander as she enjoyed her meal, all the crisp, cool ingredients, an explosion of flavor and textures in her mouth. The tide was out, exposing a wide expanse of damp sand for people to walk along. She stared out at the hypnotic, rolling waves hitting the edge of it, her mind going back to Ethel. Then Eric.

And TJ.

She thought about how incredible he'd looked all cleaned up. She almost hadn't recognized him, but that full, neatly groomed goatee and short haircut really did it for him. Or really did it for her.

She wondered how he was. Whether he was settling in, and how the job was going. She wanted him to succeed. Wanted him to be happy here. Maybe one day when he felt more comfortable, they could even be friends and hang out on occasion.

Or maybe they would even have a glass of wine and watch the sunset together.

"Will there be anything else for you?"

She blinked up at the server standing next to the table. "No, I'm—Actually, you know what? I think I'll have the dark chocolate tart."

The menu said it came with a fresh puree made of local raspberries and Chantilly cream. How could she pass up that combo? She deserved a rich, comforting dessert after the day she'd had.

"Good choice. Coming right up."

Bristol scanned the room idly as she sipped her wine, and her heart jumped when her gaze landed on a familiar figure sitting at the bar with his back to her.

She resisted the impulse to call out his name or go over to say hi, contenting herself with watching TJ instead. He seemed to enjoy being a loner. And based on their previous interactions, she was fairly certain her presence wouldn't be all that welcome.

He was sitting all alone at the bar as he finished his meal, watching a ballgame on the TV. The back of him looked almost as good as the front did, with those broad shoulders tapering down to a strong back and a tight behind. His snug T-shirt clung to the muscles across his shoulders and down either side of his spine. Construction was definitely working for him too.

"Here you are." The server set her dessert in front of her. "Enjoy."

"I will, thanks. Hey, can you do me a favor? Add that gentleman's tab to mine? The one in the black shirt at the bar." She indicated TJ with a nod. "But don't tell him it was me. Just say it's been paid for."

"Sure. I'll be right back with the bill."

Her dessert was presented beautifully and probably tasted as amazing as it looked, but she was too distracted by TJ to enjoy it properly. It was gone before she even realized it, and then the server was there with the bill and the card machine. Bristol paid the double tab and was just finishing the last sip of her wine when TJ stood and reached into his back pocket for his wallet as if he were going to pay his own bill.

The bartender leaned over and said something to him, probably that his bill had been paid.

TJ stopped, then looked around.

Oh, shit.

She quickly looked out the window. But too late. He'd already spotted her.

And when that dark gaze landed on her, she swore it got harder to breathe.

She smiled at him and raised a hand to give him a friendly wave, ordering herself to stop getting all fluttery over a guy she didn't even know. Not really.

Except it felt like she did. And she couldn't remember the last time she'd been so attracted to anyone.

His expression was just short of frosty as he slowly turned

and made his way toward her. Her heartrate sped up, every feminine cell in her body sitting up at attention. "Hi," she said before he could, because she was nervous and couldn't stop herself. "Just stopped in for some dinner?" She took the final sip of wine, her mouth suddenly dry.

He nodded, his gaze moving over her lilac-colored scrubs and lingering on her chest for an extra moment in a way that made her pulse trip. Although to be fair, maybe he was looking at her ID badge, and she was just a dirty bird. "Did you pay my bill?"

She swallowed twice to get the wine down. "I—"

"Look, I appreciate the thought, but I don't need any more charity from you. You've done more than enough already." He opened his wallet as if he was going to take out money to pay her back.

"Don't. Please." Blood rushed to her cheeks. He wasn't being rude, but she was embarrassed for making him uncomfortable. And it was so incredibly annoying to be attracted to someone who was so cold to her. "It was nothing, really. And you weren't supposed to find out it was me."

Something close to amusement warmed the inky depths of his eyes. "But I did. And it wasn't that hard to figure out."

She grinned. "No, I guess not. I'm not exactly stealthy." She waved his money away. "Seriously, please."

"All right," he relented, although she could tell he felt awkward accepting it. "Thanks."

"My pleasure. Here, please sit." She gestured to the empty chair across from her. "I promise I won't make any more demands of you."

He hesitated a moment, then pulled the chair out and lowered his long, lean frame into it. Up close, the size and power of him hit her all over again. She tried not to stare at the bulge of his biceps or the roped muscles in his forearms.

And those eyes. Dark and rich as black coffee, rimmed with thick black lashes. The full goatee looked amazing on him, framing his mouth and giving him an almost dangerous edge. It was hard not to stare at his lips, too, or wonder what they would feel like on hers. Hard and masterful, she bet.

Yep, you're a dirty bird.

She mentally shook herself, a little amazed that he'd accepted her invitation. "So, how are things? Getting settled okay? Job's going well?" She hadn't meant to fire three back-to-back questions at him like a machine gun, but she was all nervous and jittery.

"Things are good."

The answer was vague, but his voice was as gorgeous as the rest of him. Deep and dark enough to send a pleasurable shiver up her spine. "I'm glad." She was thrilled that he'd taken the opportunity to turn his life around.

"You work at the hospital?"

"Yes. I'm an ultrasound tech." And she could sure use some company after the day she'd had.

"Ah. So you…scan babies and all that."

"It's a common misconception that we do mostly OB scans. We actually do a ton of other things like check for tumors and gall or kidney stones, clots. Today I did a scrotal scan."

He winced.

"Good thing, too, because this poor guy had a testicular torsion that required emergency surgery."

Oh, God, the look on his face. "That sounds…eventful."

"Yes. I assist with prostate and breast biopsies too."

Humor glinted in the depths of his eyes. "What kind of hours do you work?"

She shrugged. "It varies. Mostly I work regular day shifts,

but we all do the occasional weekend and take on-call shifts too. I got called in last night due to a perforated appendix."

He nodded but didn't say anything more.

Now that they'd exhausted the obvious small talk topics, he didn't seem interested in keeping the conversation going, which wasn't exactly a surprise. Time to change the subject, because she didn't want him to go yet, and she was sure he was itching to.

"Isn't the view amazing?" She glanced out the window, shook her head to try and clear away the vision of that hard body pressing hers flat against the wall. Or a bed. "I'll never get tired of it. Not sure if you've had much of a chance to explore yet, but about a half mile down that way, there's a trail that winds up into the woods, and there's a fantastic lookout point at the top. Do you like hiking?"

Eric had loved it, but then Rangers were pretty much always outdoorsy-types.

"I don't mind it."

Jeez, he really sucked at making conversation. "Or the lighthouse. There are great trails leading up to it too. You should definitely check it out while the weather is good."

"I'll keep that in mind." His stare held hers, setting off a rush of heat deep in her belly.

She took a hurried sip of her water. Why was her throat so damned dry all of a sudden?

He eased back in his chair a little, finally seeming more relaxed. And good *lord* the man was nice to look at. "So how come you're eating over here in the corner all by yourself?"

She shrugged. "Needed a change of scenery and a decent meal after work, and Cassie was busy. So I took myself on a date."

He nodded once and kept studying her, and something

about his gaze made it seem like he could see inside her head. "Tough day at the office?"

Okay, he was perceptive. "Yes, actually. But the view, the meal, and the last-minute company have done the trick." She toasted him with her water glass.

"You sure it's not the wine?"

Her lips twitched at his dry humor, glad that he was thawing out a little. "A glass or two of wine never hurts on days like this."

He looked away from her to glance around the bar, and as though someone had flipped a switch, his expression shifted. The warmth she'd glimpsed in his face disappeared in an instant, replaced by an unreadable mask. "Well, I should get going."

"Of course." She tried not to feel dismissed.

He stood. Paused to look down at her for a second, and a tingle rippled through her. "Thanks for dinner."

"You're welcome. Bye." Her gaze lingered on him until he disappeared out the door.

Bristol let out a sigh and finished her ice water in a single gulp. It did nothing to cool the sudden heat suffusing her body.

TWELVE

Bristol finished up the last of her patient charts and logged out of her computer for the night, stretching her arms over her head with a satisfied smile. After the longest week in forever, it was finally Friday night. The summer weather was still glorious ahead of the storm front expected to hit over the weekend, and she had two whole days off ahead of her to spend doing whatever she wanted. Including nothing, if that's what she chose.

"Looks like someone's excited for the weekend to start."

She turned to find Brandon standing in the doorway in his paramedic uniform, grinning at her. "You know it. Are you outta here shortly too?" He'd only returned to work last year, having battled his way back from severe PTSD after being captured and held prisoner in Yemen during a deployment as a PJ. Then the whole ordeal with his partner, Jaia. She was happy that he seemed to be doing well and was certain that Jaia was a big part of the reason why.

"I wish. Nah, I'm just hanging out here waiting to find out whether we're transporting a combative patient to another hospital."

"Ooh, fun."

He chuckled. "Never a dull moment. What are you doing here so late?"

"Covered for another tech and just finished up some admin stuff I was behind on. You guys are training this weekend, right?" Their Pararescue unit was based in Portland.

"Yep. With the storm moving in, we'll be busy."

"I bet. How is Jaia, by the way? And don't say anything to her, but I'm thinking of coming to the book club event next weekend. I'm not what you'd call a hard-core reader, but I'm all for meeting up with my ladies and talking about books and life stuff over a glass of wine. Or two, I'm not fussy." She hadn't been to one of their events yet, but the group sounded really fun. Not all stuffy and pedantic like some book clubs she'd heard about.

"You should go. This next one's some kind of fancy tea party in Beckett and Sierra's garden. Jayne Eyre theme, I think she said."

"Ohh, I read that one in college. Loved it." Beckett and Sierra apparently lived in the most gorgeous Victorian heritage home overlooking the water. And who didn't love a proper tea party with scones and tea and pretty plates set in a garden? Jaia also made the best authentic masala chai in the entire universe. Once you tried it, there was no point in having chai anywhere else, because it was bound to be a huge disappointment. "All right, I'll message her."

"Good." He glanced away, lifted his chin at someone down the hallway. "Sorry, gotta go. Duty calls."

"Yes, go. And don't take any crap from that patient." Not that she was worried. With his training and experience, and after all he'd been through, he could more than handle himself with a violent patient.

"I won't," he called back, already out of sight.

She grabbed her stuff and headed outside to the parking lot with a spring in her step. It was getting dark out, and she was starving. When she got home, she was starting her weekend off right by slipping into a hot bath and then curling up on the couch with a pizza to watch a movie she'd been wanting to see that had just released to streaming. Tomorrow morning, she'd get groceries for a few days in case the storm was bad enough that they lost power.

Because she'd come in at an odd hour to cover for the other tech, her car was parked far away from her normal spot, in a little alcove tucked into an odd-shaped pocket in the southeast corner of the lot. There were no lights there, so she pulled out her phone in preparation to turn on the flashlight app.

Three seconds later, she jerked to a halt when she spotted two men standing off near the tree line edging the lot. They stopped talking, their heads whipping toward her, and her heart jolted when she realized it was TJ talking to…Mark?

Her gaze dipped to the small bag in TJ's hand. "What are you doing?" she blurted. She was not imagining this.

He shoved it into his pocket. "You shouldn't be here."

She glanced from him to Mark and back again, outrage shooting through her. He was buying drugs? Buying drugs *here*? After everything she and others had done to help him turn his life around? "Really?" she accused, fighting the wobble in her voice. Dammit, she would not cry.

"What is this?" Mark said, edging back a step.

Her gaze snapped to him. Narrowed. How dare he turn out to be a dealer? "He moved here to get his life back together," she told him, anger and disappointment flooding her in equal measure. How could TJ give up his chance and throw it all away with everything he had going for him here?

TJ's expression hardened as he stared at her. "You need to go. Now."

She held her ground, refusing to look away. Damn him. She felt sick to her stomach. "I can't believe you."

"Enough." Mark spun toward her, raising his arm.

A gasp stuck in her throat when she saw the gun pointing at her. She froze in place, too afraid to move, her gaze glued to the barrel of the weapon.

"Hey, easy," TJ said in a low voice, holding his hands up in a gesture of surrender when Mark swung the weapon toward him. "There's no need for that. She doesn't know anything."

"Did you set me up?" Mark took a nervous step backward, his gaze darting to her.

"No."

"Then what the fuck is she doing here?" He jerked the gun back on her.

"She doesn't know anything, man, just in the wrong place at the wrong time. Put it away."

How could TJ be so calm? Bristol retreated a step, mouth dry, heart beating a hundred miles an hour. *Oh my God. Oh my God—*

TJ moved so fast Bristol didn't even understand what was happening until Mark was on the ground and TJ had the gun in his hand.

He turned and raced toward her. "Run!" he shouted.

Eyes wide, she spun around and bolted, the awful crawling sensation at the back of her neck telling her she was being chased by someone else. Not daring to risk a look over her shoulder to find out, she ran straight for her car, her legs like jelly, the sound of TJ's pounding footsteps on the asphalt almost as loud as the thudding of her heart in her ears.

Her eyes had finally adjusted enough to the darkness for

her to be able to see her car. She fished her keys out of her pocket and fumbled to hit the unlock button. The taillights flashed. She raced to the driver's side, ripped the door open and jumped inside. Then let out a yelp when the passenger door flew open and TJ hopped in, slamming his door shut.

"Go!" he snapped, twisting around in his seat to look behind them.

She made the mistake of looking in the rearview mirror and saw two shadows racing toward them.

Reaching for her seatbelt, Bristol frantically started the engine and put the car in reverse. The car jerked backward. TJ grunted as he hit the dash.

She winced. "Sorry—"

"Go, go," he commanded, still looking behind them.

She yanked the transmission into drive and floored it. The tires skipped for a moment before they found traction and shot them forward. She sped for the parking lot exit, casting a terrified glance in the rearview. A pickup was swerving around some parked cars where she'd been moments before, chasing after them.

"Which way do I go?" she demanded, her heart stuck so far up her throat she was about to choke on it.

"Turn right," TJ ordered.

She put her blinker on without thinking and made the turn as fast as she dared, tires squealing in protest, speeding for the light up ahead. Thankfully it stayed green. "Which way?"

The pickup turned out of the parking lot and barreled after them.

"Head for the highway. Fast." His voice was clipped, the tension rolling off him palpable, making her heart slam harder against her ribs.

A hundred questions flooded her brain but she shelved them all, focused solely on keeping control of her car and trying to lose the truck behind them while not getting killed in the process.

Brittle silence filled the interior as she raced toward the next intersection. Every time she looked in the rearview, the truck was still back there. And it seemed like it was getting closer every second, even though she was doing thirty above the speed limit.

"Faster," TJ ordered.

She gritted her teeth and pushed down harder on the accelerator, her little car hurtling toward the intersection at a speed she was far from comfortable with. But the light ahead was still red when they got close, leaving her no choice but to ease up on the gas.

Turn. Come on, turn green!

"What the hell? Don't slow down!" he barked.

"The light's red," she shouted. "I'm not getting us T-boned!"

"Fuck the light, *drive!*"

THIRTEEN

Rattled, fighting every instinct that screamed at her to obey the red light, she hit the gas and turned her blinker on as she neared the intersection.

"What the hell are you doing?"

"Trying not to get us *killed*," she snapped back, cringing as she reached the intersection. Calling a hail Mary, she hit the hazard light button in case it might help stop someone from hitting them.

"Go, go!" TJ yelled.

She shot through the red light at a terrifying clip, cringing, and smothering a squeal as she made the turn. "I am!" Horns blared all round her, tires screeching as cars swerved to avoid slamming into them.

"And stop indicating your every goddamned move to the guys chasing us!" He punched the hazard button to shut the lights off.

"Well, I'm *sorry* if I'm not doing it right," she snapped back, gripping the wheel with white-knuckled fingers as she tore up the hill. "It's my first car chase, and I'm just a little bit stressed right now—so cut me some damned slack!"

The car directly ahead of them was moving too slow. She shoulder-checked, automatically flicked on her blinker before she could stop herself. "Shoot," she muttered, drowning out TJ's outraged exclamation as she shut it off.

Behind them the truck had run the red light too. It was speeding up the hill, its more powerful engine closing the distance at a terrifying rate.

"Cut around the green car up ahead and turn right. And don't you dare use your turn signal," TJ warned.

Huffing out a flustered breath, Bristol focused intently on the road. She passed the green car, did another quick shoulder check, and managed to zip back in front of it without indicating. She gave a mental shout and fist pump, feeling like a total badass for breaking so many traffic laws while fleeing for her life. If she survived this, Cassie would never believe what she'd just done.

"Don't stop," TJ said, his voice clipped as he looked out the back window. "They're still right on us."

But they had another problem. There was a lineup of traffic stopped at the next light, about fifty yards ahead. "Uhhh…"

"Go left. Now," he bit out.

It went against every instinct and everything she'd been taught about driving, but self-preservation took precedence. She yanked the wheel hard left.

Her little car whipped around the turn, tires screeching as the back end fishtailed slightly. Biting back a curse as she fought to regain control of the steering, she sped up the hill toward the freeway, the short side street she'd turned onto clear of traffic. So far, at least.

A glance in the mirror moments later showed the pickup was nowhere in sight. She felt a wave of mingled hope and relief wash over her. "Do you see them?" Maybe she'd lost them. Her heartrate slowed a fraction as she divided her attention between the road and the mirrors.

TJ swiveled in his seat to look behind them both ways. "No. But that doesn't mean the coast is—"

She let out a yelp and slammed the brakes when the pickup suddenly veered out of a cross street directly in front of them. Yanking the wheel to the left, she narrowly avoided slamming into the back of the truck. The sudden turn sent them careening across the other lane, barely missing another car coming in the opposite direction as it crested the hill.

But the truck couldn't handle the angle of the turn. Out of the corner of her eye she saw it flip onto its side and fly across the road to slam into a power pole.

"Oh my God…" She drove past it.

"Pull over," TJ said.

She shot him a disbelieving look. "Are you insane?"

"Do it. Hurry."

Her gut commanded her to get as far away from the situation as possible, but the urgency in his voice gave her pause. Battling with herself, she hit the brakes and yanked the car over to the shoulder. Watched in shock as he unstrapped and hopped out to run toward the truck. Maybe they were badly hurt, and he was going to try to help them?

She got out too and stood on the shoulder, phone ready, thumb hovering over the emergency call button just in case. Should she call the police? Get back in the car and the hell away from this insanity?

TJ ran up to the flipped truck. The windshield and windows were all smashed from the impact. Two men were trying to crawl out of the cab. One made it out, hit the pavement like a landed fish, and lay there while his buddy crawled out, bleeding from his head.

Bristol edged a little closer, gaze riveted on the men. They lay side by side on the road under the faint light from the broken streetlamp. TJ ran up to them, knelt and secured their hands behind their backs with plastic zip ties that he'd apparently been carrying in his pocket—because maybe he tied people up on a regular basis?

Bristol stopped a few dozen feet away and hovered there in uncertainty, not knowing what to do, still tempted to ditch TJ, just jump in her car and not look back. But thinking about her brother made her stay put. *Rangers never leave a man behind.*

Not that she was a Ranger. She was an ultrasound tech. And she was mad as hell at all three of these men, for different reasons.

"Who the fuck are you?" TJ growled to the men as he took pictures of their faces and checked their pockets.

Neither of them answered, their expressions mutinous.

"*Talk*," TJ said to the guy who wasn't bleeding, digging a knee into his back. It occurred to Bristol that it was weird neither of them seemed to have any ID or phones on them. Maybe they were in the truck.

When it was abundantly clear neither of them was interested in talking, TJ stood and stalked around to the up-facing side of the truck.

Bristol edged backward, shifting her focus back to the bound prisoners lying on the side of the road. The shock of everything was starting to wear off, rapidly being replaced by a rising tide of anger.

Her breathing turned shallow and choppy. These men had chased them. Endangered her life and forced her to take emergency evasive measures that could have gotten her or other innocent people seriously hurt or killed.

TJ rummaged around in the cab of the truck, grabbed

something, and stuffed it in his pockets. "Let's go," he said, walking toward her.

Bristol was mad at him too, but her gaze swung back to the bound men, her anger rising until it was hard to breathe. Those…those *assholes*. God knows what would have happened if they'd caught up to her and TJ, but it wouldn't have been pretty, and they were also involved in whatever illegal deal she'd witnessed at the hospital.

Her temper snapped.

"You know what? *No*." They weren't getting away with this. No way.

She stomped toward them, spotted a plastic water bottle lying on the shoulder on the way. She snatched it up, planted her feet, and hurled it as hard as she could at the man closest to her.

Instead of smashing him in the head, the nearly empty bottle bounced harmlessly off his back and rolled into the middle of the road, but she felt vindicated anyway. "I hope you have the worst whiplash *ever*," she spat at them, vibrating with indignation.

"Okay, feisty pants. Let's go." TJ grabbed her by the arm and dragged her away, hustling her back toward her car. "Gimme the keys," he said, holding out his free hand expectantly.

No traffic had come by yet. She couldn't decide if that was lucky or not.

She yanked her arm out of his grasp. "I can drive." On the one hand she didn't want to spend another minute in his company. But on the other she wanted answers too badly to leave.

"No, you really can't. And you're in shock. Hand them over."

Was she still in shock? Maybe.

Reluctantly handing the keys over, she realized her hand was shaking. Actually, all of her was shaking. Okay, yes, it appeared she was still in a bit of shock. But for sure she was still mad as hell.

"Get in," TJ said, giving her a little push toward the passenger side. She slid into the seat, fumbled to get her seatbelt on as he roared away from the accident site. He sped away up the hill, phone to his ear.

She bit back a warning about it not being safe to talk on the phone without a hands-free device, listened as he reported the accident and hung up. "Who were they? Why were they chasing us?" she asked.

"I don't know who they are."

The clipped answer made her want to scream. "That's it? That's all you have to say about what just happened?"

"Yes."

Her eyes flared wide in outrage at his dismissive tone. She absolutely wasn't going to let this go, but fighting with him now wasn't going to get her anywhere. Besides, the way he was watching behind them so closely made her afraid that more people might be after them than she realized.

"Where are we going? Am I allowed to know that at least?" she asked as he reached the freeway entrance and merged them into the light traffic heading south. Her breathing was still a bit choppy. The rush of anger on top of the adrenaline burst was fading now, leaving her a little dizzy.

Calm down. Breathe.

But the tension coming off TJ was palpable, winding the knot in the pit of her stomach tighter. "Home."

She looked over at him sharply. "You know where I live?"

He didn't answer, and she was too drained to push. She would conserve her energy for when they got to her place, because she had *plenty* more to say to him when they did. She was so angry and disappointed she wanted to shake him. After all she'd done, after all Beckett had done to help him and give him a chance at a better life, he was either using drugs or dealing them. Or both.

She swallowed against the rise of nausea in her belly.

She'd believed in him. Trusted him because of his ties to Eric. Maybe she was just stupid. Cassie was right—she should have left this alone.

TJ passed the turn to her townhouse complex. She frowned. "I thought you said—"

"Quiet."

She glared a hole through his face for a long moment, but when he didn't react, settled for folding her arms and staring through the window as he drove them to the north side of town. In a quiet residential neighborhood, he turned down a dead-end road and pulled into the driveway of a cute white bungalow.

"Where are we?" She was starting to get nervous. Mentally calculated an escape route in case she had to flee, and the odds of whether she would be able to outrun him. The answer was a disheartening no.

"My place."

He lived *here*? The place was brand new, and she knew what properties sold for around here.

Why had he brought her to his house? Too afraid to ask, she edged as far away from him as possible, her fingers closing around the door handle, preparing to make a break for it.

"For Chrissake, I'm not gonna hurt you." He sounded offended as well as irritated. But what was she supposed to think? She'd literally caught him in the middle of a drug deal and could ID him to the police, bad guys had chased them, and now he was basically kidnapping her.

He parked in a detached garage and turned off the engine. "Let's get inside." He sounded as happy about her being here as she felt.

"Just take me home."

He gave a low, humorless laugh that made the back of her neck prickle. "Oh, I wish."

Alarm streaked through her. She gripped the door handle, staring at him while her heart beat an erratic tattoo against her ribs. "What does that mean? Why can't I just go home?"

He paused to look at her, those deep, dark eyes burning with frustration in the overhead garage light, along with something that looked an awful lot like resignation. "Because you just put targets on both our backs."

FOURTEEN

"Targets? Targets for what? Who?" Bristol's voice had a shrill edge to it as TJ ushered her inside the back door and locked up behind them.

Ignoring her for the moment, he immediately moved around the house, pulling all the blinds down on the windows, then retrieved the hidden phone from his bedroom. His day had just gone off a cliff in the most spectacular way imaginable and taken him and Bristol along with it.

It wasn't her fault, but they were both in danger now, and he didn't know how much to tell her. For her own good. Goddammit, why couldn't she ever seem to leave him alone?

He typed out a quick message to his contact as he returned to the main living area of the house. Bristol was still standing where he'd left her.

She had wrapped her arms around her body, a subconscious attempt to comfort herself. "TJ, say something. You're scaring me."

He suppressed a sigh. Yeah, she should be scared. But not for the reasons she thought.

When he didn't answer right away, her expression shifted

from worried to annoyed. Her fists slid down to plant on her hips, her chin coming up. "Were you selling or buying from Mark?"

He scrubbed a hand over his face. She had no idea that she'd just blown a critical meeting that had been more than a year in the making, and he didn't know what protocol to follow now. "Neither."

"Don't you dare lie to me. Not now."

"I'm not."

She gave him a look that said she didn't believe him. "Then what did I see? You guys were just catching up, having a little chat in the shadows of the hospital parking lot? I saw him give you something, and you put it in your pocket. Was it drugs?"

Yep.

He gestured to the living room couch under the long, now-covered window at the front of the house. "Sit."

"I'll stand, thanks."

"Fine, then I'll sit." He dropped onto the couch, let out a deep breath. "I'm not an addict or a dealer."

Her posture didn't change, and he could tell she still thought he was full of shit. Which made sense, considering what had happened with her brother. Addicts were consummate liars. "Then what just happened?"

"You blew my cover."

Shock filled her eyes. "Cover?"

"Yes, and the entire op with it. So now we're both in danger."

She stared at him, her face going slack with surprise. "Op? Cover?" she repeated.

He nodded once, jaw flexing. "I'm undercover DEA. Or was, until about twenty minutes ago." What an epic clusterfuck. Everything he'd done up until now, everything the agency had put in place to get him to this point, had been destroyed the moment she'd stumbled upon that meeting.

Her face went a little pale, and her arms fell to her sides. "Maybe I will sit down," she said quietly, and walked over to sink onto the wide easy chair off to one side of the room. "DEA," she said after a minute, staring at him in disbelief.

"Yeah."

"So you were…just posing as an unhoused person?"

"Yes." It had been way rougher than he'd expected. He couldn't even think about all that time and all the hardships being a total waste. The agency *had* to get the intel they needed from the evidence he'd gathered tonight. Otherwise, everything he'd sacrificed had been for nothing.

"Why?" she asked, sounding aghast.

He understood her confusion. "Best way to see what's really going on in the drug scene at the street level is to live on them and stay under the radar."

"And why were you meeting with Mark? How is he involved?"

"He's a confidential informant who's been giving us insider intel for the past eight months." A growl of frustration built in his chest. They'd worked so hard to win his trust.

They'd been so close to getting in contact with the critical asset Mark had access to. Been within weeks of having enough intel to execute a raid on the main facility the drugs were shipped through after reaching this part of the coast. It would have put a major dent in the cartel's operations in the region and stopped hundreds of millions of dollars of potentially lethal drugs from hitting the streets of American cities and towns.

It would have saved thousands of lives.

"So he runs drugs through the hospital? For the cartel?" Bristol asked.

She looked and sounded so disappointed. "Yes."

Before she could ask anything else, his burner phone rang. "Yeah," he answered, not bothering to get up and have this conversation in another room. Like it or not, Bristol was part of this now, and at least temporarily his responsibility.

"What happened?" his handler, Diana, asked. She was one of only a handful of agents he reported to. His team was small because of a suspected leak in the DEA chain. Someone on the inside might be feeding intel to the cartel working this part of the coast.

"An acquaintance saw me meeting with the CI." He was acutely aware of Bristol watching him, hanging on his every word.

"And your cover?" Diana asked.

"Burned." To fucking ash.

"That's unfortunate. The timing especially."

He smothered a snort. "Yeah."

"Anything else I need to know?"

"Two guys working with the CI chased us in a pickup. They crashed west of the 101 near Crimson Point, with minor injuries. I secured them and called the cops." He reached into his back pocket to extract the IDs he'd found in their wallets, gave their names and listed addresses. Though chances were good they were all fake. "I've also got their phones. I haven't had a chance to look at them yet."

"Good. I'll send someone over to collect them. Where are you now?"

"Home." It still felt weird to say that. Not that it would be home after tonight. His entire world had just been upended again.

"And this acquaintance? How much does he or she know?" Diana asked.

"She knows I'm DEA. She's here, by the way."

A startled pause answered him. "You took her home with you?"

"Couldn't be helped under the circumstances." There was no way he would have left her to fend for herself in the parking lot or ditch her after the crash. Mark was still out there somewhere. If he'd reported what happened to his contact in the cartel, there could be others after them right now.

"Are you secure?"

"Secure enough for the moment."

"All right. Sit tight while I pass this intel along. I'll contact you with further instructions." She ended the call without a goodbye. Diana was always all business.

He lowered the phone to his lap, meeting Bristol's gaze. Anxiety radiated off her like a forcefield, and he couldn't blame her. He tried to think of something he could say to reassure her, but he couldn't do that without lying, and he'd already done enough of that. To keep her safe, he needed her to trust him.

"What did they say?" she asked.

Having her in his personal space felt strange. And it didn't help that his every sense was attuned to her, from the visual picture she presented to the slightly husky edge to her voice to her subtle, sweet scent permeating the air between them. Her presence seemed to fill the entire room, infusing it with her essence until there was no escape.

"They're looking into our situation. But for the meantime, we're stuck together." In this tiny house with only one bed. Though if he had to sleep before she was cleared to leave, he was definitely bunking on the couch. He was way too keyed up to trust himself to be near a bed with her.

She rubbed her hands up and down her thighs, and he

could practically hear the wheels turning in her head. "For how long?"

"Not sure." Staying here together wasn't a long-term solution. This place wasn't even remotely what he would consider secure. But for the moment the cartel network didn't know where they were. That was a point in their favor. How long that flimsy illusion of safety lasted, he didn't know. Probably not long. Days, not weeks. If that.

"How bad is this?" she said softly after a long beat of silence. "Our situation."

He felt a twinge of sympathy. He'd never dreamed of being in this predicament, and hated that she was tangled up in it with him. She was innocent, should never have wound up in this kind of danger.

And she was also a huge potential distraction when he couldn't afford to be distracted.

"You want me to be honest?"

She nodded, eyes grave behind her glasses, face pinched. He had the strongest, dangerous urge to go to her, gather her up on his lap, and hold her until she felt safe.

"About as bad as it gets," he answered instead, seeing no way around it. She was too intelligent not to piece everything together on her own, and he wouldn't insult that intellect or whatever shaky trust she had left in him by lying.

Her eyes flinched slightly. "So you mean we... Our lives are still in danger?"

He wished to hell he could say no. But looking into those sharp blue-gray eyes, he had no choice but to tell her the truth. "Yes."

She blanched a little and leaned back into the cushion behind her. "Oh, God."

Yeah. "We're safe here for now," he said, wanting to reassure her as much as possible. "The agency knows where we are and will work out another location for us if necessary until they can confirm we're in the clear." He leaned forward, stretched out a hand across the coffee table. "I'm gonna need your phone."

She shrank away from him slightly. "I need to call Cassie and let her know I'm okay."

He thought it over. Decided this once would be fine. "One call, then you give me your phone. And you can't tell her anything about what happened today, understand?"

Bristol nodded, but he shook his head, made sure he had her full attention before continuing. "Just tell her you're okay and ask her to get a bag of clothes and whatever else together for you. I'll have Beckett pick it up and bring it over."

"Why Beckett?"

"Because he was an A-Team leader, I know him personally, and I trust him." TJ would have to call him and explain everything. If anything went down, Beckett could more than handle himself and would make sure he wasn't followed on the way over.

"Cassie's a professional bodyguard and a former cop. I trust her. Couldn't I go stay with her?"

He felt even sorrier for her that she was stuck in this mess because of him. All because she'd tried to help someone she'd thought was a homeless friend of her brother's. "No. You can't involve her. Your buddy Mark knows you two are related, and after tonight the cartel will be pumping him for everything he knows. You won't be safe there, and neither would she." He didn't like it either, but Bristol was far safer being here with him.

She absorbed it all with a sober nod, then made her call. "Hi, Cas. Listen, I'm okay, and I don't want you to worry, but there's been a bit of a situation, and I need a favor." To her credit, her voice only wobbled a little. "No, I'm with TJ. But

I think I'm going to have to go dark for a while now," she said, looking at him for confirmation. Or maybe reassurance.

When he nodded, she continued, rubbing the center of her forehead with her fingertips as if she had a headache. "Can you pack a bag for me for a few days? Beckett will pick it up and bring it to me. Oh, and make sure he brings my bat."

Her bat? He could tell the conversation wasn't easy for her, could hear Cassie demanding more answers in the background. Not wanting to eavesdrop, he busied himself sending a message to Beckett to arrange delivery of the bag and bat.

"I can't give you my location, but I promise I'll tell you more when I can, okay? I'm all right, I swear." Bristol met his gaze from across the room. "TJ's got me."

Those words resonated deep in his gut, the impact of that stare cutting right through him. He heard the unspoken trust there. Felt them as both a deep connection and a solemn vow. She believed he would look out for her.

Knowing that ripped through all his emotional defenses like an armor-piercing bullet.

Yeah, he had her. Whether either of them wanted this or not. And it wasn't simply because she was Eric's sister. He had gotten her into this, and it was his responsibility to protect her.

But more than that, he wouldn't let anything happen to her because he cared about her on a deeply personal level that came with its own dangers.

He signaled at her to wrap it up. If Mark had reported her presence to his cartel contacts, it was possible they might track her phone to try and get a location.

"I gotta go now, Cass. I'll call you again as soon as I can. Love you." She ended the call, blew out a hard breath and handed over her phone.

TJ took it, shut it down and removed the battery before

setting it on the coffee table with a quiet thud that sounded loud in the stillness, then looked back up at her. "You all right?"

She was still pale. Yet still so ridiculously hot, even in her scrubs. The naughty librarian vibe of those glasses was crazy sexy on her.

"I mean…" She gave a humorless chuckle and shrugged. "I guess?"

The urge to protect her beat at him, to protect her even from her fear. "You'll be fine. I'm here, and this'll be over before you know it." He hoped.

She shook her head slowly, staring at him like she'd never seen him before.

"What?"

"Wow, you're like, *really* good at the whole undercover thing."

He would not laugh. Would not. But his lips quirked in spite of himself. She was so damned witty and sweet and unexpected.

He stood, heading for the kitchen. "You must be hungry after working so late. I'll see what I can make us to eat. Any allergies or aversions?"

"Organ meat, but unless you love liver and onions, that's probably one thing I can remove from my list of things to worry about."

He enjoyed her dry humor, especially in the face of all this. "I'm fresh out of organs."

"Good. Can I help?"

"No, I've got it. Feel free to watch some TV, try to relax."

As if either of them would be able to relax while they were sharing a roof and being hunted.

TJ busied himself in the kitchen, listening for any suspicious sounds, or for that telltale tingling in his gut that came from survival instinct. The comforting weight of his pistol pressed against his lower back as he worked, but the whole time he was acutely aware of the woman sitting just twenty feet away in the other room.

Through everything that had happened in his life, he'd never been tempted by drugs. Not once. But he was tempted by Bristol. More tempted than with any other woman he'd ever met.

Even though she was Eric's sister.

Even though he knew he would never be good enough for her.

Even though he could never deserve someone like her.

Three excellent reasons why he needed to get any intimate thoughts of her out of his damned head. Especially since they were going to be alone together in this small house until further notice.

FIFTEEN

I think I'm gonna have to go dark for a while now.

What the hell had happened? And what would Bristol even know about going dark? The very idea of it was terrifying.

Cassie hurried across the well-lit parking lot to the rear door of the Crimson Point Security building and scanned her ID. The moment the locking mechanism released she wrenched the door open and raced up the stairs, not wanting to wait for the elevator. It was after hours on a Friday night, but some of the staff would still be working.

She burst through the fire exit door and into the reception area. The front desk was empty, but down the hall she spotted the twins coming toward her.

"Whoa," Tristan said in his mellowed Kentucky accent, pausing in concern as she rushed in their direction.

"What's wrong?" Gavin asked, stopping just behind him.

They might be identical, but she knew them both well enough now to tell them apart. Their personalities were completely different.

"Bristol. She's in trouble. Is Ryder or Callum in?" She

glanced past them down the long hallway. The office doors she could see from her vantage point were all shut.

"No. Walker's here, but he's in a meeting. Here, come sit down and tell me what's going on." Tristan gestured toward the nearest office.

She didn't want to sit down, didn't want to rehash this more than once or talk about her personal business, but she couldn't very well go pound on Walker's door when he was in a meeting.

"Anything I can do?" Gavin asked her.

She shoved her frustration down. They were trying to help. "No. Thanks, though."

"Sure." He looked at his twin.

"You go ahead," Tristan told him.

Gavin nodded then looked at her again. "Let me know if you need anything."

She forced a smile. She didn't like asking other people for help, but she had no choice at the moment. "Will do. See you."

Tristan opened the office door and flicked on the lights. She went over and sat in one of the leather chairs positioned in front of the desk. He lowered his tall frame into the other one several feet away, watching her intently with concern in his green eyes. And it was genuine, which made him even hotter than he already was. It was strange, since he and Gavin were identical, but to her, Tristan was way better looking, no matter how wrong it felt to be attracted to someone she worked with.

In spite of everything, from her cynical view of the opposite sex and all the lovely trust issues that came with it, she still wasn't immune to him. It was a good thing they were work colleagues and couldn't get involved. Her taste in men was epically disastrous.

"What happened?" he asked, the overhead light making his short auburn hair glow. "Cass, seriously. Talk to me."

She relented. "I don't know, but it's bad." The hard knot in the pit of her stomach said so. It was killing her that she didn't know more, couldn't do anything when she wanted to charge over there and get to the bottom of this. "Bristol called half an hour ago to say there had been a situation. She said she was okay, that she's with TJ, but then she said she had to go dark, and asked me to pack a bag for Beckett to pick up."

He frowned. "TJ. The homeless guy who rescued Carly?"

"Yes." He saw the problem. "I don't know what happened or what she was doing with him in the first place." None of it made sense. "Going dark? Bristol?" She huffed at the ridiculousness of it. "Something's really wrong."

"Did she sound okay?"

"Mostly." More together than she should have, under the circumstances. "But I'm worried. I came straight here because I'm hoping for help with getting some answers." Before she went insane.

Tristan nodded, leaned forward and reached out for her hands. She felt a little jolt when his fingers closed around hers, heat suffusing her chilled skin. He'd never touched her before, and she didn't like the little velvet flip deep in her belly one bit. She resisted the urge to snatch her hands away, get up to pace and burn off this overload of anxious energy. He was just being kind.

"Did you contact Beckett?" he asked, now leaning close enough for her to see the light dusting of freckles across his nose and catch the scent of his cologne. Subtle, clean, and woodsy. As sexily understated as the rest of him.

She gently pulled her hands from his, feeling awkward and not liking the way her nervous system had gone haywire at the innocent contact. "Called him twice. He didn't pick up or respond to my messages. I'm hoping Walker can help."

He was CPS's intelligence expert with a million connections in the industry.

Before Tristan could answer, a door opened somewhere down the hall and voices floated out. Cassie jumped up and hurried to look out the doorway just as Walker came out of another one near the end of the hall, followed by Beckett a moment later. They both stopped when she stepped out into the hall.

"Cassie, hi," Walker said.

He was a physically imposing man in his mid-forties, his short black hair graying around the temples. He was the most reserved of the CPS management. Quiet and intensely observant, not surprising given his background in Army intelligence.

"Hi. Did you get my—" She went silent when a woman emerged from the same office. "Ivy." Walker's fiancée.

Cassie had met her several times, but didn't know her well. Though she got the feeling that very few people probably ever did. She wasn't sure what Ivy's background was, but it was also something to do with intelligence. She'd heard about some of Ivy's hacking abilities from the twins after Ivy had guided Gavin through the violent mob to save Carly during the Portland riots.

"Hey." The brunette's expression was polite enough, but it gave nothing away. Although it didn't take a genius to know what the meeting they'd just finished had been about.

Cassie's gaze swept from her to Walker, then Beckett. "You were meeting about Bristol."

"Come into my office, and we'll talk," Walker said, his deep blue eyes kind.

"I'm heading out," Beckett said, then looked over at her. "I'm supposed to pick up a bag at your place."

"I've got it in my vehicle."

"Give us a few minutes," Walker said to him, then curled a hand around Ivy's hip and kissed her temple.

For some reason, witnessing that simple gesture of affection triggered an ache deep in Cassie's chest that she quickly blocked.

"See you at home. Tell Shae I'll be there by six-thirty."

"Will do," Ivy said to him. "Although dinner might be delayed, because I heard she might be having a call with Finn."

"Ah. From Djibouti."

"The place all Marines dream of being deployed to at least once in their career," Ivy said wryly. She followed Beckett, offered Cassie an encouraging smile on the way by.

Cassie glanced over her shoulder to see Tristan still standing in the doorway of the office they'd been in. "See you."

He gave her a nod. "See you."

She followed Walker into his office. After shutting the door behind her, she took a chair in front of his desk and got straight to it.

"So, Bristol called me thirty minutes ago." She repeated what Bristol had said, still worried as hell and doing her best to appear completely calm and professional in front of one of her bosses. "Do you know anything about this TJ guy, other than he's a former Ranger who wound up on the streets?"

Walker nodded. "Beckett came in after getting a call from him around the same time as Bristol talked to you. I reached out to some contacts to verify what TJ told him, and everything checks out."

"What did he say?"

Walker waited a beat. "TJ's undercover DEA."

Shock ripped through her. It hadn't even occurred to her that he was anything but a down-on-his-luck vet, but Walker seemed convinced it was true. "You're sure?"

"Positive."

Wow. "So...that's why Ivy didn't find anything about him before when she did some digging?"

"Exactly. After he left the military, they created a whole new identity for him. But he did receive an honorable discharge from the Army, and was recruited by the DEA shortly thereafter. He's been working undercover on the streets for a while now."

Cassie leaned back in her chair and ran a hand over her face. So TJ was definitely involved with people in the drug trade. Dangerous people. "Okay, then whatever happened this afternoon with him and Bristol is related to his cover. How did she get caught up in it?" It scared her that Bristol had been dragged into whatever this was. Her stepsister was in no way prepared to deal with something like this.

"We were told he was meeting at the hospital with a confidential informant about drugs moving through the building."

Oh, God. "And Bristol stumbled right into the middle of it," she guessed.

"Looks that way. She was just in the wrong place at the wrong time and took them both by surprise. The CI got nervous, thinking TJ might have set him up. Two suspects chased him and Bristol from the hospital and were involved in a single vehicle collision minutes later. Bristol and TJ escaped without injury. The DEA is running the suspects' IDs now, looking for a match in their database."

Shit. "So where's Bristol?"

"At TJ's house."

"He has a house?" Since when? With what money? He'd barely started working.

"Beckett's company is providing it to him as part of their employment package."

Wow, Beckett really did go above and beyond for the veterans he hired. "Did Beckett know about him being undercover DEA?"

"No."

"Am I allowed to know the house's location?"

"You'll have to ask Beckett about that."

"All right, I will." She shifted in her seat, determined to stay professional and not lose her cool, but Walker was clearly only telling her certain details, and it was frustrating to say the least. "Is there anything else you can tell me?"

"That's all I know at the moment."

Cassie doubted it but maintained her composure. Whatever Walker knew, he had told her the most important things. Presumably. "Is she safe there? With him?"

"For the time being, yes."

He seemed certain about that. Cassie wasn't as confident. "She has no training."

"But he does."

Yeah, but how trustworthy was he? Just because he'd been a Ranger and served with Bristol's brother didn't mean he could be trusted with Bristol's life. "And this all means that she's currently a potential target."

"Unfortunately, yes."

"I can protect her myself."

"The CI was someone who works at the hospital with her. They know each other personally to some extent, and so it stands to reason he'll know the connection between you. The cartel involved could access your tax and financial information, including your credit card statements, and easily find out where you live. Whereas TJ's been living on the street under an assumed identity for months, without any digital fingerprints to trace."

He paused, his gaze steady and calm as she chewed on all of that. "If Ivy couldn't find much on his background, no one can. Also, the house he's staying in is registered to Beckett's company, without any way to link it to him. Not even a utility bill in his name. So Bristol is actually safer where she is. At least for now."

Cassie absorbed that for a few sobering moments. She might not like any of it, but had to agree his points were all valid and logical. Bristol's safety was all that mattered right now. "Do you have a way of contacting them?"

Bristol must have shut her phone off, because voicemail had picked up immediately when Cassie had kept calling her back.

"Just the number TJ contacted Beckett with. He used a burner."

Great. She shoved out a breath, scrubbed a hand over her mouth and chin. What the hell was she supposed to do now? Just nod, sit here, and pretend this was no big deal? Leave Bristol in TJ's questionable protection and do nothing?

"I understand this must be upsetting for you."

Upsetting? Yeah. Technically she was only a few years older than Bristol, but she was a lifetime older in terms of life experience, and she had training. "I want to protect her."

"I know." He watched her for a second. "I think you should take a few days off until this is resolved."

"No." Absolutely not. She had busted her ass to get this job, to give herself this fresh start, and as the sole female bodyguard at the firm, she had to prove herself on the daily more than the guys did. It sucked that it was necessary, but that was just how it was in this industry. "I don't want time off."

Time off would just mean empty hours for her to fill by mentally climbing the walls of her little house.

"Is Bristol close to her father?"

"Yes." Reasonably so. At least compared to Cassie's own experience.

"He'll need to be notified, then."

"Not until I know more." What was the point? It would only scare the shit out of him, and he'd barely recovered from the massive heart attack he'd suffered a little more than a year ago. There was no way she would tell him yet.

"I'm happy to inform him of the situation when the time comes if you want."

"No. It needs to come from me. Thank you, though."

"Of course. If you change your mind, just let me know." He pushed his chair back from the desk. "I don't have anything more to tell you at the moment, but let me reassure you that the firm is monitoring the situation. We'll share any pertinent intel as we get it."

If they felt it was relevant and necessary.

He didn't say that part out loud, but he didn't have to. She knew how it worked. "Thanks. I need to get going too, grab Beckett that bag for Bristol."

She rose, thanked him again on her way out and strode quickly down the hall, her mind spinning. Unable to ignore the tension in the pit of her stomach that kept reminding her that Bristol was in way over her head. And that there wasn't a damned thing Cassie could do to fix any of it.

She heard low voices down the hall and found Tristan talking to Beckett in the reception lounge. "Hey," Tristan said, pushing his tall frame away from the wall he'd been leaning against. "Everything okay?"

He'd stayed to check on her.

She forced a nod, the craziest thought passing through her brain. That if the two of them had been in Bristol and TJ's position, she wouldn't mind being forced to share a roof with him.

Which was insane and completely inappropriate, and she forcefully shoved it from her filthy mind. "What are you still doing here? I thought you left with Gavin."

"Wanted to make sure you're okay."

The little catch in her heart annoyed her. Hanging around to give her emotional support was taking the work partner thing a bit farther than she was comfortable with. He was her coworker and sometimes partner on the job. They weren't even friends. Definitely would never be more than that. Even if it wasn't wildly inappropriate, it still wasn't happening, because she was a complete disaster when it came to romantic relationships.

"I'm fine, thanks." She switched her attention to Beckett, who stood with his hands braced behind him on the counter. "You taking Bristol's stuff over to TJ's now?"

"Was planning to."

"Good, I'll go with you." She spun around and headed back to the hall before he could argue, not giving him a choice. She was going to see Bristol for herself and make sure she was okay. "Meet you out back in five."

SIXTEEN

Angel's phone chirped while he was in the middle of stirring a pot of pasta sauce on the stove. His work phone, the one only a handful of people had the number for.

He glanced over his shoulder, aware of the sudden tension in his body. Liana was stretched out on the sofa in the living room with her laptop open, busy doing more research into the latest data on experimental treatment protocols and clinical trials.

He turned the burner down as low as it would go, covered the sauce to leave it simmer, and stepped outside into the backyard, shutting the door behind him. Angling his body so that he could keep an eye on Liana, he dialed the saved number.

"Got your message," he said quietly when his contact answered. He didn't want his neighbors to overhear if they came outside.

"One of our little birdies didn't turn up for his post-meeting debrief. He hasn't made contact, and his phone's been turned off. That means he's in the wind," Hawk said. The nickname of a falcon Angel rarely had contact with.

"Which birdie?"

"Mark."

Angel called a picture of him to mind. Mid-thirties, worked a custodial job at the Crimson Point Hospital where he acted as a courier for the organization, smuggling product into and out of the place for distribution. The organization liked to "launder" its product that way, using certain healthcare professionals to help circulate it, in exchange for a healthy monetary compensation.

But Angel made a lot more than that for his particular trade.

"Any leads on his current location?" he asked.

"Yeah, but there's more. Two other birdies were arrested after being involved in a car chase and subsequent rollover near Crimson Point. One's still in custody, but the other was released. Not sure where he is at the moment, but Mark's headed up to Washington State. He made contact twenty minutes ago."

"So what do you want?" Time was ticking. If he was being tapped for this job, he wanted to handle it immediately so he could get back home to Liana as soon as possible.

"Information. I'm sending you the last location where Mark's phone pinged from. He hasn't moved in the past three hours, so it looks like he's bunking at the house. Find out what he knows and deal with him."

Deal with him.

He shot another glance at Liana, still keenly invested in whatever she was reading, a little frown of concentration creasing her forehead. They were so close to securing her the chance she needed to save her life. "What's the commission?"

"Fifty."

It was less than what he'd made from each of his last two targets, but every bit helped. And his body count was already too high for his morals to balk at adding another. All bad people the world was better off without anyway. Or so he told himself. "Are you still tracking him?"

"Yes."

"Send me the details, then at oh-two-hundred hours reverify his position. I'll handle it from there." He ended the call, ignored the prick of his conscience. This latest target was yet another lowlife the world wouldn't miss. He could almost convince himself he was making the world a better place with this work.

Even if he wasn't, it brought him one step closer to hopefully saving Liana. That made all the risks worth it.

When he stepped back inside, she looked over at him. "Everything okay?"

"Yeah, fine. Just a work thing. They're short-staffed again. You hungry?"

She hesitated a fraction of a second. "Yes."

She'd barely eaten anything over the past two days, too tired or too nauseated to be interested in food. But even feeling like shit, she would force some dinner down to make him happy. "Liar," he said softly.

Her lips twitched. "You've been working on that sauce for almost two hours. I don't want all your effort to go to waste. It smells amazing, by the way."

"Double liar."

A soft laugh escaped her, and he smiled. Thin, exhausted, and ill as she was, he could still see the gorgeous woman he'd married in her eyes and smile. "Your cooking skills have improved exponentially since you took the reins."

"That's not saying much." He'd been shit at cooking until she got sick. Must needs, and all that. "It'll be ready in ten."

"Can't wait."

They ate together in the kitchen. He helped her to the

table and served them both. She was more animated than she had been in days. They chatted about what she'd found online that afternoon, and about the plans she had for the back garden next spring.

She finished another tiny mouthful of pasta, washed it down with a small sip of water, and sat back. He prayed it stayed down. She'd lost too much weight as it was. "When we go to Zurich, let's take a week just for us to travel around first."

The comment surprised him so much he stilled with his fork inches from his mouth. "Really?"

"Yes. Who knows, maybe some clean mountain air will revitalize me." She reached across the table to grasp his free hand, a gentle smile curving her mouth. "You've been burning the candle at both ends for so long, taking care of me and the house in addition to traveling for work and taking on extra night shifts. Carrying the weight of having to make enough to pay all the bills until I can work again. Mountain air would do you some good too."

Guilt slithered through his stomach. He smothered it. Whatever lies he'd told her to hide the truth, he had made the right decision and would do it all again. And again. "I'd love that."

"Good." She squeezed his hand, sat back, and forked up more pasta. "Now polish off everything on your plate. Need to keep your strength up if you're going to be carting me all over the Swiss countryside, up and down mountains like Peter in *Heidi*."

"Sounds like fun."

Her eyes sparkled, and seeing that will to live in her galvanized him. He would keep killing targets until he had the money they needed, even if it damned his soul to hell.

After dinner, they watched a movie in the living room,

stretched out on the sofa together with her lying between his legs, her back propped against his chest and her head resting against his shoulder. Her hair smelled like the vanilla shampoo she loved.

She made it almost until the end before falling asleep. Angel stayed like that, holding her until after the credits rolled, tracking the slow, even rise and fall of her chest. Until after the screen went black and the sky outside the picture window went dark.

He carried her to bed. Tucked her in securely and left a note on the bedside table in case she woke after he was gone, though he doubted she would. The level of exhaustion she suffered would keep her asleep until morning.

Once the house was secure, he climbed into his car, checked for Hawk's latest message, and then set off north for the Washington State border.

At two in the morning, he got the confirmed location. Twenty minutes later, he parked several blocks away and went to reconnoiter the target on foot. The run-down rancher was dark. Both front windows were boarded up. One car sat in the driveway.

Out of view of anyone who might be looking out a window, he tugged on gloves and a black balaclava that covered most of his face. A dog barked somewhere in the distance as he hopped the chain link fence into the backyard.

He picked the lock on the back door in seconds and slipped inside. The house was dark and still, a musty smell mixing with the acrid stench of weed.

Silenced weapon in hand, he crept through the cramped space and found a door closed at the far end. He eased it open, saw a shadow jolt upward in bed and moved fast, pinning the man to the bed and slamming a hand over his mouth before he could make a sound.

"Heard you had an accident this afternoon," he said in a low, menacing voice.

Mark struggled, guttural sounds of rage and fear escaping his throat.

Angel silenced him with an elbow to the side of the head and quickly bound him, dragging him into a chair and tying him to it. Mark moaned softly, blood dripping down his temple.

Angel slapped the side of his face smartly. "Hey. Focus."

In the thin light coming between the slats of the blinds on the window, he saw Mark's head come up, eyes squinting at him. "Who the fuck are you?"

"Where was the meeting?"

"What?"

A backhand to the other side of his face snapped his head sideways. "Where?"

"Hospital in Crimson Point. Fuck, man! Lemme go."

"Who else was there?"

It took some more physical encouragement to get him talking. But soon enough he had solid intel to feed up the chain. The two other guys involved with him checked out. The apparent dealer he'd met with was TJ Barros. And a female bystander had definitely seen them all.

"Who is she?" Angel demanded.

Mark coughed, spat out a mouthful of blood and glared up at him with utter loathing. "Just a chick I know from the hospital. She took off with TJ. I think he knows her too, because he was protecting her."

"What's her name?" he asked again.

"Bristol. Can't remember her last name. Look, man—"

"What else?"

"There's nothing else, man. Now fucking let me go!"

Not happening. And Mark knew it as well as he did.

Angel had what he needed. Now he needed to finish this job and get home before Liana woke up.

The silencer muffled the shot. He left the body tied to the chair in the bedroom and crept out the same way he'd come in, locking the door behind him with his tool. Back at his car he sent the image he'd taken to his contact using a burner, along with a message.

I need access to the security video outside the southeast corner of the hospital in Crimson Point. He specified the time window.

On it, came the reply. *Commission transferred.*

He checked his bank account, now fifty Gs fatter, then made his way back to the highway and headed south. He had just crossed the state line when his phone alerted him with a sharp ping. Pulling into a rest stop, he watched the video footage some hacker must have found.

The video showed the southeast staff and service entrance of the hospital and that corner of the parking lot. Angel's latest victim and the others had been smart enough to at least have their meeting beyond the scope of the camera.

Suddenly a woman appeared at the right edge of the field of view, the flashlight on her phone aimed off screen. She stopped, startled. Her expression shifted from shock to anger. She said something. Appeared to be arguing with whoever was off screen. Then a man ran at her.

Tall. Big, athletic build. Dark hair, full goatee, wearing worn jeans and a plaid flannel shirt.

Had to be Barros.

He grabbed the woman's arm, and they raced across the parking lot. Angel zoomed in to try to get a look at the license plate of the car they jumped into. It tore away out of view. Seconds later, a pickup raced after them.

Angel texted the plate number, make, model and color of

the car to Hawk. He waited, thinking. The cartel didn't have any intel on this Barros guy. Who was he? Angel couldn't be sure, but it was possible that either he or Mark was the leak. Or maybe they were both involved.

He was just nodding off when a response came back.

Car registered to Bristol Moreau. It listed her address in Crimson Point.

He looked up the address, studied a map of the town as he considered his new orders that had just come in.

Find Barros.

They were desperate. That's the only reason why they would ask him to take this on right now. And it would cost them.

Tracking isn't part of my job description, he answered. That was Hawk's and the other falcon's territory.

It is now.

Yep. Completely desperate. Interesting. They must think Barros was at least somehow related to the leak.

How much more do I get? He didn't care if it was ballsy. As long as he got the job done, he was valuable to the organization. He was safe. And so was Liana. He could afford to push a bit.

Triple if you handle it in the next twelve hours.

"Yeah, that works," he murmured to himself, his heart beating faster.

This was it. The last big chunk of money he needed to get Liana her spot.

Angel started the car, pulled onto the highway and took the first exit west, driving toward the coast. He was going to Crimson Point to find Bristol Moreau. And through her, hopefully Barros.

SEVENTEEN

TJ finished washing their plates and set them on the rack beside the sink to dry, aware on a cellular level of Bristol watching TV in the living room twenty feet away. It had been more than an hour since the conversation with his handler, and there was still no obvious solution to his current predicament.

Bristol. Or rather, them being stuck alone together in this little house.

He wiped the already clean countertops, partly to keep his hands busy and partly to buy him more time before he was forced to interact with her like a human being. His time as an undercover agent on the streets had completely eroded whatever social intelligence he'd once had. He was unused to being around others now, and this place, while a luxurious reprieve for him in so many ways, was small. There was no way to avoid her while she was here.

Or the feelings she stirred in him.

Her presence seemed to suffuse the air around him. He felt her on a molecular level, could feel the weight of her stare on him right now.

The TV went silent. "Did Beckett say how long he'd be?" Bristol asked.

He dried his hands on the dishtowel, keeping his back to her. She distracted him. Made it hard to think clearly, and more than ever, he needed a clear head. "No. Just that he'd be here as soon as he can."

"They'll be checking up on you."

"I know." Without a doubt they would be. Beckett had his own connections within the intelligence industry, and also had close ties with Crimson Point Security and its management. They would be analyzing the shit out of him and his background right now, if they hadn't already.

Over the past ninety minutes, he'd been forced to accept that the life he'd been living was over. Not that it had really been a life at all. More like he'd been existing from one day to the next. Still, having that yanked away in an instant after all the effort and sacrifice was a huge adjustment.

"Okay, so, are you just planning to ignore me until this is over? Because that could be a while yet, and I'm kind of going crazy over here. I don't bite, promise."

He paused, hand tightening around the cloth for a moment before he turned to face her. Christ, she was beautiful. Every time he looked at her, it hit him. Being attracted to her was problematic to say the least. "What do you want to talk about?"

"Anything, at this point. There's nothing on TV to distract me, and this silence between us is really starting to grate on my nerves."

"I'm not much good at making conversation." As evidenced by the long, awkward silence while they'd eaten dinner. Separately. Him at the kitchen counter, her on the couch. Not that it had helped dull his awareness of her.

"With me, you mean? Or in general?" She pushed her

glasses up the bridge of her nose. It was adorable when she did that.

"In general."

A slight frown drew her eyebrows closer together. "Were you always that way?"

"No."

"Didn't think so, because my brother always made you sound like a really social kind of guy."

"I wouldn't exactly say that. And that was a long time ago." He searched for something else to say. "You must miss him."

"I do. But he's still in here and always will be." She tapped the center of her chest. Her scrubs hid the gorgeous shape of her body, but, of course, now he was looking at the curve of her breasts.

"What do you remember most about him?" she asked, pulling him out of his thoughts and his gaze from her chest.

"He was solid," he answered without having to think about it. "Team player, professional, always had his head in the game. Always had your back."

Her soft smile did things to him. "Yeah, that's what I loved most about him too."

"He was lucky to have you. "

"I was lucky to have him too." Her expression shifted, edged with a sadness he could feel. "Even if he was lost for a while, he came back to us in the end."

And then was killed. It was fucking tragic. "I'm sorry he went through all that. But I'm glad he had you."

She gave him a saucy grin. "Yeah? Even though you endured a taste of what I put him through?"

One side of his mouth lifted. This was getting a bit easier now. Talking to her this way still felt alien, but he could feel some of his walls coming down. "Even then. Not many people would go to those lengths to help someone." That kind of goodness was rarer than diamonds, and deserved to be protected. Just like she did.

"I loved him," she said with a shrug, as if it explained everything.

"I know. He had a picture of you both as his screensaver."

Her eyes welled up. "He did?"

"Yeah. He told us all about you." Shit. "Maybe we should talk about something else."

She cleared her throat. Sat up straighter. "All right, fine. Then how about your background? Will you tell me some of it now? Since you already know all about me from Eric."

Yeah, he supposed that was only fair. Although he definitely didn't know everything he wanted to know about her. "I was born in Pennsylvania. In a little town not far from Gettysburg."

Her eyes brightened. "I've been there. My dad took Eric and me when we were kids one summer. Were you close with your parents?"

He nodded. "Pretty close."

She frowned. "Your job must be hard on them too."

"No. They were both gone before I joined the DEA."

"Oh, I'm so sorry. What happened?"

He didn't like talking about it. But she'd been honest with him. She deserved to know what kind of man she was trapped here with. "My dad got behind the wheel in bad weather after a Christmas party. They went off the road into a flooded ditch on the way home. Neither of them made it out."

"That's terrible—"

"I was home to visit them on leave. I was supposed to drive them that night. But it was my last night stateside, and I was too busy having a good time with some buddies, so I bailed on them at the last minute. And they died."

The guilt over that would haunt him forever.

"Oh…I'm *so* sorry." He could tell she wanted to ask more, braced himself for it. They had both lost close family in car accidents. Another twisted quirk of fate that connected them. "How old were you?"

"It happened a few years ago." His leave had been extended by a few days so he could bury them.

She winced. "Oh God, that's so hard. Is that why you decided to do undercover work when you joined the DEA? Because they were gone, and you felt like you…didn't have anyone?"

Her perception was dead fucking on. He'd never let himself examine his motivations too closely at the time. "In a way." He'd found direction, purpose and brotherhood in the Rangers. After burying his parents and leaving the military, he'd felt lost.

And, yeah, maybe the guilt had played a big part in volunteering for undercover after joining the DEA. Some part of him wanting to punish himself.

"What were their names?"

"They both went by their middle names. Teresa and Javier."

Her gaze sharpened on him. "TJ."

He nodded. He'd chosen his new identity as a way of honoring them.

"I think it's a beautiful tribute."

Was it? They were still dead—because of him. And they both would have hated the job he'd taken on. What he'd become.

A thick silence had settled between them, but was thankfully broken by the sound of a vehicle pulling up out front. He hurried to the front window, drew the edge of the blind back a fraction to look outside. "It's Beckett." *Oh, hell.* "And your stepsister."

"Cassie's here?" Bristol jumped up and rushed for the door.

TJ caught her arm before she'd gone two steps, stopping her and earning a surprised look. "What's wrong?" she asked.

"Just being careful," he answered, placing her behind him. With things so uncertain at the moment, he wasn't taking any chances that a threat might be outside hiding somewhere out of sight.

It felt as natural as breathing to protect her, to put himself between her and any unseen threat waiting on the other side of the door. It felt right.

Beckett greeted him with a terse nod and looked past him to Bristol. Cassie stood right behind him, eyes narrowed on TJ. "You guys good?" Beckett asked.

"Yeah." TJ stepped back to let them in, and Cassie immediately breezed by Beckett to embrace Bristol while TJ shut the door.

"Hey. You okay?" Cassie asked her softly.

"I'm okay." Bristol pulled back and gave her a tight smile. "Kind of surreal, huh?"

"No kidding." Cassie bent down to grab the handles of a fancy-patterned bag she'd brought in. "Here. I packed what I thought you might need for a few days."

"Thanks. Did you bring my bat?"

"Got it," Beckett said, handing over a battered aluminum bat. "Not sure it'll do you much good though."

"I just feel better having it with me. I keep it under my bed. Have since college." Bristol stroked a hand over the barrel almost lovingly, and the sex-starved part of TJ's mind immediately pictured her stroking something else entirely.

He shoved that thought aside, put a chokehold on his

libido that seemed to go into overdrive around her. They were here because they were being hunted, for God's sake.

Arm around Bristol's shoulders and her body language screaming protectiveness, Cassie's gaze swung to him, pinning him like an insect where he stood.

He didn't blame her for her dislike or suspicion. She didn't know him. Pretty much everything she'd been told about him so far was a lie—with the exception of his military background—and now Bristol had been dragged into this mess.

"I assume you're armed?" she asked him in an icy tone.

"Yes."

"So," Beckett said, stuffing his hands in his jeans pockets and rocking back on his heels. "DEA, huh?"

TJ nodded. "You verify everything?"

"Not me. CPS."

Made sense. "I'm just waiting to hear back from my handler. Won't know what my next move is until then."

"Understood." Beckett glanced around the small space before focusing back on him. Likely checking escape and entry points, assessing security weaknesses. There were plenty. "Need anything else?"

A time machine so he could go back in time and meet his CI somewhere else? Then his cover would still be intact, and Bristol wouldn't be in danger. "Not right now."

"Left something in the truck. Back in a sec." He went back out the door and returned moments later with a long gun case, setting it on the floor. "Hunting rifle. Just in case."

"Thanks."

Beckett nodded, looked over at Cassie. "Ready?"

The set look on Cassie's face made it clear she didn't want to go anywhere, but her expression softened as she turned Bristol toward her. "This will all be over and behind you before you know it. Just lie low and be careful for the time being."

"I will." TJ had to give Bristol credit. There were no tears, no hint of fear from her. Not even a slight wobble in her voice. She was a lot stronger than she looked.

Cassie's gaze swung back to him, laser sharp. "Anything happens to her, I'll hold you personally responsible." *And then I'll make you pay dearly,* her eyes promised.

He dipped his head in acknowledgment, respecting her loyalty to her stepsister. Bristol deserved that kind of love and protectiveness.

The two women hugged and said their goodbyes. "Just shout if you need anything," Beckett said before he and Cassie left. TJ locked the door behind them, let out a deep breath and turned around to face Bristol.

EIGHTEEN

"So where am I sleeping?" Bristol asked, bag in one hand and her bat in the other.

A whole new kind of tension filled the room now that they were locked in here alone together again. It was selfish as hell, but deep down he liked the idea of having her all to himself. "My bed."

"You sure? I'll be fine on the couch."

"No. You're taking my room." It was more secure, for one. But the totally primitive part of him wanted her in his bed. Even if she was in it without him.

Jesus, he had to stop thinking about her in a sexual way right the hell now.

He turned away from her and started down the short hallway. "I just washed the sheets yesterday, but I can throw them in the machine again now if you want."

"No, it's fine."

Good, because that same primitive part of him liked the thought of her lying in the sheets with his scent on them. Getting all over her.

What the hell's wrong with you? That's Eric's baby sister you're fantasizing about.

In the bedroom, he flipped on the light and did a quick visual sweep to make sure it was tidy. The window above the headboard was small. Even if someone tried to force their way through it, it would be a tight squeeze. "Make yourself at home. Bathroom's through there." He nodded at the en suite. The window in there was even smaller.

Bristol stepped past him, leaving a trail of her scent on the way by. She set her bag and bat down next to the bed, faced him while he struggled to keep his eyes on hers and not drink in the rest of her body. "Where are the towels?"

"Here." He got some from the closet, went to hand them to her, and stopped short as he turned around.

She was standing directly in front of him, having followed him across the room. They were practically face to face. Close enough that he could see the thin ring of pale blue around her pupils that he'd never noticed before.

Their gazes locked. Neither of them moved.

His pulse surged, his blood heating instantly. The air thickened between them, and his gaze dropped to her lips. Full and plush and pink. Insanely kissable.

He could almost feel them giving beneath his own. Imagined what it would be like to slide his tongue between them. To taste her. Tease her until she whimpered and wrapped around him, demanding more. Give her enough pleasure to make up for everything else.

Her gaze dropped to his mouth in turn. Her lashes lowered. She leaned forward ever so slightly, and he realized too late that he was already doing the same.

Their lips touched. It was only the briefest contact, but a stark, primal hunger streaked through him, so strong he could barely control it.

He jerked his head back, shaken by the power of his response. He slid his tongue across his lower lip as Bristol blinked up at him, pupils dilated behind her glasses. He imagined her wearing them and nothing else, her hair gathered up in his fist while she knelt before him and—

It took every bit of control he had not to grab her and crush his mouth to hers. To take what she so willingly offered.

He ruthlessly shoved his libido back into the vault where he'd been keeping it. She didn't know what the hell she was doing. Didn't know how tightly wound he was. How long it had been since he'd...

She cleared her throat and stepped back, lowering her gaze as if embarrassed. "Thanks." She took the towels and disappeared into the bathroom, allowing him to finally pull in a breath and get hold of himself.

Jesus, if he hadn't pulled back when he had, he wasn't sure he would've been able to stop.

He ran a hand over his face. Christ, what a mess. It was bad enough that she was in this situation because of him. He needed to protect and take care of her until the threat passed, not fixate on getting her naked and under him in his bed.

"I'll let you turn in," he said gruffly from the bedroom doorway. "Been a long day, you must be tired."

She stepped back out of the bathroom, hair loose and shiny around her shoulders. And God help him, all he could think about was plunging his hands into it, fisting it as he feasted on her, plundering her soft mouth before savoring every inch of her smooth, warm skin. Every inch of each delectable curve hidden under her scrubs. "Okay. Good night."

He hesitated a second, feeling the need to leave her with something comforting. "You're safe here." As long as he remembered not to touch her again, that is. "Try to get some sleep."

"You too."

Yeah, right. Not likely with his blood running this hot and an unspecified threat hanging over them.

"Night." He shut the door, putting a physical barrier between them, and strode back down the hall. But the rush of arousal continued to pump through his system long after he walked away.

He'd never wanted anyone the way he wanted Bristol. Wasn't sure what it was about her that twisted him up inside so badly, but she did. Maybe it was the situation they were in. Or his personal connection to her through Eric.

And he damned well owed it to Eric's memory to not only keep her safe, but to keep his distance from her.

After grabbing a blanket from the hall closet, he made sure all the windows and doors were still secure, then checked his phone. No new messages. He and Bristol were officially trapped in here together at least overnight.

Ignoring the ache between his legs, he stretched out on the couch, grabbing a throw cushion to use as a pillow. He lay there for a long time in the darkness listening to the quiet hum of the fridge, his mind drifting from what actions the cartel might take against him to Bristol curled up in his bed right now, her hair tousled over his pillow and his scent surrounding her.

Even though he knew it was wrong, he'd still have given damned near anything for the chance to be in it with her.

Off limits. Get your head straight.

Eventually, he drifted into a light doze, only to wake with a start in the darkness later.

His eyes slowly adjusted to the dimness. The house was still and silent, but something had woken him, and it wasn't

Bristol. There was no hint of light in the hall coming from under her door, no indication of movement or stirring on the other side of the living room wall.

His muscles tensed when he caught the edge of a silhouette moving across the blind on the kitchen window. Someone was in the backyard.

Immediately, he rolled to one knee beside the couch, reaching for the weapon he'd left beside his phone on the coffee table. There was no time to warn Bristol. He had to intercept and neutralize the threat before whoever it was got inside.

A nearly imperceptible scraping noise at the back door raised the hairs on the nape of his neck. He hurried over on silent feet, got there in time to see the door handle shift slightly.

He waited behind the door out of view from whoever was on the other side, coiled and ready. Watched the door crack open a fraction of an inch. Waited a second longer, until a foot and leg slipped inside.

He slammed his shoulder into the door full force, crushing the leg between the jamb and the edge of the door. An enraged howl rent the air as he brought his weapon up and spun to confront the intruder, finger on the trigger.

As he turned, the door burst inward without warning, catching him off balance. He lost his footing, had to throw out his hands to catch himself and keep from sprawling face first on the floor. His weapon slipped from his grasp and hit the tile.

Before he could recover it, out of the corner of his eye he saw the assailant's arm come up. TJ quickly rolled his body to the side and swept a leg out, knocking the attacker's feet out from under him. The instant the guy hit the floor with a pained grunt, TJ dove at him.

He seized the attacker's wrist, wrenched the pistol from his grip. It fell to the floor with a clatter just as an elbow flew at TJ's face. He dodged it at the last moment, used the momentum to flip over and throw a punch at the guy's throat.

The man had good CQB training because he managed to block it and land a punch to the side of TJ's face. TJ's head snapped to the right, stars exploding in front of his eyes. He rammed his fist into the guy's diaphragm. Managed to wind him, but they were grappling on the floor now, both of them struggling to get the other in a headlock. He was bigger than TJ, and motherfucking strong.

TJ spotted the dark shape of one of the pistols lying close by. He flailed a hand out for it while keeping his other arm locked around the bastard's throat.

He barely had time to register the silhouette looming above them, just a split second for his heart to seize as he braced to be shot by the new assailant. Then the attacker's arm slashed down, immediately followed by a loud thump.

The guy in TJ's grip jerked like he'd been shot, a howl of agony ripping from him as he stopped fighting entirely and slumped to the floor, clutching his side.

TJ looked up at the silhouette, stunned to recognize Bristol standing there, face set, bat poised in her grip like she was ready to take the guy's head off.

NINETEEN

Heart hammering halfway up her throat, Bristol gripped her bat with bloodless fingers, ready to hit the attacker again if he so much as twitched. Thankfully, she didn't have to, because TJ pounced on him, wrenching the guy's arms behind him and securing them with a...sock?

The prisoner was cursing and making guttural sounds of pain but wasn't fighting anymore. She'd hit him hard in either the back or side, actually felt a bit queasy when she thought of the sound it had made. A horrible thwack-crunch that told her she'd probably broken his ribs.

"Okay, Slugger. You can put that down now."

TJ's voice wrapped around her, deep and shockingly calm considering what had just happened. She swallowed hard and lowered the bat, her nervous system still trying to decide whether it was in fight or flight mode.

She'd never hit anyone in her life, but when she'd seen this guy trying to kill TJ on the kitchen floor, a switch had flipped. Even still, she hadn't been able to bring herself to swing at his head. Just the thought of doing that made her want to throw up.

She took a step back, suddenly shaky as hell. "What do you want me to do?" Her voice was high and tight, probably because the muscles in her throat were pulled taut as guitar strings around her hyoid bone.

"Get my phone. It's on the coffee table."

She pivoted and hurried into the next room, her legs turning rubbery now that the immediate danger was over and her adrenaline level was dropping. She got the phone and hovered uncertainly in the kitchen entryway, not wanting to get any closer to the attacker than necessary, even if he was tied up and incapacitated.

"It's okay. He's not going anywhere. Trust me." Crouched next to the prisoner, TJ stretched out a hand toward her.

She gave him the phone, stood there shifting her weight from foot to foot while he messaged someone. What if this guy wasn't working alone? What if someone else was outside waiting to get them, or more were coming? "What now? Want me to call the police?" she said, trying to ignore the awful sounds the guy was making.

"No," TJ said without looking up. "Go into the bedroom. Wait there until I come get you."

It went against her gut to leave him without backup, but she did as he said, shutting the door for good measure and perching on the end of the bed. She was still on edge. Part of her wanted to clap her hands over her ears to block out the guy's sounds of pain and whatever happened next, but the rest of her was too afraid she might miss something important.

From down the hall, she could hear TJ questioning the suspect. She couldn't hear the exact words, but cringed at the sudden bellow of pain and more scuffling that told her the prisoner wasn't in a cooperative mood. She wished she could call Cassie or even Beckett for backup, but TJ had taken her phone earlier, apparently not trusting her to leave it off.

The interrogation in the kitchen didn't appear to be going well as the minutes ticked by. There were more cries of agony, more sounds of struggling. Then things got quiet. Way too quiet.

She fidgeted with her hands, one knee bouncing up and down. Then TJ's voice called down the hall.

"Stay in the bedroom. Backup's on the way, ETA ten to fifteen minutes."

It felt more like an hour while she sat there, straining to make out any sounds outside her window. Eventually, she heard a vehicle pull up out front, then footsteps and the front door opening.

TJ's voice was muted as he spoke to whoever it was. The low volume told her things must be more or less under control. She breathed a little easier.

A few minutes later she heard muffled shouts like before, then retreating footsteps. Vehicle doors opening and closing. The engine started, and the vehicle left.

A knock on her door made her jump.

"It's me," TJ said. "All clear. You can come out now."

She got up and opened her door, shooting a glance past him down the hall toward the kitchen. "Is he gone?"

"He's gone. The DEA took him."

She looked up at him, wanting to bury her face in his chest. "Do they know who he is?"

"One of the guys who chased us earlier."

Oh, shit. "Do they think he was acting alone?"

"Yes, but on orders."

A chill snaked down her spine. "How did he find us?" The truck had been undriveable, and both suspects had been lying bound on the pavement. He shouldn't have been able to move, much less track them here. It meant someone else was watching them, and that was terrifying.

"Don't know. They must have had eyes on us somehow." He searched her eyes. "You okay?" he asked quietly.

She nodded, even though she felt very much not okay. He was so composed. And tall and strong and gorgeous, his frame filling the doorway. She didn't want to seem weak by comparison. But she really wanted to burrow into him and hide for a while. "You?"

"I'm fine. Thanks to you." Grudging admiration laced his tone.

She swallowed. "I didn't know what else to do."

"You did great. You've got one hell of a swing. Remind me never to piss you off when your bat's nearby." One side of his mouth kicked up in amusement, transforming him from sexy-aloof to irresistible.

The situation wasn't remotely funny. She was still worried as hell, but an answering smile tugged at her lips anyway. Except a second later the tug inexplicably turned into a wobble.

She sucked in a breath, covered her face with her hands and squeezed her eyes shut before she fell apart, struggling to hang onto the last shred of her control. That guy had somehow tracked them down, broken in, would have killed TJ and probably her as well if they hadn't stopped him. So presumably, when the guy didn't check in with whoever had sent him, they would send someone else.

Don't cry. Don't cry.

"Hey." Long fingers circled her wrists with warm, gentle pressure. "It's okay now. It's over."

Was it? He had no way of knowing that for sure.

She sucked in a shaky breath, then another. *Come on. Stay strong. You can do it.*

When she was reasonably sure she had most of her composure back, she wiped the heels of her hands under her eyes, and he let go of her wrists. He was still so close, those dark eyes delving into hers in the dimness, pulling her in with an invisible magnetic force, and she was powerless to resist.

When she leaned toward him, he didn't pull away. His heavy arms banded around her and held her tight to his chest, her cheek resting in the muscular hollow of his shoulder. The feel of all that masculine strength surrounding her was such a relief, a little shudder ripped through her.

"You're okay," he said in that same hypnotically calm, deep voice, his grip sure and firm.

Bristol nodded, closing her eyes and breathing him in. Focusing on the feel of him holding her and blocking everything else out. He felt amazing. Warm and solid, holding her as if he'd needed it as much as she did. She forcefully cleared her mind and drifted on the sensations, holding onto the feeling of security he gave her, even if it might actually just be an illusion.

She didn't notice the change in him right away. The gradual tension that crept into his muscles until she finally noticed that his whole body was rigid. Confused, she opened her eyes, lifted her head to look up at him.

Her heart stuttered at the intense look on his face. The raw desire in his dark eyes that echoed inside her and made the breath catch in her throat.

A heartbeat later, he released her like she'd scalded him and stepped back, expression suddenly guarded. As if she'd only imagined what she'd just seen.

Except she knew she hadn't imagined it.

"We need to leave," he said brusquely.

The abrupt shift in his demeanor was like a bucket of ice water dumped over her. "Leave? To where?"

"Somewhere they can't track us. We can't stay here, this location's compromised."

It sure as hell was. "Is your handler—"

"She's handling the situation with our intruder. Beckett and Jase are trying to find us another place nearby." He turned away. And she wished she could turn the clock back to when she'd been cradled in his arms just moments ago. "Get your stuff together. We have to move."

He left her standing there, confused and aching for him. For something he clearly didn't want to give her.

TWENTY

Reeling mentally and emotionally, she hurriedly packed up the few things she'd taken out of her bag earlier, grabbed her bat, and made her way down the hall. TJ was waiting with the rifle case and several bags at his feet. He must have had them prepacked and stored in a closet somewhere. "Stay here while I check outside."

He slipped out the back door off the kitchen and returned a few minutes later. "All good. But stay behind me on the way to the garage."

Despite his assurance, she still felt horribly exposed when she stepped out of the house, staying on him like a shadow as they hurried through the darkness into the detached garage. He threw their stuff into the backseat of her car, hit the remote to open the garage door and pulled out onto the street. He waved at a man standing out front of the house, she guessed a DEA agent on guard duty, but kept the headlights off until they were halfway down the hill toward town.

"Where are we going?" she asked finally, hating that he wasn't telling her anything. He was constantly checking his mirrors like he expected someone to be following them.

"Dunno yet, but it's safer to keep moving for now."

She hated this. The uncertainty. "Does Cassie know we're moving?"

"CPS will tell her in the morning."

Technically, it was morning already, but Bristol bit back the other questions crowding her mind and turned her head to look out her window. It was the middle of the night. Crimson Point was quiet and still, the half-moon shining across the ocean, catching on the crests of the endless lines of whitecaps rolling into shore.

Normally the view would soothe her, but between the earlier attack and this constant, electrical awareness of TJ that was getting worse instead of better, she felt more agitated than ever. How was this her life now?

They had just reached the waterfront when TJ's phone buzzed in his lap. He grabbed it, glanced at the message, and handed it to her. "Search up the address when it comes through."

Another message appeared moments later. She put the address into her car's GPS and enlarged the map. "It's on the southern edge of the town, east of the coastal highway. Looks like a...townhouse complex?"

"Condo. It'll be more secure."

"Did the DEA set this up?"

"CPS. But the DEA approved it. Tell them ETA fifteen minutes."

She sent the message and received an immediate response. "Parking spot two-nineteen under the building." She gave him the gate code.

They didn't speak for the rest of the drive, and she was too tired to try to force a conversation anyway. When they arrived at the building, TJ turned into the underground parking. Beckett and another man she didn't recognize were waiting for them by the elevator.

"Been an eventful night for you, huh," Beckett said when she got out to grab her stuff from the back. "But I heard you put the bat to good use after all."

"Laid him out with one swing," TJ said before she could answer, getting his own gear from the other side.

"I put another dent in it," she said to be funny, even though nothing about this was remotely funny.

Beckett chuckled and indicated the man beside him. Tall, broad-shouldered, with golden brown hair and amazing aqua eyes. "This is Jase. He'll take you up and show you the place, but we just took a look and everything's secure. Nothing in town's open this time of night, so we just grabbed what we had from our kitchens and brought it over."

"If you guys need something else, I can get it for you when the stores open later," Jase said.

"We just finished construction and didn't have time to finish staging yet, so the furnishings are pretty bare," Beckett added.

"Is Walter with you?" Bristol asked.

"Yeah," he said, seeming surprised by the abrupt change in subject.

"Can I see him?" She needed some normalcy right now. Something happy. And animals were always the best medicine. They didn't judge or ask questions.

"Sure, he's in the truck."

She followed him over to the pickup and waited while Beckett opened the rear right passenger door. A furry little head popped up, droopy eyes half closed from being woken in the middle of his sleep, but his long, feathery tail thumped gently against the edge of his bed in greeting.

Oh, he was the most adorable old guy. "Hello, Walter."

Walter got up with a weary grunt and turned his oddly shaped little body around so he was facing her. She leaned inside to stroke his head, felt the unexpected prick of tears when he licked the back of her hand. His breath was terrible, but she didn't care. "You are the *sweetest* thing." God, why was she on the verge of crying again? She was safe.

"He's a good boy," Beckett said from behind her.

Okay. Get it together. Back to reality. "Thank you," she said, kissing the top of Walter's fluffy bedhead. When she straightened and turned around, Beckett had a slight smile on his normally hard face. "I really needed that."

"Walter's happy to oblige, anytime." He reached past her, ruffled the top of the dog's head.

When she looked past him, she found TJ watching her from next to the elevator. She felt the impact of his gaze right down to her core, and an answering heat bloomed in all the right places.

Or all the *wrong* ones.

They thanked Beckett again and got into the elevator. Jase rode up with them to show them the unit, but by the time they got there, her entire body was humming with an almost electrical awareness of TJ. Need and arousal pulsed through her, and the harder she tried to suppress it, the stronger it got. Until her skin felt so sensitive she could hardly stand it.

That brief, forbidden kiss earlier had changed something inside her, and now she couldn't shut it off.

"It's only one bedroom, but it's still peak tourist season, so we're running low on inventory right now," Jase said as he let them in.

The strong smell of new paint hit her first. The unit was small but the light buttercream paint on the walls made it seem larger and airier. Everything looked brand new and spotless, but the space was practically bare, with just a sofa and TV in the living room, and the made-up queen bed in the bedroom.

"Towels and whatever are in the bathroom."

"This is great, thanks," TJ said to Jase, standing a step ahead of her. She took the opportunity to eye the breadth of his shoulders. Imagined running her hands over his bare back, tracing all the muscles. Digging her fingers deep into them while his weight pressed her into a flat surface.

She pushed out a breath, tried to shake off those thoughts and the growing ache building inside her.

After explaining the security system, Jase left them. TJ locked the door behind him.

When he turned around to face her, her insides tightened painfully. "You take the bed," he told her, expression unreadable.

But she knew his indifference was a mask. She'd seen the cracks in his façade earlier tonight. For all he pretended otherwise, she knew she wasn't the only one fighting the pull between them.

She stood in the bedroom doorway as he walked past her to the couch in the tiny living room and started making up a bed there.

Bristol watched him, deep in thought. She had an important decision to make.

Tonight had shaken her false sense of security, had shown her just how uncertain life could be. TJ had protected her. Had comforted her.

He had also lived a life of severe deprivation on the streets for too long. He'd gone without human kindness or contact for too long, and she was sure that included any emotional connection with a woman.

The fact was, she wanted him. And she was pretty sure he wanted her too, much as he seemed determined to fight it. So even if it was completely out of character, she was going to have to be the one to make a move.

A heady surge of feminine power rolled over her as she walked up behind him. As if sensing her presence, he stilled, the blanket in his hands. He stood motionless, the air around them crackling with latent anticipation.

It was now or never.

Dredging up every last bit of courage she possessed, she stepped around in front of him. Her gaze found and held his as she brought her hands up to settle on his shoulders. She couldn't resist sinking her fingers into the thick muscles there. Testing the power of him. Reveling in it while her pulse went crazy.

His dark eyes stayed locked on hers. "Don't," he warned, his voice low. But the fire blazing there belied what had just come out of his mouth.

The heat between them intensified, igniting a delicious throb between her legs. And something in her enjoyed seeing him like this. Watching him fight the attraction and being able to push his buttons, seeing how far she could go until he snapped.

TJ didn't move, but the muscles under her hands were locked tight as she slowly skimmed them down to his collarbones, to the first button holding his flannel shirt together.

Staring up at him in the taut silence, she undid the first one.

The muscles in his jaw bunched.

She skimmed her fingertips over warm skin covering the thick pad of muscle on his chest. He drew in a sharp breath, his gaze dropping to her mouth.

Bristol slid her hands lower, arousal pumping hot and sweet through her veins. She paused for a moment, just long enough to let him wonder whether she would continue or not before slowly undoing the next button.

Then another. And another, until most of his muscular chest was bared to her gaze. Gorgeous and masculine and begging to be explored.

Holding the worn, soft edges of the shirt in her hands, she leaned in and kissed the center of his chest. Couldn't resist the urge to give a naughty stroke of her tongue right over his pounding heart.

A low growl sounded in his chest. Pure triumph shot through her when he plunged his hands into her hair, twisted her face up, and brought his mouth down on hers.

TWENTY-ONE

He purposely made the kiss hard, bordering on forceful to drive the point home. To punish her for pushing him past his limit.

She'd deliberately baited him into this. Now she was about to find out there was a price to pay for unleashing the beast inside him.

But instead of tensing in his hold or trying to stop this, Bristol melted into him. Her lips turned pliant beneath his, and she wound her arms around his back. Clinging to him, her lush breasts pressed into his chest.

Her unexpected reaction shifted something deep inside him. He couldn't help but soften the kiss, unable to hold onto the frustration and anger in the face of her response.

She was so damned soft everywhere, from her heart and generous nature, to the luscious curves he couldn't get enough of. Her pliant lips parted, allowing his tongue to delve inside and touch hers. Her soft moan went straight to his head, sending blood rushing from his brain to his groin.

It had been a long time for him. Well over a year since he'd had sex, with someone whose name he couldn't even remember. His whole body craved release. But he wanted to get Bristol off first. Needed to. Wanted to watch her surrender completely to him before he sank deep into her soft warmth and took care of his own needs.

He spun her around so she was facing away from him, jerked her back against his body and held her there, her breathless gasp fanning the flames burning inside him. She shifted restlessly in his grip, rubbing her ass against the hard ridge of his erection trapped in his jeans, her arched position pushing up the outline of her breasts farther.

His mouth found the side of her neck. He nipped the soft, smooth skin there. Soothed the little sting with the stroke of his tongue as he moved his hands up her belly to the tempting mounds of her breasts. He cupped them through her shirt, savoring the feel and weight of them, the way they filled his palms.

A soft, broken moan escaped her when he found the hard nubs of her nipples and squeezed them between his thumbs and fingers. She shuddered, reached down impatiently to grab the hem of her shirt and started to peel it upward.

TJ pushed her hands aside and did it himself, reveling in the way she raised her arms and let him drag it over her head. His hungry gaze locked on the sight of the sheer black lace bra encasing her full breasts. He teased the hard pink nipples straining against the fabric, nipped the edge of her jaw when she gasped.

Too impatient to find and undo the fastener, he tugged a lace cup down and tucked it under the curve of one breast, then the other. He bit back a groan at the way it pushed the plump mounds up higher, the tight pink centers begging to be touched.

He slid his thumbs over them. Locked one arm around her

hips when she moved restlessly, caught a nipple between his thumb and forefinger, squeezing and twisting gently.

"TJ," she whispered, rubbing her ass against his erection.

He was so hard. Half desperate to plunge into her heat, he could all but taste the release waiting for him.

With an iron will, he shoved the sharp edge of need aside, kept playing with her nipple while he slid his other hand inside the waistband of her jeans. It was a snug fit, not much room to maneuver, but he wedged his hand down until he could cup her center in his palm, adding pressure to the top of her sex with the heel of his hand.

Bristol moaned in approval and grabbed the fastener of her jeans to undo them and shove them down her hips. He looked down the length of her body to find that her panties were the same sheer black lace as her bra. He eased up on the pressure of his hand, nipped the side of her neck again when she groaned in protest and arched her hips, seeking more.

Just getting her off wasn't enough for him now. He wanted to push her past her control. Wanted her mindless with the need for release before he gave it to her, to show her without words that he was the one in control here.

He stared at his hand as he slid his fingertips up and down the center of her panties, a dark thrill shooting through him at the way she whimpered and squirmed in his hold. He could feel her dampness through the lace. Knew she had to be aching as much as he was.

When his patience thinned, he eased his hand into her panties and curved his fingers along her slick folds. She was soaked, the swollen knot of her clit peeking through the top. Breathing faster, he stroked her slowly, up and down, drawing out each motion to make her crazy before he teased the edge of her clit with a fingertip.

Bristol gasped and stiffened in his arms, a broken moan spilling free.

"I can feel you melting all over my fingers," he rasped out, rewarding her with slow circles.

Her hips followed his fingers, moving with his touch, rubbing her ass against his cock while she reached up to wrap an arm around his neck. With her head tipped back to rest against his shoulders, rounded breasts thrust out and her eyes closed, she was the picture of erotic surrender. Hotter than any fantasy he'd had of her.

He rubbed her clit until her breathing turned choppy, then eased his hand lower to push two fingers into her heat. Bristol made an unintelligible sound of pleasure and twisted her face toward his, seeking his mouth.

He released the nipple he'd been playing with to grab a fistful of her hair and plunge his tongue between her lips, his other hand working the slick flesh between her thighs. He could feel the tension building in her, feel the little tremors in her muscles as her breathing grew shallow.

"You gonna come for me?" he said against the side of her jaw, struggling to control the raging need to plunge inside her. She had stripped off his emotional armor. He wanted to do the same to her.

She nodded, grabbing hold of his wrist between her legs to hold his hand snug to her slick folds. "Don't stop," she breathed shakily.

He wouldn't stop. Couldn't, even if he'd wanted to. She had him spellbound, completely wrapped around her little finger with her incredible sensuality. But he didn't want her to know it.

"What if I did?" he said, something inside him feeding off her desperation.

"No," she gasped out, gripping his wrist harder. "Don't. I

need—" Her words cut off on a sharp inhalation when he pressed on her clit, then transformed into a beautiful moan so erotic he almost came in his jeans from the pressure of her ass against him.

Fuck.

He released her hair to cup her breast, fingers toying with the nipple while he continued his relentless strokes between her legs. Stroking her clit with exquisite care before plunging two fingers back into her heat.

Slow and tender around her sweet spot, then hard and quick inside her. Over and over and over until her upper thighs squeezed tight around his hand and her spine bowed in a beautiful, erotic curve. She shattered in his arms with a wild cry of release that sent a thrill of triumph through him.

TJ squeezed his eyes shut and pressed his face into the tender curve of her neck, holding her tight with his hand still buried between her quivering thighs. He felt every pulse that rippled around his invading fingers, his cock throbbing in desperate tandem. When she finally came back down to earth she sagged into his body, her gratified sigh music to his ears.

Easing his hand from between her legs, she turned around to face him, her eyes heavy-lidded with a deep satisfaction that had a growl forming in his chest. "I knew you'd be like that," she murmured, winding her arms around his neck and lifting on her toes to kiss him.

TJ grabbed hold of her and pulled her tight to the front of his body, savoring every single point of contact between them. He was starving for her, so fucking hungry he couldn't think straight as he backed her up and shoved her flat on the couch. Just the sight of her like that, bare breasts shoved up by her bra, nipples pointing at him and her panties wet from her release, was like a whip flaying the frayed edges of his control.

He ripped his shirt over his head rather than bother with the remaining buttons. Heard a seam pop as he yanked it over his head and tossed it aside, then yanked his jeans open and shoved his underwear halfway down his thighs. And oh, fuck, the look on her face as she pushed up on her elbows to study him, those big blue eyes eating him up like he was the most delicious dessert she'd ever seen.

There was just enough blood left in his brain to remember something vital and stop him from pouncing.

Condom.

He plunged a hand into his jeans pocket, managed to come up with his wallet and get the single condom out without fumbling it, but then her hand closed around him. He sucked in a breath, suppressed a growl as scorching pleasure streaked up his spine.

"Allow me," Bristol said, her voice as sultry as the look on her face as she took the condom from him. She wrapped one fist around the base and rolled the condom down the length of his shaft with the other.

TJ gritted his teeth and tipped his head back as he fought to hold on, feeling like he was on the verge of dying. But then her arms were drawing him down into her embrace, the soft curves of her body cushioning the hard planes of his as she pulled him into her.

Struggling to breathe, he eased his hips between her spread thighs, the head of his cock lodged against the slick, heated place he couldn't wait to bury himself in. Bracing his weight on his elbows, he stared down into her face, then entered her with one long thrust.

His breath hissed out, every single inch of contact an exquisite agony. Ecstasy burned up his spine, blazing in the pit of his belly and his groin, so hot he was already on the verge of exploding.

She was perfect. So goddamn soft and warm, melting around him, drawing him deeper, deeper until they were fused completely together. He buried his hands in her hair and gripped tight. Fisting it as the need took over.

He surged in and out of her in an unstoppable rhythm, the searing need for release blinding him. Blocking out everything but the feel of her, her scent, her soft little whimpers he gobbled up with ravenous kisses. He couldn't slow down. Couldn't get enough.

He was vaguely aware of her wedging an arm between their bodies. Realized hazily that her hand was between her thighs, fingers stroking her clit, her rising cries of excitement burning him alive.

Balanced right on the knife edge of release, he felt her tense beneath him. Heard her liquid moan of ecstasy as she clenched around him. He plunged deep, buried himself to the hilt in her warmth, and raw pleasure exploded through him.

He pulled his mouth from hers, a guttural shout of ecstasy echoing through the room. The release tore through him in agonizingly delicious pulses that left him gasping, sagging over her on trembling arms.

Bristol relaxed with a sexy, humming sound and drew him down to blanket her. He lay sprawled out on top of her like a dead weight, trying to get his breath back and half afraid he was crushing her, but he was too weak to move.

She'd destroyed him. Fucking ruined him.

Sex had never been like that before. And deep down, he knew it never would be with anyone else ever again. Only her.

This thing between them had gone way beyond physical need. And if he was honest, their connection had been anything but superficial from the start.

She'd seen him when no one else had. She'd gone out of

her way to help him so many times, had touched a part of him he hadn't known existed until her. Tonight, she'd given herself to him completely. Offered herself up to him and been completely vulnerable, trusting him with far more than her delectable body and physical needs.

She was everything that was good about the world. Everything he'd thought he didn't believe in anymore. God knew he didn't deserve it. Didn't deserve her. He didn't know what the hell he was supposed to do now, but he knew for damned sure that she deserved far better than him.

She cut off his thoughts by stroking a hand down the damp length of his back, the other playing lazily with his hair. His eyelids drooped, exhaustion pulling at him.

"You okay?" she murmured close to his ear.

No. He wasn't even remotely okay. He was in too deep, the water already over his head and rising fast—and not just because of the threat from the cartel hanging over them.

The only real way to protect Bristol was to walk away from her. But he knew in his bones it was already far too late for that.

She was the one threat he wasn't going to fight.

TWENTY-TWO

Turning the woman in his arms around to shield her from the rotor wash of the helo idling behind them on the rooftop of the luxury hotel in San Francisco, Jordan drew a fingertip down her cheek. This was their third time together, and he already wanted more. "Miss me."

"I will." Jana twined her arms around his neck and plastered her body—perfected by the best plastic surgeons money could buy—against him, a seductive smile on her shiny red lips. "When can I see you again?"

"Soon." Just as soon as they could figure out how to make it work without raising suspicion. The level of planning needed to pull off the sneaking around made the affair almost as hot as the sex. "Be good."

She smirked. "Never."

Chuckling, he put his arm around her and led her across the helipad. He opened the rear door of the helicopter and helped her inside, enjoying the view when the long slit in the two-thousand-dollar red silk dress he'd bought her parted to reveal the entire length of her leg. High enough to give him a flash of the smooth skin between her legs.

He looked up to find her smiling at him in satisfaction, that familiar, hot gleam in her eyes, her nipples hard points against the thin fabric of her bodice. She never wore a bra or underwear when she was with him. To torment him as much as for easy access.

"I'm almost tempted to roll the dice and stay another night," she said over the roar of the engine.

"Too risky."

"I know. And you love it as much as I do."

Grinning, he shut the door and walked across the rooftop to the steel access door where a bodyguard waited. Jana was stunning and an incredible fuck, but that's not why he kept seeing her.

Fucking a rival's young trophy wife right under the asshole's arrogant nose got him off in a way sex never could.

His bodyguard escorted him down the freight elevator to the private vehicle waiting in the underground parking garage. Twenty-five minutes later, he was climbing the short set of steps into his private jet. A little more than two hours after that, he disembarked at a private airfield outside of Portland and got into another waiting vehicle for the drive to his estate, answering messages on the way.

But once he was finally seated at his desk in his locked office to do some work, his good mood evaporated when he saw the message waiting on the encrypted chat program.

Call me. Urgent.

"Goddammit," he muttered. It meant the intel leak was even worse than he'd feared, and closer than he'd ever realized. No matter how much he wanted to deny the possibility after all the money he'd poured into making his part of the organization secure, it was now glaringly obvious that someone close to him had betrayed him.

Time to cull his inner circle.

Fuming, he called the IT guy back using an encrypted phone. "What've you found?" he demanded. It better be good. He was sick of not having answers, and throwing more money at the problem hadn't gotten him any closer to a name. For all the good it'd done him, he might as well have put the money in a pile outside and set it on fire.

"The files in question were definitely copied. I'm still trying to figure out whether it was done remotely or not."

Jesus Christ. A wave of cold swept through him. "How could someone have accessed my system? *How*? I pay you an ungodly amount of money to make sure no one can."

"I know, I'm not sure how this happened. I—"

"Find out. Find out now, and fix this. If you can tell me who it was, you'll get a substantial reward. If not, we're done." And Jordan would be forced to have him killed because of what he knew.

"But—"

"You've got six hours. Not a minute more." He ended the call and tossed his phone onto his desk in disgust. "*Fuck*."

His IT guy was the best money could buy. Some young prodigy only a handful of people in the world could afford, and Jordan kept him on personal retainer. The system shouldn't have been hackable, let alone his most sensitive personal files. If anything in there was leaked, he was as good as dead.

Someone knocked on the door. "Go away," he snarled, trying to think.

"It's me—"

"Goddammit, I said go away!" He dismissed Jon, accessed the program he wanted on his computer and changed the passwords. Probably an exercise in futility at this point, but he was desperate to stop anyone else from getting the information he had. Including the most recent video of him and Jana, taken last month.

As soon as he was done, Jordan sat back and eyed the rug on the other side of the room that hid the access point to one of his safes. The one where he kept all the hard copies of his ammunition in the form of leverage. It was so damn ironic it would have been funny if it wasn't so fucking scary.

For years he'd been diligently compiling material on anyone who might pose a threat to him, making digital copies of everything and storing it on his state-of-the-art system as a backup in case anyone managed to find and crack his safe to get the originals. And that accidental mistake could end up being his undoing.

His gaze caught on the far corner of the hand-woven Persian silk rug. The edge of it was crooked.

He got up, walked over and crouched down, his pulse beating faster. It was slight, but the corner wasn't straight. As if someone had pulled it back and then hurriedly tried to fix it.

The exact part of the rug that needed to be moved to access the secret panel in the floor.

He stared at it, a sinking feeling taking hold. It wasn't the cleaners. They weren't allowed in here. The only people who had access were him, and the few people he allowed inside with him. People like Hawk. Angel. Jon—

The phone on his desk rang, shattering his concentration. He grabbed it and saw his lawyer's name come up on the display. "Roger. You need something?" he said brusquely, not in the mood to deal with any more headaches. Someone had moved that rug. Someone he trusted.

"We've got a potential problem."

His mood soured further. "What kind of problem?"

"I got an emergency call first thing this morning from my

new client. He's currently in jail for breaking and entering and assaulting a man in Crimson Point last night. He's been telling everyone he works for you."

Jordan's blood pressure jumped, his hand tightening around the receiver. "Is that right?"

"Everyone at the jail knows. I think it's his way of trying to protect himself from the people on the inside."

"What's his name?" He would have the idiot dealt with. "Never heard of him," he lied when Roger told him.

He recognized it as one of the men who had accompanied his inside man Mark at the hospital in Crimson Point to the meeting there last night. The one who was supposed to take care of the surprise fucking *DEA agent* Jordan had just found out about from a trusted source within the network, and make him disappear to protect that part of the operation.

Moving product in and out of the hospital was surprisingly easy, and lucrative. Losing that conduit would impact business in the region until another stable place could be set up.

"What do you want me to do with him?"

"Nothing." Both problems needed to be eliminated immediately. The inept assassin, one, for having the colossal stupidity to publicly link himself to him and the organization, and, two, because he clearly didn't know how to keep his mouth shut and posed a security risk. Then the DEA agent, for obvious reasons.

But that still didn't tell him who the leak was. He stared at the crooked edge of the rug, fury welling up. Who would dare, knowing the leverage he had against them, and the price of betrayal?

"What's the address of the place he broke into?" Jordan typed it into his computer and a map popped up with a red pin marking a small house on a residential street. "I've got it. Let me know if there's any more information."

The instant he disconnected he called his IT guy again. "Find out who owns the property at this address in Crimson Point." He could do it himself, but he had a lot on his mind at the moment, and things like this were what he paid this asshole for. He gave the street and number.

"All right, give me a minute. Accessing county property records now."

Jordan drummed his fingers on his desk, mind racing as he planned out his next steps. Thinking about all the people he'd allowed into this room the day before he'd left for Seattle.

The guy in jail was a dead man walking. But if Jordan didn't find and stop whoever had accessed his files, so was he.

"The property's owned by a construction company in Crimson Point."

"No individual name attached to it?"

"Not that I can see. Do you want me to keep digging?"

"No." It was enough to know the DEA agent had been there last night. Surely there would be some thread to pull on now. "But I need you to find and hack any potential security cameras facing that address. See if there's footage of anyone coming or going from there last night from seven p.m. onward."

He ended the call and wiped the sweat beading his upper lip, debating his options. This mess was partly his own fault. He shouldn't have risked sending someone else to kill Barros. He should have had Angel deal with it in the first place.

And Angel had also been in this room the day Jordan left for Seattle.

He shot off a brief message to him. *New task for you. Critical.*

Angel called back within five minutes. "What's the job?"

"New target. DEA agent named TJ Barros. I'll send you a picture. He was last seen at a residential address in Crimson Point as of six hours ago."

"Usual procedure?"

Meaning locating and eliminating the target. "No. Find him and bring him to me."

"That's it? Nothing else?"

"No. I want to question him in person. I need whatever intel he has. Then you can finish up." By sending Barros to his maker and giving the DEA a clear message.

That he wasn't afraid of them, and anyone who fucked with him would die.

Then he would deal with Angel.

"Got it. I'll be in touch when I find something."

Jordan battled to keep his voice calm. "This is time sensitive. Handling this quickly will be to your advantage." Angel was motivated by money. Jordan understood and respected that. He might even let him live after this job—if it turned out he wasn't the source of the leak.

"Understood."

He set his phone down, struggling to curb the rage burning inside him. First, he would meet individually with the handful of people who made up his inner circle. Once Angel brought Barros in, Jordan would squeeze the bastard for intel on all his CIs using whatever means necessary. Then he would track all of them down individually if necessary.

One of them had to be the leak. And someone had stolen his files.

When Jordan found out who was responsible, he would kill every last one of them to protect himself.

TWENTY-THREE

TJ woke up on the couch with bright morning light filtering into the room around the edges of the blinds on the windows. And he was alone.

He sat up and looked around, trying to clear the cobwebs from his sleep-deprived brain. Bristol was nowhere to be seen. They'd fallen asleep here curled up together on their sides hours ago, with her tucked into his body. It was the best sleep he'd had in forever. And apparently deep, because he had no recollection of her leaving.

The bedroom door down the short hallway was shut. He pushed aside the stab of disappointment. Probably best that she'd gone to her own bed. Made things neater, avoided the whole awkward morning-after thing.

Unless she'd left because she regretted last night and wanted to avoid him.

He ran a hand through his hair and dragged on his clothes, feeling strangely unsettled and a little raw. Last night was wrong on so many levels, he knew that, but there was no changing it now. Part of him was mad as hell at himself for caving to his baser nature and making this whole situation even messier.

No. That was just a bullshit excuse. What he hated was how off-balance she made him feel. Bristol had woken something elemental in him that he couldn't ignore, and he didn't know what the hell to do about it. Or her.

He went into the kitchen and started a pot of coffee. Shaved off his full goatee in the powder room sink while it brewed. He'd worn a beard or part of one for so long, his clean-shaven face was like a stranger staring back at him in the mirror.

Back in the kitchen, he popped some bread in the toaster. It was still early. He had no news, and last night had been a lot.

He'd let Bristol sleep a while longer. When she came out of the room, he would play it cool. Act like last night hadn't happened so they could just put it behind them and move on. Last night never should have happened. Ending their physical relationship now before things went any further was the right thing to do.

Way too late for that, and you know it.

Yeah, he did know it. Because somewhere along the way, he'd caught feelings for her. Big ones.

Didn't matter, he told himself sternly. He had to end it. Once their current predicament was over, he would get a new assignment somewhere else. Or maybe he'd leave the DEA for good. Either way, he and Bristol would be going their separate ways soon. She was too good. Too kind. She deserved a hell of a lot better than a burned-out, emotionally closed-off guy who'd spent the better part of the past year living on the street.

He snatched his phone from the counter when it rang. He

didn't recognize the number, but it was local. "Yeah," he answered, relieved by the distraction.

"You're in danger. He knows who you are."

TJ's spine went rigid. The male voice was somehow familiar, but he couldn't quite place it. "Who's this?"

"We've never met. But you know me. We've spoken before."

Woah, shit. He'd been trying to meet this guy in person for *months*. He'd been feeding them bits of intel for that long. He was the reason TJ had been granted permission to move here to the coast, in the hopes of making enough inroads with him through Mark so they could finally meet in person.

TJ had thought the botched meeting last night had shot that hope to hell, so to say this call was a surprise was an understatement. "So you called to warn me?"

"Partly. But I'm also willing to trade sensitive information in exchange for a favor."

"What kind of information?" Warning bells clanged in his brain. Who the hell was this guy, and why was he making contact now? The timing was suspicious.

"Sensitive, personal information on Jordan Leandro."

"How personal?"

"Enough to destroy him."

This was everything they'd wanted and more. Except it felt too good to be true. TJ kept talking. "Why are you reaching out now?"

"Because I know you're DEA and your cover's burned. The only way to protect yourself is to take him down before his people get you. I can help."

Fuck. Word traveled fast. And his take on the situation wasn't wrong. "What's the favor?"

"Federal protection."

"You'd need to talk to the Feds about that."

"I'd rather deal with you."

"Why's that?"

"Because I don't trust anyone else, and I'm on a tight timeline. Leandro knows his personal files were copied. It's only a matter of time before he finds out it was me. And he's got his falcons out looking for you right now."

"How do you know that?"

"Because one of them just asked me about you. I threw him off your trail, but it's only going to buy you a little time."

TJ looked over at the closed bedroom door. He thought of Bristol asleep in there, oblivious of the mounting danger.

Oblivious that he was a threat to her.

This building should be secure enough for her if he left. For now, anyway. "What kind of deal are you looking for?" He had no reason to trust this guy. But this might be the only way to salvage this entire operation. And, if they got really lucky, to take Leandro down.

That was the only real way to make sure Bristol was safe, and maybe even save himself.

"Immunity and a new identity. The Feds offered me WITSEC before, but I turned it down. Timing wasn't right."

"What intel do you have?" he pressed.

"Digital files full of blackmail material on his rivals. As well as evidence showing what Leandro's been up to with another lieutenant's wife."

Oh, shit. Yeah, this guy getting his hands on all that could definitely get him killed if Leandro ever found out. "What evidence?"

"Text messages. *Video*. Along with other evidence directly linking Leandro to recent shipments in the Pacific Northwest, and several murders."

All of that should be more than enough to put him away —if it was legit. "To qualify for federal protection, you'd have to turn all that over, cooperate fully with investigators from various agencies, and testify against him if it went to trial. That would be the minimum for any sort of deal. And going into WITSEC means giving up everything and everyone in your life, starting over."

"I'm aware. But I'm not going into WITSEC until my family's brought up from Mexico and set up here."

"You know the Feds could use that leverage against you."

"Yeah, but I want Leandro taken down as bad as they do. And like I said, I'm short on time."

If Leandro knew the files had been copied, he would have people hunting the person responsible. From the sounds of it, the countdown had already begun. "If I can get the Feds to sign off on a deal, you'll send me the evidence?"

"No. I'll only give it to you in person. Just you, no one else. Then I'll turn myself in, on the condition that my family is guaranteed safe transport and citizenship in the US. I won't cooperate further until that happens."

It was a tall order. There were so many things that could go wrong with that plan. And there was also a good chance that this whole thing could be an elaborate setup. "Let me see what I can do. I'll contact you from this number as soon as I have an answer."

"Fair warning—if you try to fuck me over, I'm gone. And you'll be dead."

The threat was real. It was possible this guy could track his location using this call and report it to a falcon or enforcer.

The sooner he got Bristol away from him, the better.

"Understood. I'll be in touch soon." He ended the call and took the battery out of his phone, even though it might be too late to stop the guy from tracking him. Taking another burner from his bag, he immediately dialed his handler.

"Morning," Diana answered. "You both still secure in the condo?"

"Yeah, but I just had an interesting conversation with the asset connected to Jordan Leandro."

"Did you? Do tell."

He explained everything. "He'll only meet in person. Just with me."

"Do you have a name for me?"

"No, but it's him. I recognized his voice. He used a burner."

"Of course." Her interest was clear. "Where does he want to meet?"

"He didn't say, but this has to happen fast. I told him I'd contact him once I had an answer about a protection deal."

"I'll contact my person at the FBI and find out what we can offer him."

"No bullshit. He'll see right through it, and if he bolts, he's gone." Either because he disappeared somewhere off the radar or one of Leandro's enforcers got him. "He also confirmed that Leandro has falcons out looking for me." His gaze strayed to the bedroom door. "Bristol needs out of here ASAP."

"Agreed. I'll call my people, make it clear this guy is priority for us. What do you want to do about Bristol?"

"I need you to arrange for CPS to pick her up here and take her to a new secure location. I can't leave her without protection." It was safest for her to be away from him, at an undisclosed site he didn't know about. When he walked out that door, he wouldn't be coming back. And if he was captured, this way he wouldn't be able to give up her location even if they tried to torture it out of him.

Leandro was fanatical, wouldn't risk leaving any loose ends. Bristol would only be safe once he was eliminated.

"All right. Give me some time to see what I can do. I'll get back to you as soon as I have an answer," Diana said.

"How soon?"

"Soon as I can."

He set the phone down on the countertop. Forced himself to eat the cold toast he no longer wanted. The coffee was almost finished brewing, but he didn't want that either. He wanted...

His gaze strayed back to the closed bedroom door, and his whole body tightened with renewed urgency. He should just let her sleep. It would be kinder and easier for them both if he just slipped out and went to the meeting without seeing her. Cleaner that way.

Then he heard the faint sound of water rushing through the pipes in the en suite bathroom. The shower was running.

An image of her standing naked beneath the flowing water filled his head. Rivulets of it sliding down her smooth skin, tracing her curves.

His resolve to keep his distance wavered. He'd made up his mind to leave, but right now everything in him was screaming at him to stay. To steal as much time left as he could with Bristol.

He walked over to the bedroom door. Stopped in front of it with his hand on the knob, telling himself not to go any farther. That he needed to walk away now.

But the need to see her, touch her one last time was like a living thing inside him.

He twisted the knob while his heart hammered in his ears, his whole chest burning with a raw hunger he couldn't contain.

He caught a glimpse of rumpled sheets as his eyes swept past the bed to the bathroom. Faint wisps of steam floated out of the partially open door.

He pushed it open.

Bristol stood with her back to him, arms raised as she washed her hair. Her pose showed off the exquisite lines of her back, the muscles on either side of her spine that flowed all the way down to her rounded ass.

Her head snapped around, her hands still in her hair. Their gazes locked.

A powerful, territorial feeling coiled through his body.

His pulse continued to pound in his ears, all but drowning out the rush of the shower. Touching her again was dangerous. Like taking another hit of an illicit drug that he knew would turn him into an addict and maybe even kill him. He should leave.

Except he couldn't. Seeing her like that, naked and only ten feet away, knowing he would have to leave her within the next hour…

There was no way in hell he could walk away without one last taste. Without one final chance to make her feel the same way he did.

Holding her gaze, he stripped off his clothes and pulled the glass door open to step inside the enclosure with her. Ready to claim the woman who had turned his world upside down and changed him forever.

TWENTY-FOUR

Heart thudding, Bristol lowered her arms as TJ stepped in behind her, the sheer size of him dwarfing her and making the shower suddenly seem cramped. Her pulse raced out of control at the intense look on his face, the unmistakable heat in his dark eyes. He looked so different clean-shaven, all the planes and angles of his face revealed.

God, he was gorgeous.

He wrapped a steely arm around her stomach and drew her back against his equally hard body, his mouth dropping to kiss the spot where her neck and shoulder met. "You left."

Yes. Sometime in the middle of the night she'd woken up, realized she was already falling too fast and hard for him, and decided to make her escape. She had planned to walk out of the bedroom and pretend last night had been a casual, one-time thing. No big deal, just a momentary lapse in judgment caused by all the fear and stress of last night.

It would all have been a lie. And she was pretty sure TJ knew that.

"I have to go," he said, interrupting her thoughts.

"Go?" The way he said it sounded so final. She pushed down the spurt of panic. "Where?"

"I need to meet in person with another CI."

"What about me?"

"You'll stay here. CPS will move you to a new location."

She turned around to face him, ready to ask what would happen after that. But she already knew. The guarded look in his eyes told her everything she needed to know.

She'd been right to leave the couch, because it was clear where she stood with him.

"Okay." She was proud of how steady her voice was, how nonchalantly she said it. With no hint of the disappointment and devastation filling her.

Oh, but he didn't like her answer.

He frowned, wrapped his other arm around her and drew her close. "It's not okay. It's not even remotely okay," he ground out, frustration pouring off him. "I told myself to just walk away. Told myself not to touch you again, but I can't do that. Not after last night. And there's no way you don't feel this too."

She stared up at him, hope forming a burning knot in the middle of her heart. "What makes you so sure?"

"Because I know you. I know what kind of person you are, and there's zero chance you would've let me in that far if you don't have feelings for me."

He was eerily on point about that. All of it. It shook her.

He slid one hand into the back of her hair, squeezing the wet strands gently. "If you don't feel anything for me, then tell me to walk away right now. Say it." His eyes burned like fire, challenging her to deny it.

She couldn't. And he knew it as well as she did.

He growled low in his throat and captured her lips in a searing kiss that made her head spin. A heartbeat later she was pressed flush against the cool, wet wall, pinned in place by more than two-hundred pounds of hard, hungry man.

Bristol wrapped around him, clung tight to his slick shoulders while his tongue stroked hers. He tasted of desperation. Radiated it from every pore as he held her there, imprinting her with his scent and the feel of his body.

He slid his hands down to cup her breasts, eyes darkening as they fixed on the tight points of her nipples. His mouth closed around one, sucking gently, the flick of his tongue bringing her up on her toes, a gasp slipping free. He stayed there for another few moments before treating the other to the same attention, each luxurious pull of his talented mouth intensifying the need inside her.

His hands moved to her waist. Slid down to grip her hips and squeeze while he sank to his knees in front of her.

Bristol steadied herself on his shoulders, struggling to catch her breath, and thankful she was nearsighted so she could see every glorious detail of him even without her glasses. The sight of him like that, on his knees before her with his water-drenched hair slicked back from his face, the muscles in his arms, shoulders and chest standing out in sharp relief...

And the raw hunger on his face, his gaze dropping to the juncture of her thighs where she was already wet and throbbing.

His fingers flexed on her hips, holding her with a possessive grip while he leaned in and nuzzled between her legs. She made a garbled sound and plunged a hand into his short hair, widening her trembling legs to give him room.

He accepted the invitation instantly, his mouth finding the top of her sex. The warmth of his tongue dragged a high-pitched moan from her as he slid it over her swollen folds to find her clit.

Her head dropped back against the shower wall, her eyes slamming shut as pure sensation streaked through her. It was so decadent, so incredibly erotic to have a man so powerful kneeling before her, worshipping her with his tongue.

It was surreal. Each warm, languid caress of his tongue sent tendrils of pleasure spiraling through her. She climbed higher and higher, and when he licked inside her, her knees went weak. He held her there, keeping her firmly in place while his tongue drove her to the edge of release. She made a pleading sound, somehow opened her eyes to look down at him.

TJ stared back at her for a long moment, his tongue buried inside her. She quivered, fingers digging into his shoulders. It was so insanely erotic. More intimate than anything she'd experienced before.

He surged to his feet, his hands gripping her rear as he lifted her off her feet and pinned her back against the wall with his weight. With the hot length of his erection trapped between them, he wrapped one arm around the small of her back to secure her there and lifted his free hand to cup the side of her face.

"Are you protected?" he rasped out, searching her eyes.

"Yes," she gasped, half-blind with desperation. Being so close to the edge and having release taken away was torture. "And I'm clean."

"Me too. You trust me?"

Staring into those dark, hungry eyes, she felt her heart soften and expand. He had lied to her before to protect his cover. And himself. But he would never lie about this. That wasn't the kind of man he was. "Yes."

With a dark sound from deep in his chest, his mouth came down on hers. She opened for the thrust of his tongue, fought to get closer when he reached between them and positioned the head of his cock against her core.

The sudden pressure took her off guard. She was wet and swollen, more than ready for him, yet he felt too huge and hard. Unyielding as he penetrated her, her body struggling to adjust to the invasion.

She hissed in a breath and tensed, trying to wriggle free. Or maybe trying to wriggle closer, she couldn't decide, her brain unable to process the knife-edge of pleasure/pain.

TJ stilled, his gaze searching hers. "Okay, Slugger?"

She licked her lips, the nickname undoing another tiny lock in her heart. "I…" She wasn't sure. It was just so intense, the angle and force of gravity heightening her inability to get any leverage to ease the pressure inside her.

He lifted her slightly, giving her a second or two reprieve before slowly lowering her again. Sinking him deeper inside her. Deeper still, his eyes locked with hers. Until he was buried to the hilt inside her.

Bristol whimpered, her body gripping him, ripples of pleasure spreading out from where they were joined. She locked her ankles behind his back and rubbed her aching clit against the hard plane of his abdomen, seeking relief from her torment.

TJ leaned his weight into her, holding her there with shocking ease. His arms and chest flexed with each slow surge of his hips while he worked in and out of her.

The tempo was maddening. The angle was perfect. She ground herself against him, orgasm looming sharp and devastating just at the edge of her consciousness. She threw her head back when it hit, her high-pitched cries filling the steam-filled enclosure.

TJ held her tight while the waves pulsed through her. When she was able to open her eyes again, she looked down and saw the tension on his face. His mouth was pulled tight, his jaw muscles standing out.

As if he'd been waiting for that eye contact, he picked up his pace, thrusting faster. Harder.

Just when he reached the edge, he suddenly pulled out of her body, grabbed her hand and wrapped her fingers around him. With their hands locked around his erection, he came against her belly, a strangled groan coming from between his clenched teeth.

Gradually the tension bled out of his body. He released her hand and opened his eyes to look at her, the hot water still pouring over them. His grip eased and he slowly lowered her feet back to the floor.

Feeling weak all over and even more vulnerable than when he'd stepped in here, Bristol tucked her face into the muscular curve of his shoulder. She leaned her weight against him, never doubting that he would keep her from sliding to her knees.

"TJ," she whispered. She felt so raw emotionally.

"Yeah," he answered quietly, and she knew he understood.

He rested his cheek on the top of her head and held her. Cradled her, his big arms sheltering her while the water rained down on them. She didn't know why he'd pulled out at the last moment like that, but guessed it was to add another layer of protection for her. Because he would never have entered her if he hadn't trusted her.

She wasn't sure how long they stayed like that, but all too soon he eased his hold and ran his hands over her, washing the last of the shampoo from her hair before moving to her belly and gently between her thighs. When she was all clean, he shut off the water and got out first, moments later wrapping her up in a big towel.

Neither of them spoke while they dried off and got dressed. Bristol didn't know what to say anyhow, the feelings inside her impossible to put into words. As impossible as their situation was.

"You hungry?" he asked, pulling his shirt down over that sculpted body that had just been plastered to her.

"I'm... A little." She tucked a lock of wet hair behind her ear.

"I made coffee if you want some."

"Sure." She watched him go to the kitchen, wondering what the hell to do or say now. Were they really going to leave it like this? After everything he'd said and everything they'd just done?

He poured her a mug and handed it over. Their eyes met, and she saw the indecision in his. The regret.

Her stomach dropped like a concrete ball.

A phone rang on the counter. He snatched it up, spoke to whoever it was on the other end. She could see the tension building in his shoulders as the conversation went on.

"Yeah, got it," he finally said, and turned toward her with that same look in his eyes. "Is CPS en route?"

For her, he meant. He must be talking to someone with the DEA.

Bristol tightened her fingers around the mug. She wasn't going to blurt out her feelings if he was about to leave.

"Okay, good. I'll be there in twenty minutes," he said, and the words echoed with a terrible finality. One that told her this was probably the last time she would see him.

Ending the call, he tucked his phone away into his jeans pocket and faced her from across the room. "I have to go."

She nodded. "I know." She wouldn't beg him to stay. Or to take her with him. Or ask him to come back to her when this was over. No matter how much it hurt to watch him walk away.

"I have to leave now. This is our one shot. If I'm not there in time, deal's off."

Don't go. Don't do it. "What about me?"

"CPS is on the way here now. You won't be alone for more than a few minutes, but I can't wait..." He looked so torn.

She dug down for the courage to ask more. "And then what?"

"Then you stay safe."

To her horror, tears flooded her eyes. She blinked fast. Tried to nod again, hating that this was going to end with her humiliation.

TJ cursed under his breath. A moment later she was being crushed in his arms, his voice low and urgent next to her ear. "Don't cry over me, Slugger. I'm not worth it, believe me."

She jerked her head back to glower up at him, gave his shoulder an angry shove. "Sh-shut up. I'll c-cry if I w-want to." Because he definitely *was* worth it. Whether he saw it or not.

His hold eased. He cupped her face between his hands, his thumbs wiping her tears away. He shook his head, a rueful but almost proud look on his face. "I knew you would be trouble the first time I saw you."

She frowned, struggling to process his meaning. "What? I was t-trying to h-help you."

"I know." His expression sobered. Turned deadly serious. "You stay safe, understand? I have to know you're safe."

"W-what about y-you?" He wasn't meeting this CI alone, was he? His cover was blown. Surely the DEA or some other agency would back him up for safety reasons.

"Don't worry about me."

Screw that. "Too late."

Something shifted in his eyes at her response. Something unguarded and vulnerable that was there and gone before she could decipher it, replaced by a veil of indifference.

"Be safe," he said quietly, the finality in his tone sending a chill through her.

This was it. This was goodbye.

Then he confused her even more by bending to give her one last heartbreakingly tender kiss before walking out and locking the door behind him.

TWENTY-FIVE

A new message from Hawk came through just as Angel got into his car. He'd spent last night in it, sleeping in little snatches in a pullout on the highway. Liana thought he was in Portland on a job for the next few days. He hated leaving her alone for so long, but she'd been in good spirits when he'd spoken to her this morning, and their elderly neighbor across the street was going to check on her.

Possible target address.

He looked it up on a map. It was a condo building just off the coastal highway on the other side of town.

Heading there now, he responded, and started the engine.

It was still early. The traffic was light, but as he drove, he found himself glancing out to sea. The forecasted weather front was already moving in from the west. Overhead, the sky was a solid leaden ceiling of gray, the clouds growing ominously darker on the horizon. Huge waves kicked up by the wind were crested with frothy whitecaps that exploded into tall fans of foam and saltwater when they crashed against the rocky shore.

A strange sense of foreboding grew inside him as he

approached the target building. Something about the storm had him on edge.

No one had seen Barros yet, or the woman he'd been with last night. Bristol Moreau. But maybe, if Angel was lucky, there would be some sign or clue about them at this new address. With him and several falcons out hunting Barros right now, it wouldn't be long before they had a lock on his location.

As he drove along the street the building was on, he scanned all the parked cars for a match with the vehicle Barros had been driving last night, then continued around the block to check the side streets. None of the vehicles he saw matched Barros's. The underground parking garage to the building was gated and accessible only to someone with the entrance code. He would have to check on foot once he got inside the building.

He parked a block away and walked to it while the rising wind gusted around him, stopping at the front entrance to read the menu board that listed the unit numbers and surnames of the tenants. None of the names matched any of the three he had been given for the construction company that owned the target unit.

But there was one unit on the board without a name, indicating that it was newly available. Exactly as it would be if renovations had just been completed.

That blank space was like an arrow pointing at a bullseye.

His phone buzzed in his pocket. He pulled it out, saw a new message from Hawk.

Found suspect vehicle near a marina close to Crimson Point. Called around and a guy matching Barros's description just showed up there a few minutes ago. They sent this image as he was leaving. Moving in for a closer look.

Angel still hadn't seen a clear image of Barros. He

enlarged the picture showing a thirty-something male with dark hair. The brim of a ballcap shadowed his face. The image was too grainy for him to see any facial features clearly, except that the guy was clean shaven. Barros had been reported as having a goatee last night but could easily have shaved it off.

What was he doing at the marina? He had to either be meeting someone, or looking to escape by water.

Is the woman with him?

No.

Keep me updated, he texted back. Sliding the phone into his pocket, he stepped back to look up at the fourth floor of the building where the unit with the unlisted tenant was located.

There was no point in trying to race to the marina. If the guy there turned out to be Barros, he would probably be long gone by the time Angel got there.

But there might be a way to make Barros come to him.

With any luck, the best chance of making that happen might still be on the fourth floor.

∾

TJ PULLED his hoodie down over the brim of the ballcap to help keep the wind-driven rain out of his face as he strode up the small hill at the edge of the gravel parking lot, heading away from the marina. The storm front had moved in fast on the drive here, the wind gusting hard enough to rock Bristol's car on the highway. He'd left it parked a couple blocks away and smeared mud over the license plates in case anyone was looking for it.

He still had no idea who this CI was, or if he was walking straight into a trap. His only reassurance was the weight of his weapon against the small of his back, and that his handler was en route with two other people from the Portland office.

No one else knew what he was doing. So if shit went sideways before that, backup was too far away to save his ass.

Once again, he was all on his own.

The stark reality of it hit him in a way it never had before. Until moving to Crimson Point, he'd managed to convince himself that he preferred being alone.

Bristol had changed all that.

The depth of his feelings for her were undeniable, had taken him completely off guard. He hadn't made any promises to her when he'd left because he didn't know what the future held, and he refused to lead her on or give her false hope. But seeing her cry for him just before he'd walked out the door… Dammit, he missed her already, and the thought of spending the rest of his life without her was too bleak to contemplate.

He pushed all that aside, going on alert. At the crest of the hill, he paused. A lone figure stood on the other side of the quiet dirt road. Tall, rangy, with a hoodie pulled over his head.

TJ took a cautious look around. It seemed like the guy was alone, but the hilly landscape made it impossible to see where any other potential threats might be hidden. And the telltale tingle at the nape of his neck confirmed that his subconscious sensed something was up.

The guy spotted him, pulled his hands from the front pouch on his hoodie and held them up in front of him, palms out. TJ continued toward him, watching him closely and ready to draw his weapon if the guy made a wrong move.

When he neared the far edge of the road and got close enough to get his first good look at the man's face through the slanting rain, shock ripped through him.

Holy shit. It was Leandro's right-hand man.

"You alone?" Jon said.

"Yeah. You?" This was unbelievable. Nobody, not even him, would have guessed someone so high up the chain would be feeding them bits of intel all this time.

Jon nodded, glancing around furtively. "I wasn't followed, but no guarantee we're alone out here. Let's do this fast and go our separate ways."

"Sounds good. They've agreed to a deal for you."

Jon looked back at him sharply. "And to getting my family set up here?"

"Yeah. Just as long as this isn't a setup, and the evidence you turn over is legit."

"Of course, it's legit," he snapped, blue eyes shooting sparks. "You think I'd put myself in this position, risking the worst kind of torture and death imaginable by doing this, risk the lives of my family by making shit up?"

"Standard procedure." Now he was dying to see what the evidence Jon had gathered contained. But that wouldn't happen until after TJ turned it over to his handler and let the agency do its thing to verify the contents were authentic and useful.

Jon started to reach one hand toward the hoodie's front pouch. TJ tensed and shifted his stance, his hand reaching toward the small of his back. Jon stilled instantly. "The drive's in my pocket," he said.

"Move slow." TJ's fingers curled around the grip of his pistol.

Jon slowly reached his hand into the pouch and came up with a thumb drive held in his fingers.

"Is this everything?"

"Yeah. Texts, photos, receipts, video. It's all there." He made no move to hand it over. "So what now?"

"You come with me. We meet up with my handler, and you turn yourself over. Once they verify what's on there…" He nodded toward Jon's hand. "They'll start the process rolling to bring your family over."

Jon's jaw tensed. For a moment TJ thought he would argue, but then he relented. "Okay." He handed the memory stick over.

TJ shoved it deep into his right front jeans pocket, the tingle at the back of his neck spreading down between his shoulder blades. He couldn't see anyone else out there, but he could feel eyes on them.

They both needed to get the hell outta here, fast. "Let's go."

TWENTY-SIX

In the backseat of his luxury SUV, Jordan stared at his phone screen as the live feed showed a figure stepping out onto a deserted dirt road near a marina close to Crimson Point. Rain pounded on the roof as the vehicle sped down the highway heading south toward the marina, the wind gusts pushing it sideways.

The man on screen wore a hoodie over a ballcap, the shadow cast by the brim concealing most of his face from view. "Where is this?" Jordan demanded. He'd had Hawk go to the marina to look for Barros and get a precise location on him.

"Just up the hill from the marina," Hawk said quietly. "Wait. There's someone else waiting across the road. They must have set up a meeting."

Jordan's attention sharpened as Hawk moved to a different position and another figure came into view across the road from Barros. "Can you see his face?"

"Trying to get a better angle, hang on." A minute later Hawk cursed. "You're not gonna believe this."

Jordan was aware of his heart rate climbing as Hawk's

phone zoomed in on the two men. The man Barros was meeting turned toward the camera slightly, allowing a clearer view of him.

All the blood drained from Jordan's face, shock detonating like a bomb. "No." His guts clenched, nausea gripping his belly. "No, I don't believe it." It couldn't be.

"It's him, boss. Sorry."

Jordan couldn't answer. Could only stare, transfixed with horror as the man he'd trusted more than any other these past three years spoke to Barros and handed him something small. Something that looked like it could be a flash drive.

The betrayal cut deep. He sucked in a painful breath, an involuntary wheeze escaping, like he'd just been stabbed in the lung.

He'd hand-selected Jon from the beginning and promoted him through the ranks. Had eventually made him his second-in-command. Had traveled with him. Shared countless meals and bottles of the best whiskey money could buy with him.

Jordan had made Jon rich beyond his wildest dreams, given him protection and power and influence... And in return Jon had turned on him. Spied on and stolen from him.

Then betrayed him by handing over things to the DEA that would end him.

Why? A howl of rage and agony clawed inside his chest.

He swallowed. Struggled to push back the red tide of rage suffusing him that squeezed his lungs and blurred his vision. This wasn't some sick prank or a misunderstanding. There was no way to refute what he'd just seen with his own eyes.

Jon had sold him out to the DEA.

"I'll kill him." His voice was raspy, hands shaking. "I'll motherfucking *kill* him for what he's done." Him and the goddamned DEA agent.

Who had Jon been working with? Jordan didn't believe

for a moment that he'd pulled this off all on his own. There had to be others. How far had the rot spread?

No one could be trusted now. He had to cull the herd, implement maximum and immediate damage control if he was going to have a prayer at saving himself. Couldn't risk letting the infection spread any further.

"Where's Angel?" he snapped at Hawk, his breathing ragged.

"Last I heard, getting himself some insurance to ensure Barros cooperates."

Jordan didn't give a shit about the girl anymore. "Tell him to get his ass to the marina and deal with this. *Now*."

"You want both Barros and Jon captured?"

"N—" He stopped himself. He wanted them to die for what they'd done, but that was just his wounded ego talking. Better to have them captured so he could have them interrogated and find out the extent of the damage.

And that way he would have Angel there as well. He would have to be dealt with too, of course. No loose ends. Three birds with one stone. And Jordan also wanted to be the one to demand answers. See the terror in their eyes when they realized he knew what they'd done and that they would die for it.

"Yes. Tell him to bring them to me and I'll double his fee." Angel would want to know the compensation up front before agreeing. It was just smart business. Too bad he'd never collect a dime of it. "I'll meet you and him at the marina. Keep an eye on everything until I get there." He was only twenty minutes away. Half that, if the driver really pushed it.

"Boss? You sure you want to risk—" Hawk said.

"Fucking *do* it," he snarled. He ended the call and ordered his driver to take him straight to the marina as fast as he could. His next call arranged to have a boat waiting there for him. A fast one. And then he made one last call to arrange his getaway vehicle.

Timing was critical. He wasn't leaving anything to chance this time.

He couldn't trust anyone now. Not Jon. Probably not Angel. Or even Hawk. He wondered if any of them guessed that.

He opened a hidden panel in the floorboard and began loading some weapons. It was time to take matters into his own hands. He'd clawed his way up through the shit of this world and through the deadly web of the cartel to get where he was. He'd survived everything they'd thrown at him, the might of the cartel and government law enforcement agencies combined.

He wouldn't let anyone take his empire from him now. Let alone a fucking undercover DEA agent and some assholes he'd made the mistake of placing his trust in.

∽

ANGEL PAUSED in the stairwell when another buzz in his back pocket signaled a new message from Hawk. He pulled out his phone.

Shit is going down. Jon is the leak. He just met with Barros near the marina.

His eyebrows shot up. Jon had been leaking intel to the Feds? Wow. Ballsy. He hadn't seen that one coming.

Okay, he responded. *And?* He wasn't sure what that had to do with him. *I'm busy.*

Boss wants you to ditch the girl and deal with this instead. Pronto. Capture them both and bring them to the marina. We'll meet you there. He says he'll double your usual fee.

A rush of elation flashed through Angel. This was it. This should be enough to pay for what he needed. It was a huge risk going after two men with training, but if he pulled it off and lived, he could walk away and leave this all behind him. He and Liana could leave for Europe as soon as the money hit his account, with the fake passports he already had stashed with the go-bags she didn't know about.

He was tempted to turn around and head straight for the marina immediately, but paused, his gaze on the fire door ahead of him that led to the fourth-floor hallway. He was already here. And if the woman was inside the condo, she could prove highly valuable to him on this op by guaranteeing Barros's cooperation. A DEA agent wasn't likely to sit back and let an innocent woman die. Especially if there was any kind of connection between them.

Angel was banking that there was.

Got it, was all he said to Hawk in answer, and tucked the phone away. Nobody needed to know how he captured Jon and Barros, they only cared that he got it done.

He pushed open the steel fire door and glanced both ways. The hallway was empty, the building silent except for the sound of the wind moaning around the edges of the windows. It was built of concrete and rebar and had good soundproofing. That would work in his favor.

On silent feet, he made his way to the target unit. Keeping his eye out for anyone who might step out into the hallway, he reached a gloved hand back for his lockpick kit. In seconds he had it picked.

He stepped inside, ready to collect his insurance.

TWENTY-SEVEN

Bristol washed her face in the bathroom sink and patted it dry. Hands curled around the edges of the sink, she stared at her reflection in the mirror. Eyes red and puffy. Nose pink. Heartbreak etched into every feature.

"Pull yourself together," she ordered herself, and straightened. She was a big girl. She would get through this.

Yeah, it hurt that TJ had just walked away after everything they'd shared and that she probably wouldn't ever see him again. But he'd made no promises. She'd done this to herself by getting attached to a man who clearly had intimacy issues and plenty of other baggage that made a healthy relationship impossible. This awful ache in the center of her chest would fade. She would get over it.

She had to keep telling herself that, or she would fall apart.

To keep busy while she waited for someone from CPS to come get her—she was hoping Cassie—she wiped down the bathroom, stripped the sheets from the bed and threw them into the washing machine with the dirty towels. Kind of like getting ready to check out of a VRBO, only worse, because her heart was hurting, and she had no idea where she would be going after this. Or for how long.

She just wanted her life back so she could heal and then make everything go back to normal. Or at least as normal as possible, since it could never go back to the way it had been before this.

In the kitchen entry, she stopped, another wave of pain washing over her. The coffee TJ had made them was still in the pot, her now cold mug sitting on the countertop. She dumped them both out and washed them by hand before wiping down the work surface, trying not to think. But even the stupid crumbs on the counter from his toast put a lump in her throat.

He felt something for her. She knew he did, no matter how much he wanted to pretend he didn't. For him to say what he had in the shower—

Men say a lot of things when they're having sex, a cynical voice in her head scolded. *It doesn't mean anything.*

"For him it does," she said out loud, refusing to believe otherwise.

Little good it did her.

She went into the living room, ruthlessly smothered another surge of sadness when she saw the rumpled blankets she and TJ had curled up beneath together on the couch last night. She shook them out. Folded one, then the other. Still not satisfied, she picked up the dented pillow and shook it too. Punched it a couple times for good measure.

She heard the front door handle turn.

She spun to face the entry as the door opened, and an unfamiliar man stepped inside. Tall. Muscular. Brown hair cut short in the back and a bit longer in the front. He stopped just inside, staring at her as he closed the door.

A faint tingle of alarm ran through her that he hadn't said anything. "Are you...with CPS?"

He hesitated just a fraction of a second too long. "Yes. You ready to go?"

The warning tingle became a blaring siren.

Her gaze darted to her bat where she'd left it propped against the TV console table. She whipped around and lunged for it.

Too late. Her hand had barely touched the handle when he knocked it from her grip and grabbed her around the torso from behind.

She shrieked and tried to bash him with her elbow. He clapped a steely hand over her mouth and clamped his arms tighter around her, the force compressing her ribs until she couldn't breathe.

"I don't want to hurt you." His low voice was so calm it sent cold corkscrewing up her backbone.

She fought harder. Twisting and thrashing. Trying to bite his palm or fingers, fighting to wrestle free of his hold.

But he was too strong. Before she could even suck in enough air to let out another scream, he had a wide piece of tape across her mouth and her hands wrenched behind her back.

He secured her wrists with more tape, her continued struggles having no effect whatsoever.

The instant her arms were secured, he reached into her back pocket and plucked her phone out, then dragged a hood over her head, plunging her into instant darkness. Terror exploded through her. Blind, bound, and gagged, she kicked at him, lashing out with all her strength.

She missed him, hitting nothing but air.

A heartbeat later, her world turned upside down as he

flung her over his shoulder and started carrying her toward an uncertain fate.

TWENTY-EIGHT

After what seemed like at least fifteen minutes of driving, the car finally stopped, and the engine turned off. Bristol's heart pounded so hard against her ribs it felt bruised. She couldn't see, couldn't speak, couldn't move her hands or arms with her wrists tied behind her, and he'd strapped her legs to the seat.

She had no idea who this guy was or where he'd taken her, except that he had to be with the cartel, and she was terrified that he was planning to use her as bait to lure TJ to him.

He unstrapped her legs, gave a quiet grunt when she managed to plant her foot in his middle, then pulled her out of the backseat. His grip was like iron on her wrists as he forced her to walk with him across the uneven surface, gravel crunching under their feet. Bristol scrambled to keep up with him, the angle he was holding her wrists at meaning any attempt to drop to the ground to try and get free would risk dislocating her shoulders.

The wind whipped over them, rain pelting their clothes. The tiniest hint of gray light filtered through the tiny gap at the bottom of the hood where it fell against her collarbones.

She could hear the faint cries of seagulls and a continuous metallic clanking sound in the distance. Like a line flapping against a flagpole. The gulls and the briny scent to the air told her they had to be near the water.

"Step up," he said, and practically lifted her off her feet when she did.

Her shoes came down on something flat and hard, and when they started walking again, the hollow sound of their steps told her they were walking on wood. Were they at a marina maybe? The clanking could be lines flapping against masts.

There was no resisting him as he drew her across the wooden planking, turning left and then right, then left again. They'd barely stopped when he suddenly swung her up in his arms and set her back down on her feet a moment later. He kept a tight hold on her upper arm to steady her as she swayed, the floor seeming to move beneath her.

A boat. Shit, where was he taking her now?

He ushered her a short distance across the deck, then put a hand on top of the hood, angling her face downward slightly. "Stairwell. Watch your head."

It was such a weird thing for a kidnapper and probable murderer to say and do, but she did as she was told before awkwardly going down a short set of stairs with him. Outside, the wind and rain continued to lash the boat. But here inside, an awful hush surrounded her as he put her in a chair, ripped the tape off her wrists and secured her hands to the back of it with rope.

Without warning he yanked the hood off her. Her glasses slid down her nose and fell to the floor with a clatter.

She blinked at the sudden shift in light, flinched when a strobing flash seared her retinas. Realized he'd just taken a picture of her.

He was focused on the phone in his hand. Her phone, that he'd taken from her pocket at the condo, and used her thumbprint to unlock it. He was busy typing a message to someone. Probably sending the picture along with the message. His boss? Or TJ?

When he finished, he lowered the phone and raised his head to look at her. Her insides shriveled.

He'd gotten what he needed from her. Proof that she'd been captured, and was bound on a boat. Bait to try and make TJ come for her.

Bitterness and resentment swamped her. If her mouth wasn't taped shut, she would have told him to go to hell and that he was wasting his time. TJ wouldn't come for her. He'd made his feelings clear when he'd walked out earlier. She was terrified for him.

Her uneven breaths sounded loud in the enclosed space, her gaze glued to the man who held her life in his hands. She couldn't look away from him, her muscles pulling tight as guidewires.

"I'm not gonna kill you," he said in an almost bored tone. "I just want him."

She didn't buy the first part for one second.

He took a step toward her. She sucked in a sharp breath through her nose, shrank back in the chair and instinctively flexed her knees to bring her feet up, ready to drive her heels into whatever part of him she could reach.

But he thwarted her attack with laughable ease, pinning her thighs in place with one forearm while he tugged the dark hood back over her head with his other hand. "Keep still. This will all be over soon." He walked away.

She waited until his footsteps climbed the stairs up to the deck and disappeared under the noise from the storm, gave it another few seconds just to be safe, then began to struggle in earnest to get her hands free. He'd tied them firmly but not so tight that they cut off the circulation, and the rope gave her a better chance at freeing her hands than duct tape would have.

An engine purred to life somewhere close by. Then the boat started moving.

A fresh surge of fear swept through her.

Hurry, hurry, she ordered herself, fumbling desperately to find any knots or points of laxity in the ropes keeping her hands prisoner. Was he taking her out to sea to dump her?

He hadn't hurt her yet, but that didn't mean he wouldn't when he didn't need her anymore—which she guessed was when TJ showed up.

If he showed up.

Oh, God, she didn't want him to die, or to be the reason he did. But if he didn't come for her, she was dead for sure.

TWENTY-NINE

TJ was partway back to Bristol's car when his phone buzzed in his pocket. He pulled it out, stopped walking when he saw an image sent from Bristol's number.

When he opened the picture file, his heart seized.

It showed Bristol, sitting in a chair in what looked like the cabin of a boat, with her hands tied behind her and a strip of duct tape across her mouth. Her face was pinched with fear, her big blue eyes wide with it.

His guts clenched. Then a message came through beneath it.

Bring Jon out to the Sea Siren *in the next thirty minutes or she dies.*

"Jesus Christ," he breathed, raw panic tearing at him.

Mother*fucker*. This was his fault. He should have pushed Bristol away harder in the beginning. Then this never would have happened. But he hadn't. Deep down he'd been too fucking selfish to sever contact, and now she was facing torture and execution by one of the cartel's enforcers.

Beside him, Jon stopped too. "What?"

"They've got Bristol."

Jon frowned. "Who?"

"Someone connected to me. The message says to bring you to the boat she's on within thirty minutes, or they'll kill her."

Jon's face tightened. "An enforcer."

"Yeah. No one else is close enough to get to her in time. You gotta come with me."

"No way in hell."

"You have to. She's an innocent civilian, she's got nothing to do with any of this."

"Fuck that. I go anywhere near that boat, I'm dead."

TJ whipped out his weapon, aimed it at him. He wasn't fucking around. "*Move.*"

Jon stared at him for a long, tense moment with a cold expression. "I'll get you close enough to board the boat. But that's it."

"Just move. *Go.*" Keeping his weapon in one hand, he dialed CPS with the other as they ran for the marina. CPS were way closer than the DEA team, and they were the only ones he trusted to provide backup. He wasn't going to risk Bristol's life by waiting for the cops to respond. "I need to talk to Ryder, Callum or Walker immediately," he said when the receptionist answered. There was no time to explain. "This is an emergency."

"Putting you through to Walker now," the woman said without asking questions.

"Walker," a deep voice answered a few moments later.

"It's TJ Barros. I need backup at the Shelter Cove Marina ASAP. Bristol Moreau has been taken hostage on a boat by a cartel enforcer."

"Ah, shit."

"Yes." He quickly ran through the rest of the pertinent intel, his weapon still trained on Jon's back.

They skidded down the slick grassy slope leading to the marina parking lot, the wind whipping over them. "This way," Jon said, heading left.

TJ followed, giving Walker updates as they went. Together they ran down the wet dock, then Jon jumped aboard a speedboat and checked the ignition. "Here," he called out, and began fiddling with the wiring.

TJ jumped aboard, steadied himself in the stern and gave Walker the name of the boat. The engine roared to life. He and Jon quickly untied the lines from the cleats on the dock, then Jon eased them out of their berth and started through the marina.

"Do you have a visual on the target vessel?" Walker asked TJ.

"Negative." He wiped the rain from his face, gaze sweeping the open water beyond the harbor mouth. Where the hell was it?

There were no boats out there, no surprise given the stormy conditions. Beyond the breakwaters at the mouth of the harbor, the waves churned, restless and angry as they rushed at the shoreline. The storm was already more intense than predicted, the winds whipping over the water from the southwest.

Jon picked up speed as they exited the harbor, the rain hitting TJ's face like needles. Squinting, he spotted a vessel ahead. He saw a pair of binos near the helm, grabbed them. The vessel bobbed in the waves, moving slowly out to sea. He tightened the focus on the stern.

Sea Siren.

"I have a visual. About half a mile out of the harbor, heading out to sea."

"Roger that. I've got a team of four en route to the marina now, including Cassie."

"Copy. We're in pursuit. Request you contact the DEA."

"Wilco. Watch your six."

"Roger." He ended the call, shoved the phone into his back pocket and adjusted the binos. The *Sea Siren* appeared to have stopped. "He's waiting for us. Hit it."

Jon opened the throttle. The bow of the boat lifted, bouncing hard enough on the crest of each wave they hit to jar TJ's bones. His watch said they had less than ten minutes until the deadline.

They closed in fast, nearing the other boat in minutes. Jon cut the throttle when they were within a hundred yards away, the bow plunging down with the sudden shift in momentum. "Closer," TJ ordered.

"No way."

"I said *closer*," he growled, feeling the seconds slipping away.

"Are you fucking insane?" Jon gave a humorless laugh. "That's Angel out there. He never misses."

"Neither do I." A meaningful pause followed. "And if he'd wanted to kill us, he could easily have taken us out with a rifle already at this range. He wants us alive."

"Yeah, so he can torture us for information about what I just gave you, *then* kill us." He shook his head. "This wasn't part of the deal. I held up my end already."

Bristol's life was hanging in the balance. TJ had no choice.

He snatched his weapon from the holster and aimed it at Jon's chest. He could still deliver Jon to Angel with a bullet wound. "Get me to that boat. *Now*."

Jon's jaw tightened. For a moment TJ thought he might try to disarm him. But then he reached for the throttle, resentment burning in his eyes. "You wanna die, that's your choice. But I don't. I'm not coming within pistol range."

"*Go.*" Poised on the starboard gunwale, TJ eyed the distance to the target vessel. There was no sign of Angel yet, but the danger didn't matter. He had to get to Bristol.

"It's your funeral, man," Jon said.

TJ kept his weapon steady on him as Jon reluctantly turned the bow toward the *Sea Siren* and started forward slowly. Their boat hit a trough between waves, plunging the bow down sharply. TJ shot out a hand to catch the edge of the gunwale.

Jon hit him full force in the back, knocking him sideways over the side.

THIRTY

The shock of the cold water made his lungs constrict. TJ surfaced, sucked in a breath an instant before a wave hit him right in the face. It took him under, pushing him down like a giant hand.

He kicked hard, his arms slicing through the water to get back to the surface. His head broke through. He turned his face just in time for the next wave to break over his shoulder instead. Somehow, he'd managed to keep hold of his weapon.

That motherfucker Jon had already turned the boat around and was making his escape, abandoning him and Bristol. TJ had no choice but to swim for the *Sea Siren*.

Turning onto his belly, he swam flat out for it. Behind him he heard Jon throttle up the other boat and speed away. Raw anger boiled in his gut. If Bristol died because of him, TJ would hunt him down like an animal and kill him—if he didn't die out here himself.

Fighting through the waves made the relatively short swim exhausting. His muscles were already tiring when he finally reached the other boat. He grabbed hold of the folded-up ladder at the stern and hauled himself out of the water. It sluiced off him in a wave, covering the rear deck as he stumbled forward while the boat rocked with the angry waves.

His numb fingers tightened around the grip of the pistol. Even after being submerged in saltwater, the Glock should still fire.

He hoped.

Jon was gone. Now it was going to come down to a fight to the death between him and the enforcer. With Bristol's life hanging in the balance.

A figure appeared at the top of the forward hatch, still mostly hidden from view. TJ raised and aimed his weapon at him, shivering from head to toe, filled with steely resolve.

This asshole wanted to take him alive, or he would have shot him the instant he came out of the water. But TJ would save Bristol or die trying. "Where is she?" he demanded, feet spread apart to keep his balance on the rocking deck.

Angel stayed where he was. TJ had to assume a weapon was trained on him right now too. "Below."

"She's alive?"

"She's fine. I wasn't gonna hurt her. I presume that was Jon?"

The calm tone threw him. He opened his mouth to demand something else, but a sudden jolt of the boat sent him stumbling back. He caught himself just in time to keep from falling on his ass. "I need to see—" His words cut off when "Angel" stepped into full view. And froze just as TJ had.

Across the length of the boat they stared at each other, weapons aimed.

For a split-second TJ thought he must be hallucinating. Couldn't believe what he was seeing. "Nico?" he finally blurted. Nico Angelopoulos. *Angel.* Jesus Christ.

Nico's face was blank with shock. "Tomás." He lowered his weapon slightly. "What the *fuck*?"

Yeah.

TJ couldn't find the words to reply. They had met in BATP training at the DEA Academy in Quantico, the first phase to becoming an entry level special agent. Nico was a former Marine and had been one of the best in their class. They'd been roommates for several weeks. Then, one day a few months in, Nico was suddenly gone.

The cadre had told them he'd dropped out for personal reasons. TJ had never seen or heard from him again. Until now.

Nico shook his head in disbelief. "Shit, man. I didn't know."

"That makes two of us."

"They told me your name was..."

TJ Barros. "Legally changed it for my cover."

Nico looked a little pale. He lowered his weapon slightly.

TJ eyed him. "You still gonna shoot me?"

If he didn't, the cartel would come for them both.

"I—no. *Shit*." He dropped his hands, weapon dangling at his side.

"Good. I don't wanna shoot you either." How the hell was this going to play out now? Nico couldn't just let him and Bristol go. He lowered his own weapon, leaving the rest of their predicament for later, his gaze slicing to the covered cabin. "I need to see her."

"Yeah, of course—" They both turned at the sound of a boat approaching them fast from behind.

The same one that Jon had brought him out here in. It was coming straight at them.

"What are the odds he changed his mind?" Nico said.

TJ tensed. "Zero." This could not be good.

The boat raced at them, skimming over the rough waves. He desperately wanted to check on Bristol, but he believed

Nico that she was okay, and for now she was safer down below with the added protection of the cabin. "Got a rifle?" He crouched down near the stern.

"Yeah." Nico ducked back inside the hatch. No sooner had his head reappeared a few moments later, shots cracked through the air. A burst of semi-auto fire.

The rounds sliced into a wave less than twenty yards from their stern. TJ ducked down lower, struggling to keep his balance in the rough seas. Even if it managed to fire, his pistol was utterly useless at this range, and the smaller, faster boat was catching up way too fast. He needed to protect Bristol.

He got up and ran for the bow. Nico was kneeling there with his rifle to his shoulder. "Drive," he shouted at TJ.

TJ barely made it two steps toward the helm when more shots rang out. This time rounds punched into the stern. The sound of the idling engine changed. It sputtered. A big wave hit them on the port bow, spinning them halfway around to face the oncoming boat.

TJ flung out a hand to grab the railing and stop himself from sliding across the water-drenched deck, managed to stop his momentum and stay in the boat. When he flipped over onto his front and looked over the water, he saw with a jolt how close the other boat was. Close enough that he could see the two men standing at the helm. One driving. The other aiming a rifle.

Jon wasn't one of them. No, it was much, much worse.

"It's Leandro," he called out to Nico, who had repositioned himself.

"Yeah." He had the scope to his eye. Took aim and fired before the other shooter could adjust his aim. Blood spattered the windscreen and one of the men dropped out of sight. The other boat veered sharply left, whoever was shooting at them firing in a wild arc.

TJ heard Nico grunt. Turned to see him slide to the deck, holding his chest.

Fuck.

TJ dove at him, knocked him flat as more rounds punched into the fiberglass hull. Their boat kept turning, then, without warning, another big wave hit them from the other side, pitching them sharply to port.

One moment TJ was pinning Nico to the deck. The next they were both sailing headlong over the edge and into the rough water.

THIRTY-ONE

She never should have left Bristol with him.

The angry thought kept rolling over and over in Cassie's mind as she sped north on the soaked, windswept highway, heading for the marina where Bristol had been taken more than half an hour ago.

She kept veering between fury and being scared sick. He'd fucking sworn to her face to protect Bristol, and at the time, given the situation and the DEA involvement, Cassie had felt she'd had no choice but to comply and leave her in his care. And what had he done? Left her alone without protection while she and Tristan were en route to get her at the condo, resulting in Bristol being taken hostage by a contract killer for the cartel running this entire region.

She eased up as little as possible on the accelerator as they neared a steep curve in the wet road, taking it fast enough that Tristan set a hand on the dash to steady himself. But he didn't say anything as she sped up to exit it.

Smart man. Driving was one of her strongest skills. She knew exactly how far she could push this vehicle in these conditions and maintain control, so she wasn't letting up an inch. Not when every second counted.

"How far now?" she asked him.

"Just under three miles until the turnoff." He was texting someone. "Gavin and Decker are a few minutes behind us, and the Sheriff's Department has been notified. Along with the DEA and Coast Guard."

"Good." She and Tristan would be the first ones on scene, and they had no idea what to expect. "Anything else from *him*?" She refused to say his name. Bastard.

"Not that I know of. CPS is in the process of gaining access to security cameras at the marina—" He paused. "They're saying the footage confirms that Bristol arrived at the marina with the same guy who took her from the condo. Five-ten, early-thirties, brown hair, muscular build. She still had the hood over her head. He took her aboard a boat named *Sea Siren* and headed out of the harbor."

"Then we're gonna need a boat to go after her."

"Yeah, on it." He kept texting.

"No identity on him yet?"

"No."

"What about the other guy?"

"He's in pursuit."

Cassie clenched her jaw. If he got Bristol killed, she would end him even if it meant spending the rest of her life in prison.

The rest of the drive passed in a tense silence, her anxiety mounting as she took the turnoff for the marina and headed toward the water. Was Bristol okay? No, she *had* to be. It made no sense for the enforcer to go to the trouble of kidnapping her in broad daylight and dragging her out on a boat in the middle of this storm if he'd just planned to kill her.

He had to be using her as bait. To lure *him*.

An evil part of her hoped *he* got what he deserved for putting Bristol in this situation. Just as long as her stepsister wasn't hurt in the process.

She sped down the road that curved toward the water. The marina appeared up ahead, the parking lot mostly empty. Beside her, she felt the change in Tristan. He was on full alert, weapon already in hand, ready to face whatever awaited them.

She was glad they'd been assigned together for this.

"Anything else from CPS before we do this?" she asked, looking out to sea. She didn't see any boats out there.

"A handful of people arrived at the marina in the past ten minutes."

Well, that was helpful. "Probably boat owners wanting to secure their vessels in this storm."

She turned into the parking lot, did a quick visual sweep before driving to a spot near the gates. "Ready?" she asked, killing the engine.

"Yep."

They got out together, each of them automatically taking their own half of the field of view. She spotted one person at a berth close to the entrance, securing the lines on his boat. In the distance, two men were walking away from them along the wooden planking. One other stood on the deck of a boat berthed two rows over from them.

Stepping onto the closest dock, she raised her high-powered binos to scan beyond the breakwaters. A pleasure craft was powering back toward the harbor mouth. And beyond it in the distance, a small cabin cruiser rocked with the waves. "Vessel inbound, and one heading out to sea." The name on the stern was fuzzy. She squinted, tightened the focus. "It's them."

"I'll alert CPS."

She didn't answer because her throat was suddenly too tight to speak. She stared at the distant boat, thinking of Bristol bound and terrified inside it. "There's no way we'll catch up to them in this storm." Even if they'd had a boat ready.

"CPS is updating the Coast Guard."

As sick as she felt to admit it, that was probably Bristol's only chance.

She lowered the binos, adrenaline pumping through her, with no available outlet. There wasn't a damned other thing she could do to help Bristol at the moment. "Now what?" She wanted to scream. Held it back, buried it deep down.

"Keep tabs on the boat and give updates until we hear more. That's all we can do."

Yeah, and it fucking sucked. She swallowed, fear twisting her stomach. "Do you know she doesn't even swear?"

Tristan glanced at her. "Who? Bristol?"

She nodded. "I can count on one hand how many times I've heard her curse in all the years I've known her. And never the F word." She shook her head, telling herself her eyes were watering because of the wind. She was too professional to ever break down while she was on the clock. "She didn't deserve any of this."

"No. But we're going to do everything we can to help get her back safely."

Cassie raised the binoculars again. The *Sea Siren* was still heading slowly out to sea, her silhouette bobbing up and down between the wild waves. Meanwhile, the pleasure craft was now at the harbor mouth. It cruised toward the end of the farthest dock.

The occupant jumped off to tie up the boat. A man. He straightened, turned to face the parking lot. A shot cracked out. The man crumpled to his knees, clutching the bright red stain blooming on his chest.

She and Tristan both darted for cover, weapons up.

Pop, pop.

A boat motor roared to life. She and Tristan both peered around the edge of the boat they were crouched behind. "Shit," Cassie breathed. The two men she'd seen on the dock earlier were driving the boat back toward the mouth of the harbor.

The wounded man was lying on his back beside the berth, his legs moving slowly.

She called it in, racing with Tristan toward the downed man with weapons in hand, their feet thudding over the slick wooden planks. The guy was still alive, clutching the wound in his chest.

Tristan got there first and crouched beside him. Leaving him to try and stop the bleeding, she turned her back on them, guarding their six while she quickly relayed everything to Ryder. Beyond the end of the harbormaster's office, she saw a CPS vehicle pull into the parking lot and stop next to hers. Gavin and Decker stepped out.

She tapped her earpiece. "Suspect down. Bring a first aid kit."

"Copy," Gavin answered. She raised an arm and waved at them to get their attention. They spotted her and broke into a run, a bright red first aid kit in Gavin's hand.

"Did you get a good look at the shooters?" Ryder asked her.

"Negative. I didn't see their faces close up."

"We'll check the security footage. Are they still heading out to sea?"

"Affirm. Gavin and Decker just arrived on scene."

"Good. Do you still have a visual on *Sea Siren*?"

She turned around and looked through the binos again. The shooters were speeding in *Sea Siren*'s direction. The boat was much smaller and faster and must have had a more powerful engine because it was gaining ground fast.

"I can still—" She stopped, her insides freezing.

"Cassie? What do you see?"

"Smoke," she answered, heart slamming in terror at the dark plume rising from the stern. "*Sea Siren*'s on fire."

THIRTY-TWO

The sound of her own harsh breathing filled the sudden, eerie quiet.

What the hell was happening? The shooting had stopped. There were no more voices. No more sounds of another boat nearby. Just the wind and waves battering this one.

Where was TJ? Her kidnapper had told her he had come for her. She thought she'd heard his voice before.

Her thoughts scattered when she noticed a strange smell. An acrid, chemical smell.

Smoke. Something was on fire.

The rush of terror gave her a burst of renewed urgency. With her fingers bleeding, she finally managed to pry the knot she'd been working apart enough to put some slack in the rope around her wrists.

She yanked her aching arms up and down and back and forth to get free, desperate to escape. The toxic smoke was already thickening in the air, filtering in through her hood. She coughed, kept her eyes shut to protect them.

One last hard jerk, and the ropes gave enough for her to slide one wrist free, then the other. Her shoulder joints hurt as she brought her hands up to grab the hood and tear it off. Opening her eyes to slits, she got her first look around the interior. The air was hazy with smoke, the dark color telling her it was probably from oil.

Unable to spot her glasses through the haze, she shoved to her feet, ripped the tape from her mouth, and rushed for the short set of stairs that led topside. The boat rolled hard to the right before she reached the deck. She grabbed hold of the metal railing to steady herself, moved up the last two stairs, and crouched there in the hatchway to take a cautious look around.

The deck was deserted. She was the only person still aboard.

"Ohmygod," she cried, and ran for the bow. Blood was spattered across part of the port wall and deck. Her heart lurched. TJ...

She spun around, squinting through the driving wind and rain to scan the roiling ocean. The boat that had attacked them was speeding away. There was no sign of TJ or her captor anywhere. Had TJ been killed? Was he aboard the other boat?

Fighting tears, she continued searching the water, looking frantically in every direction. Her distance vision was shit without her glasses, but she thought someone's head and shoulders appeared between the waves off the port stern.

TJ!

Not knowing for sure if it was him, she spun back around, spotted a life ring tied to the side of the seating area and fumbled to get it undone. The person in the water was too far away for her to get the ring to him. She rushed to the helm, turned the wheel to steer back toward him, but after ten seconds nothing had happened and the dot in the waves was even farther away. Either the wind and waves were pushing her out to sea, or the fire had disabled the steering mechanism.

She rushed back to the railing. "TJ!" she shouted, praying it was him, and that he could somehow keep his head above the surface. Dammit, she couldn't see him anymore.

She cupped her hands around her mouth. Leaned her stomach against the railing to yell with all her might. "Swim for the life ring!" It was his only chance.

She gripped it with both hands, turned her body sideways, and hurled it as hard as she could away from the boat. The wind caught it. It hit the top of a wave and slid down the other side at least twenty yards from where she'd seen the person. But it was all she could do.

The boat pitched sharply to port. She grabbed the railing, managed to catch her balance just in time to stop from falling overboard, but a big wave crashed over the edge, knocking her backward and soaking her from head to feet. Sputtering, she climbed to her feet and staggered through the ankle-high water covering the deck to the helm. The smoke at the stern rose in a tall black column into the thick clouds above, the wind whipping it out behind the boat like a banner.

Bristol gripped the helm and tried to turn back toward shore, shaking from a mixture of shock and fear and cold. Her teeth chattered, rain pelting her head and face.

The boat didn't respond. She tried turning the other way. Nothing.

More waves crashed over the deck, rushing down the open hatch into the cabin. And she prayed it was just her imagination, but it felt like the boat was listing to the rear.

Glancing behind her, a new shockwave of fear hit when she realized the boat was slowly sinking at the stern. She looked around frantically, finally spotted a compartment marked life jacket in the helm station and ripped it open. She grabbed the first fluorescent orange vest she found and quickly put it on.

There was a radio nearby. She didn't have a clue how to use it, but if she could perform and read medical ultrasounds, she could damn well figure out how to operate this thing. And she'd just seen a show a couple weeks ago about a sinking fishing boat in Alaska. There was a specific frequency they used to call the Coast Guard. She was sure the channel was somewhere in the teens.

She found the power button to turn it on, then grabbed the handset and started looking for the button to switch channels. There was a red one with sixteen printed on it. She hit it, then pressed the key on the mic.

"Mayday, mayday, mayday." She knew that much. "Can anyone read me? I'm on board a small boat…" There was a fancy painted wooden sign hanging near the helm, and the name on it matched what was on her life vest. "*Sea Siren*. It's on fire and taking on water. Unsure of my location. Over."

She released the key, her pulse thudding in her ears as she awaited a response from someone. Anyone.

"This is US Coast Guard Air Station North Bend," a male voice said. "Mayday relayed, *Sea Siren*."

Thank you, God.

The pressure of tears burned the backs of her eyes, her throat as she kept going. "Another vessel shot at us." Her words came out fast, as fast as the gunfire earlier, her jaw trembling. Her whole body was, her breathing rapid and shallow. "Two other people aboard went overboard a few minutes ago. I spotted one in the water about twenty or thirty yards from the boat before I lost sight of them. I don't think either of them were wearing a life vest."

She was shaking all over, trying to keep her teeth from chattering so they could understand her. Wanted to cry at the thought of TJ lost in the water, drowning. Maybe already gone. The other guy? Fuck him. She hoped a passing shark ripped his limbs off and left him to sink to the bottom. "Please help," she added, voice wobbling. "Over."

"We read you. What is your current location? Over."

She grabbed hold of the ledge as another wave tipped the boat sideways, stumbled before finding her balance. "I'm n-not sure." *Don't cry. You have to be strong.* She looked behind her. "I was taken aboard as a hostage with a blindfold on. But I can still see the marina behind me, and it's close to Crimson Point." The coastline was to her right. "I think I'm drifting northwest."

The boat tipped again, the sharpest yet. She dropped the mic, grabbed hold of the back of the seat to stop from slamming into the wall. The stern was sinking faster now. A gust of wind blew thick, oily smoke into the cabin. She coughed, covered her nose and mouth with the inside of her elbow and looked frantically through the windscreen toward the bow. It seemed to be rising out of the water.

The Coast Guardsman was saying something else through the radio, but the smoke was too thick in here. She grabbed hold of the doorframe and fumbled her way back out onto the deck, forced to lean forward to stay on her feet as she made her way toward the bow.

She looked around, squinting and throwing a hand up to try and shield her eyes from the pelting rain. The other vessel that had attacked them was long gone. Off to her right, the shoreline stretched out in a fuzzy haze of browns and grays. It might be closer than it looked, but without her glasses she couldn't be sure. Behind her, she could just make out the harbor and the masts of the boats moored there.

But there was no further sign of anyone in the water.

A powerful gust of wind kicked up a giant wave over the

bow. It hit her hard enough to knock her to her knees. She managed to keep hold of the railing, both feet braced against the edge of the deck to stop from sliding into the water.

Her muscles shook all over as the cold wind raked over her, making the water feel like ice. The stern continued to sink lower into the water. She didn't have much time left before she would be forced to abandon ship.

Icy fingers clenched around the metal railing, she huddled up into a ball to try and conserve body heat, and shut her eyes. She'd done everything she could to save herself. The Coast Guard was sending someone. She would hold on here, stay aboard as long as she could before resorting to jumping in the water.

She shuddered and curled up tighter, struggling not to cry as she thought of TJ probably floating lifeless just out of view. Waves smashed into the boat, spraying her and threatening to tear her numb fingers from the railing. Then, over the gusts of wind, she heard a new sound. A rhythmic thumping.

She looked up, shielded her eyes with her hand as she searched the heavy gray clouds. The noise grew louder, then suddenly the silhouette of a helicopter appeared off in the distance. She shot to her feet, stumbled back toward the cabin. Smoke was still thick in the air, but not quite as bad as before. She hurried inside, started rummaging through compartments.

There! A flare gun.

She hurried back to her spot near the bow, sat down to mitigate the chance of toppling overboard, and tried to figure out how to fire it. There was a row of plastic cartridges on top that looked a bit like Nerf gun ammo. She took one of them, shoved it into the open barrel and closed it.

"Now what," she muttered, frantically studying the thing.

When nothing came to her, she raised it toward the sky and just pulled the trigger.

Nothing happened.

"Dammit," she whispered, examining it more closely. Did it have a safety switch on it maybe?

There was a button on the side. She pressed it once, raised the barrel to the sky and pulled the trigger.

Still nothing.

"Come *on*," she shouted, beyond frustrated and on the verge of giving into the tears that were right beneath the surface. She could hear the helicopter but didn't know if it could see her yet.

Raising the gun one last time, she held the button down and pulled the trigger at the same time. There was a whooshing sound. A flare shot out of the barrel, bright red, like a burst of fire against the angry gray clouds. It shot up into the air, ran out of steam and then began to fade as it fell.

She watched the helicopter, praying it had seen her by now. But her heart sank as she realized it was heading to the left and behind her, heading somewhere between her boat and the marina.

THIRTY-THREE

TJ sucked in a gulp of air an instant before another wave crashed over him. It took him under, tumbled him around like he was in a spin cycle. Just when he was sure he was dead, it shot him upward, almost spat him out on the surface.

He heaved in another breath, his heart slamming out of control, blinded by the stinging rain and wind raging across the top of the water. He couldn't feel his hands or feet. His limbs were numb, heavy as lead as he dragged them through the water.

He spotted something on the crest of a wave nearby. Realized there was a body floating in it.

Nico.

He turned around, forced his exhausted muscles to propel him through the raging water. A wave picked him up, carried him closer and dumped him down the far side.

He flung out a hand just as the body came back into view. His fist managed to catch fabric but his grip was weak, his muscles sapped by the cold. Kicking hard, he managed to move closer and hook an arm around Nico's chest. He flipped around, hauling Nico over onto his back and put him in a rescue hold. "Nico!"

Nico's head lolled on his shoulder, eyes closed, mouth partly open.

TJ didn't know if he was dead. But he wouldn't let go. His legs churned, desperately fighting to keep their heads above water. He caught sight of the *Sea Siren*. It was moving farther away from them, a plume of smoke rising from her stern.

Bristol! No! She was tied up and helpless, alone, and the boat was on fire.

His insides turned to ice, anguish slicing him like a blade. He was too fucking far away. She would never hear him yelling over the storm. And he would never be able to swim back to the boat to help her.

He sucked in a breath to scream her name. A wave hit him from the side, catching him mid-inhalation. It dragged him under.

His throat clamped shut. Lungs burning from lack of air.

He lost his grip on Nico. Kicked violently, fighting his way to the surface.

His head broke through. He coughed. Thrashed in the water, his body desperately trying to clear the water from his lungs.

Some air finally got through. He sucked it in greedily. Something bumped his shoulder.

He grabbed hold of it. A leg.

Managed to snag Nico before they were separated again. Cast a desperate look toward shore.

It was getting farther away by the minute.

He flung his head around, stared at the column of smoke rising from *Sea Siren*.

Bristol! The scream burned in his aching throat.

More waves battered him. Tossing him and Nico around, pounding them with relentless fury.

He couldn't keep this up much longer. His legs were already slowing, refusing to obey him.

In desperation he flattened out on his back, clinging to Nico as they drifted with the waves. He shook all over, gasping in shallow breaths. He squinted up at the ominous gray sky, the raindrops pelting his face.

Bristol...

His mind raced but his body was beginning to fail him. His numb limbs were uncoordinated, weak.

He blinked at a red flash in the sky above him. Before he could focus on it, a wave slammed over his head and enveloped him in darkness.

~

"GODDAMMIT, COME *ON*," Bristol snarled.

She loaded another flare, was just getting ready to fire it when another helicopter suddenly appeared out of the clouds to her right.

She caught her breath. Held it. *Oh, God, please...*

She loaded another cartridge, aimed the gun away from the helicopter, and fired. This one didn't seem to go as high.

But the helicopter had to have seen her, because it dipped low and headed straight for her. Staying huddled in place, she raised an arm to wave up at it while it circled above her. Eventually it dropped down to hover directly over her.

She squeezed her eyes shut and curled into herself as the powerful wind from the rotors pounded down on her, coating her in freezing sea spray. When she cracked her eyes open to risk a peek, the side door was open and someone in a uniform and helmet was coming down toward her on a cable.

Bristol scrambled to her knees, keeping hold of the railing. Whoever it was swung back and forth with the combined force of the rotors and the gusting wind. Slowly, slowly, he descended toward the shifting deck.

His feet touched down. He signaled the crew in the helicopter, unclipped from the cable and signaled again. The cable began to retract, and he turned toward her.

She barely resisted the urge to launch herself at him, stayed where she was as he came to her and crouched down. He pushed up the visor on his helmet.

A pair of familiar hazel eyes stared at her. "Hey, Bristol. You okay?"

"Travis," she cried, flinging her arms around him. "Oh, my God." The tears she'd been fighting broke free.

"Are you hurt anywhere?" he asked, easing her away from him to check her over.

"N-no. But TJ and the guy w-who took me... They w-went overb-board. One was shot."

"The other helo's looking for them right now." He shifted his grip on her. "Can you stand up?"

"Y-yeah." She wasn't sure if she was crying or if it was just the salt water all over her face.

Travis helped her stand, signaled for the cable. "I'm going to put this safety harness on you," he told her as the crew lowered it. He held her steady around the waist with one arm as he caught the end of the cable with his free hand, his feet braced wide apart on the rolling deck. "I'm going to hook us together, and then Whit'll winch us up."

She looked up, clinging to his shoulders. She wanted TJ. Her heart was cracking into pieces that he might be dead. "Brandon's there?"

"Yeah. And Groz and Grady are on the other bird." He

quickly helped her into the harness, got them clipped together on the line and signaled Brandon.

Bristol clung to him as the cable pulled them off the deck. The pulse of the rotors was almost deafening. When she looked up, she saw Brandon leaning partway out of the open door, feeding the cable through his gloved fists.

The instant she neared the doorway, he reached out to grab her. Within seconds, he and Travis had her aboard with the door shut. Travis unhooked them, started relaying information to Brandon. "She's alert and responsive. No obvious injuries, other than shock and cold."

"Hi, Bristol," Brandon said, giving her a smile as he took her life vest off. "How you feeling?"

"C-cold," she answered. Scared. Grieving the probable loss of the man she'd fallen for. "W-worried about T-TJ."

"If he's still in the water, Groz and Grady will get him out," Travis said with absolute confidence that she desperately wanted to believe. She couldn't accept the alternative. "Now let's get you out of those wet clothes so we can make sure you're okay and get you warmed up."

She swallowed and didn't answer because she was afraid she would break down completely and embarrass herself in front of these brave men. Her limbs and hands were too cold and numb to help much as Travis quickly helped get her top and soaked jeans off. She squelched the wave of shyness. They were her friends, professionals, and she wasn't even naked.

Brandon wrapped a mylar blanket around her before laying her out on a stretcher on the floor. "Just gonna check your vitals to make sure you're okay," he said, sticking a temperature probe in her ear while his fingers found her radial pulse. After thirty seconds he stopped. "Your pulse is high, and your core temp's a bit low."

"Let's sit you up," Travis said, reaching beneath her with one arm and pulling her upright. He handed her a thermos top of something with steam coming from it. "Hot, sweet tea. It'll help until we can get you aboard the ship."

"Sh-ship?" she said, wrapping her hands around his to bring the cup to her lips. It was hot and sweet just like he'd said, but without him steadying it she would have sloshed it all over her.

"Coast Guard cutter about nine miles out. What happened?"

She swallowed her mouthful of tea. Felt the blessed warmth as it spread down into her stomach. "He t-took me as bait to get T-TJ."

"Who's TJ?" Brandon asked, tucking the blanket around her more securely.

"He's..." Tears rushed to her eyes. "A DEA agent," she managed to get out. "It's...it's c-complicated."

"Yeah, sounds like it." Brandon was rubbing her back and arms to get the circulation going. She almost started crying again. Couldn't believe that both of them had been the ones to rescue her. Without them, she'd probably be fighting for her life in the water right now.

Just like TJ was.

He *had* to still be fighting.

THIRTY-FOUR

Cassie's patience had run out more than an hour ago.

About to come unglued, she barely kept herself from pacing up and down the dock as the Coast Guard cutter made its way to the berth at the far end. The only thing stopping her was Tristan, standing silently beside her while holding an umbrella over them. For whatever reason, probably some misplaced sense of loyalty, he'd insisted on coming here with her after they'd been released from the marina.

This whole thing had been one giant shit storm. But at least Bristol was alive.

"Not long now," he said quietly, the rain drumming so hard on the umbrella it poured off the edges of it. The storm had turned out to be much more intense than forecasters had predicted, and showed no sign of letting up. The latest models showed it raining and blowing until early afternoon tomorrow.

"Not soon enough," she grumbled, shoving her hands deeper into her coat pockets, her left one curling around her personal phone. She'd switched it off because it had blown up with calls and messages from her mom and Bristol's dad as soon as she'd texted them what was happening. Thankfully, calling hadn't been an option because things had been too chaotic at the time.

She'd been careful not to make it sound that bad, but their concern was completely understandable. Her final message to them was that the Coast Guard was bringing Bristol to shore and that Cassie would personally contact them once she had Bristol back safe and sound.

After a small eternity, the ship finally finished docking. She headed straight for the gangplank at a rapid clip, Tristan right beside her, keeping her dry. She'd thank him for everything later. Right now, she was one-hundred-and-twenty-percent focused on Bristol. Anyone who got in front of her or slowed her down was going to wind up on their ass.

A few people began disembarking. Her heart leapt when she spotted Bristol at the top of the gangplank wearing navy blue sweats, a blanket wrapped around her shoulders.

As soon as she reached the dock, Cassie caught her in a huge hug and held on tight. *Thank God.* Now she could finally breathe again.

Bristol smelled like seawater, her dark hair still damp and crusted lightly with salt crystals. "You okay?"

Bristol nodded, hugging her just as hard in return. "You?"

"I've aged thirty years since the last time I saw you, but... yeah, now that you're back safe and sound." *Jesus.* The past twenty-four hours had been a complete nightmare. She gave Bristol one last squeeze and eased back, belatedly realized that Tristan was getting soaked, standing there in the pouring rain covering her and Bristol with the umbrella.

"Vehicle's parked just ahead," she said to Bristol. "Up to a quick run in the rain?"

"Yes. Hi...Tristan? Or are you Gavin?" she asked him.

His gentle smile turned Cassie's heart upside down. No man that big and strong and deadly should also be that sweet. "Tristan. Good to see you."

"You too."

"Come on. Let's get outta here," Cassie said, sliding an arm around Bristol's shoulders.

The three of them made a dash to the SUV. She put Bristol in the back right passenger seat, started to go around to the driver's door, and stopped.

Tristan stopped too, watching her with those intense green eyes that made her feel things that scared the shit out of her. "You mind driving this time?"

"Love to drive for a change." His grin was both endearing and outrageously sexy at the same time.

She rammed that thought into a deep, dark closet at the back of her head, jammed a broom handle under the latch for good measure, and got in the back with Bristol. Her stepsister was huddled beneath the blanket, looking pale and a bit like a lost little girl.

It broke Cassie's heart to see her like this, to think of all she'd been through.

"Can you tell me what happened?" Cassie asked gently once Tristan was driving for the exit. "Or do you need time before we talk about it?"

"No, I can talk now." She wrapped the blanket tighter around herself. "I was at the condo waiting for someone from CPS to come—"

"Tristan and me."

"Oh. Well... A stranger walked in. At first I assumed he must be with CPS, but at the last second, I realized he wasn't. And by the time I got to my bat—"

"You and that stupid bat."

"It's a *great* bat, but I was too late. He secured my hands behind me, put duct tape over my mouth, and yanked a hood over my head. Next thing I knew, he was practically carrying me down the stairs to a car. He drove for a bit, put me on the boat and then…" She paused, seemed to gather herself before continuing. "I heard another boat approach. Then it left. Soon after that I heard talking. One was the kidnapper, and I'm pretty sure the other was TJ."

Cassie was still livid that he'd put her in danger.

Bristol pressed her lips together as tears filled her eyes. "Another boat came. It shot at us. I heard the bullets hit the back of the *Sea Siren*. Then the other one sped away, and it was just quiet. I didn't hear anything or anyone. When I finally got untied, I could smell and see the smoke. I went up on deck, but there was no one there, just a bloodstain near the bow. The other boat was still racing away. I spotted someone in the waves. I don't know if it was TJ or not," she finished hoarsely. She looked down at her hands, twisting them in her lap.

It was clear she felt something for TJ, and it was more than obligation or gratitude for him trying to rescue her. "Then what?" Cassie asked.

"My boat was sinking. I called the Coast Guard."

"You did?"

She nodded. "Figured out the radio, but the smoke was too thick. I went out on deck, and that's when the helicopters came. So I found a flare gun—"

Cassie laughed softly. She couldn't help it. "Look at you, you dark horse little badass."

Bristol's lips quirked in an ironic smile. "Took me three tries to figure out how to fire it."

"But you did it."

"Yeah. And guess who was on the helicopter?"

"Who?"

"My friends Travis and Brandon, from the hospital. They're both PJs—"

"I know." She shook her head. "That's incredible."

"Yes." She twisted her fingers some more. "They got me onto the Coast Guard cutter. Travis and Brandon got called out right away on another mission. There was another helicopter out looking for TJ and…the other guy, but no one would tell me if they'd found them." She searched Cassie's eyes anxiously. "Have you heard anything?"

Cassie took a deep breath. "Our information is that they pulled two people from the water."

Bristol stiffened. "Alive?"

"I don't know."

Tears flooded her eyes. She looked away, blinked fast, but tears dripped onto the blanket. "I want TJ to be okay," she whispered.

"I know. I'm so sorry, babe." She rubbed Bristol's back, not knowing what else to do or say. Tristan, thankfully, wasn't saying a thing, and she trusted that the only other person he would tell about any of this was Gavin.

But there was more to the story than Bristol knew. "The boat you heard? We think the guy driving it took TJ out to you initially, then left him there. But when he got back to the harbor, someone shot him dead just after Tristan and I got there. Then the shooters took off back after you."

Bristol frowned. "Do you know who it was?"

"The victim? We're not sure yet, the cops and DEA are dealing with it now, but he died a few minutes later at the scene. And from what I've heard, one of the guys who attacked you might be a cartel lieutenant he was working for."

Her eyes widened. "What? And who was the guy who kidnapped me?"

"One of his enforcers."

Bristol paled.

Cassie took her hands in hers. "That's all I know right now. But you're safe now, and that's all that matters. We'll get you home—unless you want to come to my place?"

"No. I want to go home."

"Okay. Once we get you there, I'll start making calls and get an update." She hesitated before saying more. She didn't like the guy, would give half her salary for the chance to kick him in the nuts for what he'd done to Bristol, but it was clear her stepsister felt deeply for him. Whether it was gratitude, Stockholm syndrome, or something else, she wasn't sure.

"It's the middle of summer. The waters here don't get much warmer than this. So if TJ was a decent swimmer, there's a good chance the other crew found him and got him out in time."

"Unless he'd been shot."

Yeah. There was that.

Cassie squeezed Bristol's hand in silent support, then fished her phone out of her pocket, switched it on and shot off a quick text.

"Who you talking to?"

"Just reassuring our parental unit that I've got you safe and sound."

She groaned. "You told them?"

"Had to. But don't worry, I'll handle everything for tonight. If we're lucky, they'll wait until tomorrow before they descend on you. They were scared as hell for you, Bris. We all were."

She nodded. "Me too."

In Crimson Point, Tristan pulled up in front of the walkway leading to Bristol's townhouse. Cassie got her safely inside, then carried the umbrella back to the SUV where he waited. He rolled down the front passenger window.

"I'm gonna stay with her," she said.

"Then I'll just park this for you and catch a ride home."

"No, you keep it for tonight." She reached through the window to set the dripping umbrella down on the floorboard. When she straightened, her eyes locked with his. "Thank you. For…today."

She had a disturbingly strong urge to get in the car and curl up in his lap, bury her face in the side of his neck and absorb all that quiet, controlled strength he radiated. But that was as forbidden as all the other illicit things she'd imagined doing with him—she shoved those into the rapidly-filling closet in the back of her mind too—and would lead to guaranteed disaster.

She'd worked her ass off to get this job and the reputation she was proud of. She wanted to be seen as equals with the guys, had something to prove to the firm, and wouldn't risk it all by getting involved with a coworker.

Not even a green-eyed, six-foot-something redhead who made her ache with the loss of everything she could never have.

"Don't thank me. Just glad she's okay. Hey, before I forget." He reached into his inside jacket pocket, pulled out a folded piece of paper and handed it to her. "This is for you."

She unfolded it, saw it was two tickets to the concert she'd mentioned a while ago. "What did you do?" She couldn't believe he'd done this, let alone remembered about the concert.

He frowned slightly. "I told you I would." He shrugged. "It's not a big deal, a friend comped them."

She wasn't sure she believed that. Was he for real? He couldn't be. There had to be some fatal flaw in him she was missing. Like maybe he was actually a serial killer. Shit, what was he trying to do to her?

"One thing you should know about me?"

It wasn't lost on her that he was echoing the exact same wording she'd used with him this past spring when they'd headed to Portland before the riots had broken out. "What's that?" she made herself ask.

"If I say I'm going to do something, I do it." His green stare was so direct. Unflinching. Cutting through all the protective layers she had purposely wrapped herself in. "Text or call if you need anything."

"Will do." She wouldn't, because he was now the last person she trusted herself with for anything outside of professional reasons. "Thanks again."

The hint of a smile tugged at the corner of his mouth. And God help her, all she could think about was tracing that spot with her tongue before delving inside to taste him.

"You're welcome."

She spun around and rushed through the rain for the door, heart tripping all over itself. This was a work-life complication she didn't need. She'd sworn off men for damned good reasons, was still trying to pick up the pieces of her life and build a new one she could feel proud of.

Tristan Abrams tempted her in too many ways to count. Worse, from everything she'd seen and heard, he seemed like a genuinely good guy. Which practically made him a damned unicorn.

She didn't trust it. That saying about if something seemed too good to be true, it probably was? One-hundred-and-fifty percent true in her experience.

Given her history and shitty judgment when it came to men, it pretty much guaranteed that Tristan was probably also a raging narcissist.

THIRTY-FIVE

An indistinct voice became audible somewhere in the background. Muted, as if he were underwater.

"Can you hear me?" It was closer now. Clearer.

He struggled to home in on it. Somehow identify where it was coming from.

"Mr. Angelopoulos."

Nico dragged his leaden eyelids open. Squinted against the line of bright lights that hit his retinas.

"Can you hear me?"

He blinked, struggling to focus on the blurry face hovering above him. His tongue felt thick and heavy in his mouth. His chest was on fire. Every breath hurt. "Yes." It came out barely a whisper.

"You're in the hospital."

His surroundings slowly registered. More pain bloomed in his upper back and shoulder, yet he remained strangely detached from it, as if it was happening somewhere in the background. A middle-aged woman was standing over him, wearing scrubs.

"You just came out of surgery. You're in the recovery

room. I'm just going to check your temperature. Are you warm enough?"

He nodded. Or tried to as she slid a thermometer into his ear.

"How's your pain level?"

"Okay," he croaked. At least he was still alive.

"Do you remember what happened?" She withdrew the thermometer to check it. The reading must have been normal because she didn't say anything about it as she made a note in his chart.

The boat. Barros. Leandro and Hawk coming at them. The bullet.

Searing pain. The icy shock of the water.

"Who...who pulled me out?" he managed. His throat was dry and sore. He guessed either from nearly drowning or the intubation during surgery.

A shadow fell over him.

He turned his head on the pillow, blinked up at Barros.

"Hey, man. Good to see you. Glad you're gonna be okay."

"Hey. What...happened?" The last thing he could remember was sucking in that last mouthful of water on his way down. The certainty that he was seconds from dying.

"I grabbed you right after you went under. Then the Coast Guard pulled us out."

It was still so hard to believe it was real. That he was still here. But fear gathered in his gut. "So what happens now?" He wasn't cuffed to a railing. Maybe that was a good sign.

"It depends."

"Did they get Hawk and Leandro?"

"Not Leandro. But Hawk's dead."

He'd shot him. He wasn't sorry. But he was deeply sorry

that he was facing life in prison for all the lives he'd taken. "Liana. My wife."

"What about her?"

"Promised her." He was so damned weak.

"Promised her what?"

Nico held back the rest of it. But he needed help. Needed Barros to understand. "Have to get her help."

Barros was watching him closely. Nico looked past him, fixed his gaze on a cabinet on the wall marked with a red cross. He stared at it pointedly for a second before looking back at Barros. Barros followed his line of sight.

"Gotta get her help there," Nico repeated.

Barros turned back to him, frowning. "Yeah, we'll help her." He glanced over his shoulder toward the door and nodded at someone.

The doors opened, and an instant later, the most beautiful sight in the world appeared. A nurse pushing Liana toward him in her chair. Her eyes red from crying, but a smile wobbling on her lips.

He reached a hand out for her. She grabbed it, squeezed it between her own. "Li…," he whispered, his throat closing up. He didn't know what to say. Didn't want to tell her all the terrible things he'd done, or for her to know she was married to a contract killer.

"Baby," she whispered, leaning over to cradle his face in her hands and kiss him.

Tears burned the backs of his eyes. He buried his hand in the nape of her neck, holding on tight.

"I'll let you two have some privacy," Barros said.

Nico looked up at him. How much did she know? Had they told her anything?

Barros darted him a warning frown and shook his head

slightly. "She knows you were on a job when you were shot and wound up in the water."

"I'm so glad you're still here," Liana choked out.

Nico expelled a painful breath and pulled her closer, cradling her head on his chest. "Thank you," he said.

Barros nodded. "Take care of yourself, man." He stuck out a hand.

"I will." Nico caught it, squeezed. "You too."

Barros released his hand and walked away, leaving them alone in the private room. Nico closed his eyes and kissed the top of Liana's head. He'd just been given another unexpected reprieve. He still had time.

He had to figure out a way out of this. And he had to do it fast.

~

TJ EASED the recovery room door shut and turned toward the elevators at the end of the hall, only to come to an abrupt halt.

His handler Diana was leaning against the wall between him and the elevator, arms folded across the blazer of her navy pantsuit. "Well? How was the romantic reunion?"

"So far, so good." It wasn't often he got to witness nice things on the job. Or for him to be kept in any kind of loop by Diana and the rest of the agency. But given Nico's involvement, his history with the agency, and the complicated shitshow they now all faced, Diana had fast tracked a deep dive into him.

Everything she'd found over the past several hours, including intel from Nico's waterlogged phone, had revealed his probable motivation for becoming Leandro's enforcer.

His wife Liana had a terminal illness. Western medicine's

limitations, or maybe shitty insurance coverage, had made Nico desperate enough to resort to taking on contract killing to make enough money fast enough to pay for private treatment. They hadn't found any specifics on his targets or evidence of accepting large payments. He would have discarded any burner phones he'd used for those kinds of communications, and probably an offshore account somewhere.

Personally, TJ hoped they never found any of the evidence.

He'd managed to convince the agency to get Liana and bring her here to see her husband. He couldn't imagine being in Nico's position. If it had been Bristol, TJ would do everything in his power to save her too.

The op to meet with Jon had been blown to hell—along with Jon on that dock—but the memory stick he'd retrieved had somehow stayed in his pocket throughout his unplanned, prolonged swim in the ocean. Leandro had valuable intel on the inner workings of the lynch pin of the Pacific Northwest operation of the cartel that they couldn't get from anyone else. The agency's techs were trying to retrieve the information on it now.

Hopefully the thing was waterproof.

His hands and feet were still freezing, even though they'd pumped him full of warmed fluids on the emergency helo flight here and he'd changed into dry clothes. "Any word on Leandro?"

"Yeah." Her pale brown eyes glittered with annoyance. "Another flight crew spotted him and his passenger climbing into the hatch of a small sub about six miles off the southern Oregon coast."

"You're shitting me."

"Oh, I wish I was, believe me."

He shook his head, anger punching through him. They needed to find that asshole and drag him into a hole so they could extract every single thing he knew about the cartel and its PNW operations.

"We've got everyone in the region and then some hunting him right now. We'll get him." She shook her shoulder-length brown hair back. "What about you?"

"What about me?"

"What are you gonna do from here?"

"Haven't had time to think about it." That was a lie. He'd been thinking of almost nothing else in every free moment since he'd been pulled from the water.

"You're a shit liar."

His lips twitched. "No, I'm not." Lying was part of the deal with going undercover. "But since you want me to be real… I'm done with undercover."

This whole thing had changed him forever. He couldn't go back to who he'd been or to the life he'd been living before it. Because it hadn't been a life at all. Or living. Bristol had forced him to see that clearly.

She was a ray of light in the darkness. He couldn't lose her now. Whatever sacrifices he had to make from here on out, he would fight for her.

"Agreed. And I figured as much anyway." Diana cocked her head. "No other thoughts? Ideas?"

"Not yet." He was acutely conscious of the minutes ticking past, the rising frustration at being kept here. He needed to see Bristol. Given that they'd told her practically nothing, she probably thought he was dead. He couldn't do that to her. And, yeah, it confirmed he was a selfish asshole, but he needed to see her for personal reasons that were entirely unprofessional.

"Fair enough." She pushed away from the wall and

straightened. "You're restless as hell. You got somewhere you need to be?"

"No."

A grin quirked her lips. "Like I said. Shit liar." She shook her head, something almost like fondness glinting in her eyes. "Take the rest of the night off. We'll pick this up tomorrow. Hopefully by then I'll have an update on Leandro's location. Now, get outta here and go see her before you burst."

He grinned back, not surprised that she'd already figured it out on her own. Nothing got past her. "Yes, ma'am."

THIRTY-SIX

Jordan gritted his teeth, sweat pouring off his face as the orthopedic surgeon examined the bullet wound in his shoulder. His right shoulder and arm were on fire, the pain so intense it stole his breath. "Well?" he ground out.

The surgeon straightened and shook his head. "The humeral head and glenoid fossa are completely destroyed. Even if I'm able to reconstruct the joint—"

"If?" he snapped, ready to choke him. He was suffering. Unable to stand the pain, and nobody seemed to give a shit. He'd passed out soon after climbing down the hatch of the sub. Didn't remember anything else until they'd carried him to a vehicle and put him in the back. The driver had hit every fucking bump between the coast and here.

The surgeon's steely gaze met his, expression set. He was willing to take the money and perform the surgery in this private operating room Jordan had reserved, but he wouldn't be intimidated. At another time and place, Jordan might have respected him for it. "The median and ulnar nerves are severed, and the radial has sustained damage too. Even if I'm able to reconstruct the joint, the chances of you regaining any function after recovery are slight. You would need a neurosurgeon—"

"Get one," he panted, his vision going gray around the edges. It was getting harder to breathe. He was so weak, had lost so much blood.

"I recommend amputation."

"*No*." Ice swept through him. Never. "I don't care what it costs. Just get him here." He couldn't bear the thought of not being able to use his arm again. Fucking Angel. At least he and Barros had drowned. No way they could have survived being in the water that far from shore.

The surgeon's mouth thinned. "I'll make a few calls while they prep you, but I'm not guaranteeing anything. My priority is to stop the bleeding and to try and preserve what function I can."

He nodded, desperate for the pain to stop. But the idea of being paralyzed, of never being able to use his arm again, was terrifying. "Do it. Just do it," he gasped.

One of the nurses placed an oxygen mask over his nose and mouth. Whatever gas they were pumping out of it had a weird chemical smell. "Just breathe in deeply."

He closed his eyes, clenched his teeth when someone stabbed the IV into his vein. Then everything went dark.

He woke in a bright white room. For a moment he feared he'd died, but then he was able to move his head. A nurse was at his side in an instant, checking some equipment they had him hooked up to. His right arm still burned, but not as bad as it had before. He looked down at it, bandages covering him from chest to elbow.

"How's your pain level?" the woman asked. "If you need more pain relief, you can press the blue button on the line next to you. But only once every hour or so. No more than that, you've lost too much blood to risk taking more."

"The doctor," he ordered, not giving a shit about what she was saying. "I wanna talk to the doctor."

An annoyed frown appeared above the bridge of her nose covered by the surgical mask, but she nodded. "I'll go get him."

The surgeon entered the room, still dressed in scrubs. "How are you feeling?"

"Well?" Jordan demanded. "What happened?"

He hesitated, and Jordan's heart plummeted. "What?" he snapped.

"I did what I could to repair the bones and joint surfaces and stop the bleeding. A neurosurgeon was able to repair the radial nerve."

He remembered him naming three before. "And the other two?"

"He did his best. But it's unlikely that the medial and ulnar nerves will heal. And it's also unlikely that you'll ever regain full range of motion in that shoulder. You were lucky we could save the arm at all."

A cold sweat broke out across his skin. "What does that mean?" he rasped out.

"It means you've lost function in your arm and hand."

"It's...permanent?"

"Yes, in all likelihood. I'm sorry."

Sorry? Sweat beaded his face, his heart racing out of control. "I'll have more surgeries. I'll find someone else who can actually fucking *fix* me."

Those steel blue eyes chilled to chips of ice. "You're welcome to try. But it's not likely to change your prognosis." He straightened, his expression dismissive. "My staff will take care of the billing before you leave. Best of luck to you."

Jordan was left lying there, helpless, while a chaotic

tornado of emotion tore through him. Denial. Rage. Bitterness. Hatred.

Jon was dead. Barros and Angel, probably. But he wasn't certain. He needed to be certain. Needed to fix this mess.

He glanced down at his bandaged arm, felt a wave of terror and grief break over him. Paralyzed. Never able to play the piano again. Never hold a phone or a glass of whiskey. Or wipe his own fucking ass with it.

And now that he was a liability, the cartel would come for him.

His only chance was to leave everything behind. Escape the country and start over somewhere else. Live out the rest of his days a hunted man, always looking over his shoulder, caught between the cartel and the US government.

He opened his mouth, let out an enraged scream that echoed off the terrifyingly sterile white walls surrounding him like a tomb.

When it faded, exhaustion hit. He listened to the beeping of the instruments. The sound of the pump working quietly near his head.

Jordan startled when the door opened. His heart seized, a wave of terror washing over him when a man stepped inside.

The man walked up to his bedside. Stood there for a long moment staring down at him with cold, black eyes. "You don't look so good, Jordan."

Jordan swallowed convulsively, the monitor next to him beeping faster along with his galloping heart. He wished he was hallucinating, that this was just because of the drugs. But the ice spreading through his veins told him otherwise.

How the fuck had the head of the cartel found him here?

That awful black stare continued to bore into his. "We've got an unfortunate situation here, Jordan. You and I both know there's only one way this can go." He glanced down at

Jordan's bandaged arm. Shook his head and made a *tsking* sound that was completely devoid of empathy. "Damned shame. But lucky for you, your other one still works."

Before Jordan's terror-stricken brain could process that, his boss reached up and placed something on Jordan's lap. "It's your choice, of course." His dispassionate expression made Jordan's guts congeal. "You've got fifteen minutes to do the right thing, or we handle it for you." He walked out, the door closing behind him with a metallic click that seemed to echo through the cold room.

Jordan stared at the thing on his lap, a sense of dread taking hold as he picked it up in his fingers, feeling like he was in a waking nightmare.

A plastic baggie full of pills. A hysterical laugh snagged in his throat, escaping as a strangled sound.

Fentanyl.

He had fifteen minutes to take this lethal dose of the product he'd built his piece of the empire with, or he would be turned over to an enforcer and disposed of in a much less humane way. Starting with the removal of body parts.

Cold sweat bathed his skin. His heart hammered a bruising rhythm against the inside of his ribcage. There was no choice to make. They'd even left the bag open for easy access.

He choked back a sob, tears blurring his vision as he raised the bag to his mouth with a shaking hand. The pills spilled into his mouth. They were bitter on his tongue.

A rush of defiance swept through him. Fuck them. Fuck *all* of them.

He crunched the pills between his molars for good measure. Forced them down his throat with a convulsive swallow and laid back against the pillow, closing his eyes. Fighting back the fear through sheer force of will.

In his mind, he was seated at his Fazioli. His fingers rested on the cool, polished surfaces of the keys. So familiar. So comforting. They moved effortlessly, the beautiful notes filling his head.

He felt the haze settle over him. Growing thicker. Heavier.

In his mind he kept playing. Drifting on the music just as he began to drift on the tide of the chemicals flowing into his veins.

A heavy blackness closed in around him, obscuring the vision even as he kept playing.

But the music grew softer. Quieter still.

Then stopped for eternity.

THIRTY-SEVEN

Bristol swallowed the last of her wine and set her glass on the end table with a ragged sigh. Her second big one in the past half hour. "Still nothing?" she asked Cassie.

"Not in the last ten minutes, no."

Had it only been ten minutes since Cassie had checked in with CPS again about TJ's status? It felt like well over an hour.

"Maybe we should watch a movie or something. Or do a puzzle. It'll at least pass the time."

"You can throw on a movie if you want." She wouldn't be paying attention to it.

The only thing she cared or could think about, was TJ. Her mind kept circling back to being intimate with him last night and in the shower this morning. Knowing he'd come for her on the boat. Losing sight of him in the water. Being told later that Groz and Grady had pulled two people from the water. Then nothing since.

Cassie turned on the TV and found a streaming service. "*Ocean's Twelve* okay?"

"Sure." She really didn't care. This had been the worst

day of her life, right up there with the day Eric had died. She kept veering between hopeful, nauseated, and sad.

Her time on the Coast Guard ship had been a whirlwind of medical attention, answering questions, and giving a formal statement. As soon as she'd arrived home, she'd jumped in the shower. Cried the whole time she washed the salt from her skin and hair. Dressed in her soft, thick robe, she'd come downstairs to find Cassie's phone blowing up.

She'd talked to her dad first, to reassure him she was okay. It was a miracle he'd been satisfied with a phone conversation instead of a face-to-face one. She'd thought for sure he would be over there in thirty minutes, tops, banging on the door like a madman. Only Cassie being with her, and the argument that she needed rest had held him off.

That was Cassie's doing. Bristol was grateful, because she didn't have the emotional strength to cope with that right now.

After that, there had been calls with the cops, DEA, and CPS, all asking her the same questions. No one had been able to give her answers about TJ.

It infuriated her. Was he dead? If he was dead, why wouldn't they just tell her?

She leaned her head back against the top of the couch cushion, took her spare pair of glasses off and put a hand over her stinging eyes. "God, why aren't they telling us anything?"

Cassie shifted on the other end of the couch, tucking her feet under her. "I don't know." She was frustrated too. They both wanted answers. "Babe, you're exhausted. You really should go to bed and at least try to get some sleep."

Bristol gave her an incredulous look. "Are you kidding me? I can't sleep right now." Her arm flopped down to her side, glasses dangling from her fingers. The only way she would sleep tonight was because of drugs, or staying up until she just couldn't keep her eyes open any longer.

She hadn't told Cassie about her and TJ, but she was pretty sure Cass knew something was up. This level of distress was due to far more than being worried about a former teammate of her brother's. Or because she had tried so hard to help him before she'd known the truth.

Cassie watched her for a long moment, as if considering her words carefully. "You don't have to tell me if you don't want to. But did you guys get together last night?"

What was the point in lying? Cassie already suspected. "Yes."

Cassie sighed. "I was afraid of that."

"It was more than just sex, okay?"

"Okay." Cassie didn't look convinced.

Bristol wrapped her arms around herself. "It was."

"I said okay."

She was saved from saying something defensive by a knock at the door.

"I got it." Cassie jumped up and went over to check through the peephole. "It's your neighbor."

"Which one?"

"The one that looks like a fairy." She opened the door.

Bristol sat up as Everleigh walked in, her silvery-blond hair wet from the short walk over. "Hey, I just heard you were rescued at sea by the guys." She toed off her shoes and came over to sit next to her, concern in her pretty blue eyes. "Are you okay?"

"Not really." The words came out rough, almost a whisper.

"Oh, honey..." Everleigh pulled her into a hug. "I know how scared you must have been."

Yes, she really would. Everleigh had had her own near-death experience during an outdoor concert at The Gorge last summer. "You talked to Grady?"

"Yeah, he called me right before I came over. They've been flying sorties all day, pulling people off boats up and down the coast."

Bristol pulled back to look at her. "Did he say anything about TJ? I heard he and Groz pulled him from the water, but I don't know if he was alive or not."

Empathy filled her eyes. "He didn't say anything about that, sorry. He can't tell me details about any of the missions he goes on."

She tried to hide her disappointment. Probably failed miserably. "Right." Of course he couldn't. Military and legal protocols and all that.

Everleigh searched her eyes. "You want to talk about it?"

Her voice was so gentle, her expression so understanding, Bristol couldn't say no. "Yeah." She needed to rehash everything, get it off her chest. The waiting was killing her.

By the time she was done pouring out everything, the wine bottle was empty, she was tipsy, and crying in little jags that made her hiccup. Everleigh rubbed her back, offering silent sympathy and support.

Cassie was texting someone.

"Are you asking again?" Bristol asked.

"Yes. But you're done for the night. Everleigh, please take her upstairs and put her to bed."

Bristol frowned. "But what if someone calls—"

"If I hear anything about him, I'll come tell you right away. Pinkie promise." She looked at Everleigh. "Can you…"

"Sure." Everleigh wrapped an arm around her. "Come on. Let's get you upstairs."

"Not tired," she said, feeling like she was dying inside.

This was torture, but that little flame of hope inside her refused to die.

"What about a nice warm bath?"

She stood and moved with her to the foot of the staircase, thinking about it. "I just had a shower."

"A soak in a warm bubble bath might help you sleep after."

She doubted it, but Cassie was on top of it, and Everleigh was so sweet for trying to help. "Okay."

Everleigh drew a bath for her in the en suite. "I'll leave you to it. Can I do anything else before I go?"

Bristol shook her head.

"You know where I am if you need me."

"I know. Thank you."

"Of course." Everleigh hugged her again. "Hang in there," she whispered.

Alone in the bathroom, Bristol took off her robe and slid into the hot water. She had no choice but to hang in there. Everything else had been stripped from her control.

She heard the front door shut as Everleigh left. Bristol leaned her head back against the rim of the tub and closed her eyes, trying to empty her mind.

The front door opened a few minutes later. She thought she heard voices outside. Faint.

She sat up, listening. "Cass? Is someone here?" Had her dad shown up after all?

What if it was someone here about TJ?

Heart pounding, she yanked the plug from the drain and stood up so fast the water sloshed onto the floor. Yanking her discarded robe over her wet skin, she rushed out of the bathroom, heading for the stairs.

THIRTY-EIGHT

TJ took a step back as Cassie came out onto the front doorstep. She shut the door behind her and folded her arms across her chest, barring the entrance. "So, you are alive."

He got the distinct feeling she wasn't too happy about that. "Yeah." He looked up at the second-floor windows through the veil of rain. Wondered if Bristol was up there. "She here?"

"Maybe. What are you doing here?" Cassie demanded, her voice just above a whisper.

He looked at her. "I need to see her."

"What for? Because from where I'm standing, you've done *more* than enough damage already."

Guilt pierced him. "Is she all right?"

Cassie's stare was so cold it burned. He could practically feel the tips of his ears starting to sizzle. It was amazing he wasn't incinerated under the force of the glare she was giving him. "What do you think?"

No, of course she wasn't okay. "Is she hurt?" They'd told him she was fine, physically. But he needed to know for sure.

"She's been frantic about you. Do you understand? Frantic. Even after everything she went through today, all she was worried about was you. Because no one at the DEA would tell her anything. She's been sitting here for the past twelve hours without knowing whether you were alive or dead. In all that time, you couldn't even have someone send her a single message to let her know you're alive? What the hell is *wrong* with you?"

"I would have called her myself if I could have. They had me in debriefings and meetings until thirty minutes ago, and everything's under wraps because the investigation's still active. I didn't want to tell her over the phone. That's why I'm here."

She raised a dark eyebrow. "For how long?"

He opened his mouth. Closed it. Because she was tough as hell, and if he told her a lie right now, he was pretty sure she would knock his front teeth out. "For as long as I have."

A hard, humorless smile curled her mouth. One that told him he'd just confirmed her opinion that he was a piece of shit. "Nice. After all she did for you. After the lengths she went to just to help you, and everything she went through today, you're just gonna show up, use her again—"

"I didn't use her," he snapped, his temper slipping. He got that Cassie was trying to protect Bristol, but he didn't appreciate the gatekeeper role right now. "I wouldn't do that. I care about her, okay? More than I've cared about anyone in... Ever," he finished. "If I could go back and undo what happened, I would. I would never have left her alone if I'd thought she was in immediate danger. Why do you think I went after her out there? I would have traded my *life* to protect her." It was true. He'd gone out to that boat willing to die as long as it meant saving her.

Cassie's stare thawed, and her posture lost its defensive edge. "That's good to know," she said quietly.

Good, because he was done with this conversation. The need to see Bristol was a burning coal under his ribcage, searing a hole in the center of his chest. "I need to see her."

"Cass? Is someone here?" Bristol's muffled voice called from somewhere upstairs.

Cassie's lips compressed. Then she sighed and shook her head at him. "You hurt her now, I'll rip your heart out." She walked past him toward the street, knocking him with her shoulder on the way by.

He wasn't forgiven, but she had grudgingly accepted that he wasn't leaving without seeing Bristol.

He walked through the front door, locked it behind him. Didn't notice a single thing about the layout or interior of the place, because Bristol appeared on the staircase in front of him.

She stopped halfway down it, wearing a robe, her hair up in a bun, no glasses. His heart did a painful roll. He opened his mouth to say something, but she made a choked sound and rushed at him.

TJ caught her, pulled her tight to his chest, relief flooding his body so hard and fast he felt dizzy. "Hey, Slugger."

"Oh my God, I thought you'd died," she whispered shakily, her arms squeezing him tight. "I thought I saw you in the water, and then later they told me they pulled two people from the water, but no one would tell me if you were alive." She buried her face in his chest.

The pain in her voice sliced through him. "I'm okay." It had been close though. So close that after the third gulp of water he'd sucked into his lungs, he'd thought it was over. He'd had a moment where he'd thought about his dead parents. Then he'd thought about Bristol.

And she had given him the last bit of strength he'd needed to fight like hell for this moment.

"I'm glad you're okay too," he said. Holding her felt like a miracle.

She sniffed, shuddered lightly and lifted her head. Stared up at him with those big, tear-drenched blue eyes that tied his guts in knots, and took his face in her hands. "Are you staying? Please tell me you're staying."

TJ buried his hands into her hair and kissed her. Hard. Pouring everything he felt for her into it. Yeah, he was staying.

THIRTY-NINE

Bristol was just as desperate as he was, making hungry, needy sounds as she stroked her tongue along his. He slid his hands under her ass and lifted her. Her legs wound around him as he started up the stairs, still kissing her with all the bottled-up longing, fear, and frustration he'd felt since the moment he'd learned she'd been taken.

Her bedroom was on the next floor. He carried her straight to the bed, laid her on it, and came down on top of her. Pulled her robe apart while she shoved at his shirt. In seconds, he had her naked.

He caught her hands, held them down at her sides while he feasted on her smooth, creamy skin. The blended scent of her soap and arousal went straight to his head. He sucked on her nipples, waited until she was whimpering and writhing before moving down her belly. Using his shoulders, he pushed her thighs wide to reveal the pretty, flushed folds between them.

He put his mouth to her, making love to her with his tongue. Teasing and tasting, swirling and stroking while she panted and rocked against his mouth.

"Please get inside me," she demanded in a breathless voice.

He growled against her wet center. Giving her one last slow caress with his tongue that brought her hips off the bed, he let go of her hands and quickly stripped off the rest of his clothes.

Bristol surprised him by grabbing his shoulders and pushing hard as she took control. He rolled onto his back, his heart trying to punch through his ribcage at the sight of her straddling him. Her eyes glittered hungrily, cheeks flushed. Her dark hair spilled down her back, her round breasts thrust upward, nipples pink and tight from his mouth. His gaze settled on the dark hair between her legs as she fisted his aching length with one hand and eased her core down onto him.

They both gasped at the contact. TJ seized her hips in his hands, torn between wanting to make this last and wanting to take over. It was clear she needed to be in control right now. Bristol rocked forward, a throaty moan spilling from her throat while she rode him slow and easy. So mind-blowingly sexy he could barely breathe.

Sweat broke out on his skin, his heart beating out of control. The insane intensity of the pleasure as she engulfed him made it hard to breathe. Her slick walls stroked him with each undulation of her hips. The erotic enjoyment on her face, the way her fingers slipped down to find the swollen knot of her clit…

"TJ," she whispered, eyes half-closed as a shiver ran through her.

Oh, Christ. "Take it," he told her, his voice almost a growl.

He watched the pleasure wash over her beautiful face, knew that image would be burned into his mind for eternity as she shattered, her cries of fulfilment the sweetest sound he'd ever heard.

Somehow, he held on as she clenched around him, breathing hard and fast, the muscles in his thighs and belly twitching with the need for release.

Bristol shuddered one last time and relaxed above him with a thoroughly satisfied sigh, then opened sated, storm-blue eyes to gaze down at him. She sat up taller, clamping down on him and moving her hips in a way that made him see stars.

"I'm close," he managed to get out.

"Good," she murmured, lifting her arms to draw her hair up behind her head, giving him the hottest view of his life. "Because I want to watch your face while I make you come."

He sucked in a breath. Four more sinfully erotic moves of her hips, and he was gone.

He dug his fingers into her hips, holding on for dear life as the most intense orgasm of his life ripped through him. Breathing erratically, he sank down into the bed and unlocked his fingers from her hips. That was the second near-death experience he'd had today.

"Be back in a sec," she whispered, sliding off him and disappearing into the en suite he hadn't even noticed before. She came back out a minute later with a cloth for him to clean up with, then crawled back on top of him, a warm, naked, weighted blanket.

He growled and wrapped his arms around her, hugging her close. His possessive side was going crazy. She was his. He didn't want to let her go. "I'm sorry I couldn't let you know earlier."

She lifted her head from his chest to look down at him. "About your cover, or that you were alive?"

"Both." He slid a slow hand up and down her spine,

enjoying the feel of her silky soft skin. Then he rolled her to her side, caught her hands gently and examined them. Her wrists had faint red marks around them, and some of the pads of her fingers had raw spots. He kissed each one. "He didn't hurt you?"

"No, he just terrified me. Who was he?"

He lowered her hands but kept hold of one. "A cartel enforcer."

"Did he get shot?"

"Yes."

"Did he die?"

"Almost." He took a deep breath, wondering how to tell her the rest. But he needed to. "His name's Nico Angelopoulos."

Her gaze sharpened. "And you…recognize it?" Her perception was dead on.

He gave a slow nod. "We were actually roommates for a while during initial DEA training."

Her eyes widened. "You *know* him? He was an agent?"

"He dropped out a few months into training. I never knew why, until tonight." He told her about Nico's wife and the theory about his motivation. "He told me he would never have hurt you."

"He told me that, too, but I didn't believe him," she muttered. "Is he… What's going to happen to him?"

"I don't know." There was still a chance he could die from blood loss or infection. If he made it, the FBI and DEA were going to have to duke it out for jurisdiction. After that, he was looking at a life sentence, possibly in a Supermax facility.

Unless he turned over enough evidence for them to make a solid case against the cartel. Then they might give him a sweet deal and relocate him in WITSEC.

"What about the guy who shot him?" Bristol asked.

"The local cartel lieutenant the agency's been trying to bust for the past two years. Jordan Leandro."

A shadow of fear moved through her eyes. "Did they catch him?"

"No. He escaped in a submarine."

"What?" Her eyes flashed with outrage. "How could he have done that in this storm?"

"They're trying to find out. But between the intel I got from the CI today, and whatever Nico knows, hopefully it'll be enough to nail him."

"Let's hope." She laid her head back down on his chest. Sighed. "I'm gonna have nightmares for weeks about hearing those shots, seeing the blood, and then you drowning in the water. I threw a life ring at you. Not that it did much good." She shivered.

TJ tightened his arms around her. "Heard you called the Coast Guard. And fired a flare gun too."

"I did. Pretty proud of myself for that, actually."

"You should be. I'm damned proud of you too."

She snuggled in closer. "Travis and Brandon pulled me from the boat."

"I heard that too." He combed his fingers through her hair, tried to shut out the image of her scared and tied up and alone on that burning boat in the middle of the storm, thinking he was dead. "I'm so damned sorry, Bristol. For everything."

She nodded, her cheek rubbing against his chest. "I know. I forgive you."

Just like that. No hesitation. God, he didn't deserve her or her soft heart.

Then she sniffed, and her shoulders jerked.

"Hey." He cupped her jaw, tried to tip her face up to his, but she curled tighter into him.

"Don't you dare t-tell me not to c-cry," she blurted. "Cry if I want to."

Yeah, she could. And at least he could hold her through this storm.

When her tears finally faded, he reached down for the throw blanket on the end of her bed and spread it over her, kissed the top of her head. "You need anything?"

"Just you," she whispered, and his heart squeezed painfully. "God, how can I feel this way when I barely even know you?"

"You do know me." All the most important things.

"No, I don't."

He traced a finger down her cheek. "You know I'd die for you."

Shock flickered across her face. "Don't say that," she whispered, looking aghast.

"Why not? It's true. Also, I love your fire and your quick mind. I love your bravery. I love your big, tender heart that scares the shit out of me."

"Why does it scare you?"

"Because I don't want you to get hurt." He loved pretty much everything about her he'd seen so far. Was pretty sure he was more than halfway in love with her already, as unreal as that sounded. "Your body is hideous though. Utterly disgusting." He squeezed her sweet, round ass.

Bristol snort-laughed and gave him a mock glare, a smile tugging at the edges of her mouth. "So you do have a sense of humor after all."

"Yeah. It's rusty," he admitted, "but it's still in there somewhere. Maybe you can help polish it up a bit."

"Hmm, maybe. I wonder what other mysteries I can uncover?"

"Like what?"

"Your favorite foods, and music, and what you like to do for fun. Plus a million other more important things that make you, you."

"Some of that's pretty deep. Finding all that out might take a while."

"It could, depending on how difficult you are."

He suppressed a grin. "Could take days. Weeks. Months. Longer, even."

"Let's hope not *that* long." She looked up at him. Went still. "But that would mean you'd need to stick around long enough to give me the chance." Her eyes searched his.

"Yeah. That's the plan. As long as you want me to." After what she'd gone through, he wouldn't blame her if she wanted him to go. But he desperately hoped she would give him a chance.

"Really?" The hope on her face squeezed his heart.

"Yeah, really. Because I want to get to know you too. Every single thing that makes Bristol Moreau tick. For instance, why you don't seem to curse."

"I do, sometimes. I think Jordan Leandro is a fucking asshole, for instance."

A laugh burst out of him. He hugged her close, unable to stop chuckling. "God, you're precious." And adorable. And sweet, and brave, and loyal. And kind. So damned kind he wanted to make it his mission to protect her from the rest of the world.

"And to be honest, I'm not so keen on your old buddy Nico, either," she continued as he chuckled more. "Even if he does love his wife enough to commit heinous murders for a cartel." She sniffed, then her lips curved in a tender smile that had his whole chest tightening. "I wouldn't have believed it was possible, but you're even more gorgeous when you smile."

What was this woman trying to do to him? She was already wound tight around his heart. "I haven't had much to smile about until you came along."

"Good to know I amuse you. Would hate for you to get bored this early on."

"Oh, I don't think boredom'll be an issue."

"Yeah, you're probably right." She was quiet a moment. "So, what happens now?"

He kept stroking her hair. "It'll be a few weeks before I can clear everything up on my end with the investigation and the agency. But I already told them I'm done with undercover."

"You did?" She sounded surprised and relieved.

"Yeah. To be honest, I'm not sure I want to go back at all." This assignment had taken a huge toll on him. He was exhausted and ready to make a big change.

"That's understandable."

"Maybe I'll apply at CPS. I hear it's an okay company."

"I heard that too."

"Cassie would love to work with me."

Bristol chuckled. "I think you'd grow on her over time. And Crimson Point's a great place to live."

"Oh, completely. Super safe. Absolutely no drug lords or traffickers or hitmen of any kind for hundreds of miles."

"None. Well, not after today."

He grinned, then sobered. It felt like he'd just been given a second chance at life. He didn't want to waste a day of it. And he wanted to spend it with her. "Come away with me for a while."

"Where?"

"Wherever you want, just as soon as I can get everything wrapped up. The agency owes me a shitload of vacation time."

She made a thoughtful sound, drawing a pattern on his chest with one fingertip. "I've always wanted to go to Europe."

A familiar ring tone broke the cozy little bubble they'd been in. He groaned. "I gotta answer that."

"Yeah, answer." She eased away.

He dragged his jeans off the floor, fished out his phone. It was Diana. "Hey," he said.

"Sorry to call, so I'll get right to it. Leandro's dead."

Whoa. He sat up, swung his legs over the edge of the bed. "How?"

"Looks like he intentionally overdosed on pain meds after emergency surgery at a private clinic in Bellevue, just outside Seattle. Oh, and also your old pal Nico is gone."

He frowned. "Gone?"

"Missing. His wife too."

"What?" That wasn't possible. Nico had barely survived the surgery, and Liana was wheelchair bound. "What the hell happened?"

"We don't know for sure, but he somehow dragged his half-dead self off the recovery room bed and out of the hospital without anyone noticing. Maybe she put him on her lap and wheeled him the hell out the back door, I don't know. But we can't find them, and neither can the cops or FBI. Anyway, that's the update. Now I gotta go. Talk to you tomorrow."

TJ lowered the phone to his lap, stunned. Bristol shuffled over behind him to wrap her arms around his chest, her warm body pressed against his back in silent comfort. He laid a hand on her forearm.

"What happened? What's wrong?" she whispered.

He told her.

"Wow," she said softly. "Do you have to go in? Help them find him?"

"No. I'm staying here, with you." He turned, pulled her around and into his lap, cuddling her close. He felt so at peace with her like this.

"You okay?" she murmured, one hand rubbing between his shoulder blades.

"Yeah." He was silent for a long moment, trying to put the puzzle pieces together.

Where would Nico go? He'd only been concerned about his wife when he'd come out of the anesthesia. It was possible he was still high on meds, but Nico was damned smart, and it had almost seemed like he'd been speaking to him in some sort of code in the recovery room.

Gotta get her help there, he'd said while staring at that cabinet on the wall with the red—

Oh, man. Oh, of *course*.

"Europe, huh?" he murmured against Bristol's hair, already looking forward to exploring it with her. "How do you feel about starting in Switzerland?"

EPILOGUE

"It doesn't look real. Can you believe this is real?" Bristol wanted to pinch herself.

She had always dreamed of going to Europe someday, had imagined what it would be like to experience all the different cultures, the cobbled streets of ancient towns and villages with their historic buildings. But nothing could have prepared her for this view.

"I feel like I'm in a postcard or a movie or something." She was trying her best to focus on that and stay in the moment, rather than give in to her growing anxiety about what was coming up next.

"It's not bad," TJ agreed, helping himself to a warm pain au chocolate from the napkin-covered basket between them at the wrought-iron table on the hotel terrace. He had gone all out booking the trip for them. This hotel overlooking the lake was breathtaking, and easily ten times more luxurious than anywhere she'd stayed before.

"Not bad?" She shot him an incredulous look. "It's breathtaking."

In the distance, the mountain peaks were dusted with

snow. Below to her right, Lake Zurich glittered in the golden late-September sunshine. Their hotel was right in the historic heart of the old city center, nestled just inland from the lake's northern tip.

They'd arrived yesterday afternoon after a few days in London and had explored a bit. Zurich was a vibrant mix of old and new, a center of heritage, a financial and industrial powerhouse. Especially the banking, tech, and medical sectors.

Which was why they were here.

TJ's phone beeped, face down on the table. He picked it up, read it, and texted someone. "It's your dad. He says hi."

She shook her head in disbelief, tried not to feel offended. "Say hi back."

"Already did." He put the phone away, carried on eating as though nothing had happened.

It was surreal that TJ and her dad were texting buddies. They had met the morning after that horrible day she'd been taken hostage. Their initial meeting had been chilly and stiff, but over the past few weeks her dad had thawed toward him considerably. They both loved the NFL, which helped, and her dad was always watching those NatGeo documentaries about drug smuggling or law enforcement operations against dealers and cartel members. Now he called or texted TJ about them, asking him questions for "expert insider info." It seemed to amuse TJ.

As for him and Cassie, their relationship was still very much a work in progress. Cassie had grudgingly accepted him into the family circle, but still gave him the hairy eyeball occasionally. Though to be honest, Cassie had trust issues with men. And Bristol secretly loved how loyal and protective Cass was with her.

But it would be nice if her dad would text her as often as

he did TJ now. She glanced at her phone to check that she'd turned off silent mode. No messages from her dad or Cassie. Jeez. "What time are we leaving for the hike?" She was wound up, could try to blame her jitteriness and fatigue on jetlag, but that wasn't the real problem.

She was nervous.

"Around ten should give us plenty of time to get to the pickup spot."

A shuttle bus was taking them from the center of Old Town up to the base of a mountain to meet the rest of the group for the three-hour hike. "Okay."

It was just before nine now. Only a few minutes until...

She busied herself with spreading butter and jam on bits of a flaky croissant and tried her best not to give away how anxious she was.

"You okay?" he asked, somehow picking up on it anyway.

"Yeah, fine."

Life had felt like a whirlwind since the day she'd blown his cover, and they were just now coming to the other side of it. TJ had officially given his notice to the DEA last week before leaving on their trip. He was taking these few weeks with her as a break from everything before deciding what to do after this. Once they got back and he officially moved into her place, he was thinking about applying at CPS.

Turned out the memory stick he had gotten from Leandro's right-hand guy had contained all kinds of juicy and incriminating evidence on it. Those documents, videos, and files had allowed the DEA to dismantle the cartel's operations in the Pacific Northwest.

Their trip so far had been wonderful. After the chaos of their early relationship and the whirlwind of the official investigation that followed, this time together was a gift. She'd learned so much about him over the past few weeks.

He loved rock music and Thai food. He had a dry wit that came out when she least expected it. He was tidy and brooding, although he brooded less and less since leaving the DEA. He was sexually intense in a way that got her body humming with a single heated look. And he snored a bit if he slept on his back.

Maybe later on she'd want to smother him with a pillow, but right now during the honeymoon stage, she found it sort of endearing. Mostly.

"Hey." TJ reached over and grasped her hand. Tugged her toward him.

She blew out a breath, got up and allowed him to pull her into his lap. He engulfed her in a firm embrace, his chin resting on the top of her head. "It's gonna be fine," he murmured.

She sure as hell hoped so.

"I wouldn't have asked you to be here for this otherwise."

She nodded, her cheek rubbing against his chest. He would never do anything to hurt her. And this was important to him. "I'm trying."

"I know you are. Trust me about this."

"I do." It was the only reason she'd agreed to this.

"Good." He kissed the top of her head. "Hey, there they are." He released her.

Bristol scrambled off his lap and braced herself at the sight of her kidnapper coming toward them, pushing a woman in a wheelchair along the terrace. TJ rose and stepped in front of her to greet them warmly, shaking hands with Nico and then the wife.

"Glad you could both make it," TJ said to them. "And this

is Bristol." He turned to her, curled a heavy arm around her in reassurance.

She stared at Nico, feeling stiff and awkward, the disquiet inside her growing. How did one greet their former kidnapper? "Yes, hi," she said to him. She was doing this mainly for TJ, but also a little bit for herself. For closure. Because TJ cared about him, and had convinced her that Nico was actually a decent guy in spite of everything he'd done.

The wife seemed sweet though. "Hello." Bristol gave her a genuine smile, relieved that the initial shock was behind her.

"I'm Liana," the other woman said. She was bundled up in a thick, cream sweater and lap blankets to keep her warm in the crisp morning air. Her cheeks were rosy, her long blond hair twisted into a single braid over one shoulder, and her sky-blue eyes were friendly.

Bristol liked her instantly. Wondered if she knew she was married to a cartel contract killer.

"How are you feeling?" she asked. Liana looked great, but that could be deceptive. Primary progressive MS was a terrible disease that stripped away quality of life along with function and dignity over time.

"Leave it to a medical professional to go straight there," TJ said wryly.

Bristol couldn't help it. She was far more comfortable focusing on Liana than Nico, and yes, she was incredibly curious about the medical treatments Liana was receiving here.

"It's fine," Liana said with a light laugh. "Nico said you're an ultrasound tech?"

It was still weird to think of him as Nico and not Angel, the cartel hitman. "Yes, that's right."

"Best they've got," TJ said.

Bristol raised her eyebrows. "Well, that's lovely of you to say, but he's exaggerating," she said to Liana.

"I'm not. Everyone at the hospital thinks so."

She raised her eyebrows at him. "Really? Like who?"

"Travis, Grady, and Brandon for starters."

"What? When did you talk to them?"

His eyes twinkled with amusement. "You'd be surprised who I've talked to."

Yeah, she probably would be. He was still so damned mysterious in a lot of ways. She was doing her best to peel back all his layers one at a time.

"Here, sit down and eat with us," TJ said, gesturing to the table.

Nico pushed Liana's chair close to the table, then moved around to take the seat beside her next to TJ. Bristol sat across from him, aware of the weight of his stare as she studiously avoided looking at him.

This was still bizarre and uncomfortable. The man had literally broken into the condo and taken her hostage. Now they were sitting at the breakfast table together in Switzerland.

TJ slid an arm around her back, his large hand wrapping around her shoulder in reassurance. His fingers squeezed gently. She released a slow breath, drawing strength from his presence.

"Bristol." Nico's voice was quiet. Calm.

She forced herself to look at him. Her pulse skittered. TJ tightened his grip slightly. She could almost hear his voice in her head.

It's okay, Slugger, promise. I'm right here. It's gonna be okay.

She drew in a breath, pushed the residual fear aside. "Hm?"

Nico's gaze was steady on her. "I'm sorry about what I did. And I'm sorry you were scared."

Whoa. Bristol blinked at him. She hadn't expected him to come right out and say it, let alone in front of the others. But he seemed completely sincere, and maybe even a little regretful.

She darted a look at Liana. How much did she know about what her husband had done?

Liana was watching her silently, with sympathy and kindness.

Bristol cleared her throat, reaching for grace and understanding. She didn't know what he'd told Liana, but couldn't imagine he'd told her the whole truth—for her own protection as much as to preserve her image of him—and she certainly wasn't going to bring it all up in front of Liana.

"Rumor has it you had good reason." Acting out of desperation to save his wife had a certain element of nobility to it. A twisted nobility.

And he hadn't hurt her, though he could have at any point. He could easily have killed her to prevent having a witness once TJ had boarded the *Sea Siren*. Instead, he'd left her out of harm's way in the cabin and had even tried to reassure her a couple of times.

Whatever else he was, he wasn't a monster.

"I did." Nico glanced at Liana, and the adoration on his face went a long way toward convincing Bristol that TJ was right. Nico seemed like a good person.

Her nerves eased. She'd come to this meeting hoping for closure and to satisfy her curiosity about Nico and his wife. She hadn't expected to get both within the first five minutes of meeting them, or to start *liking* the guy.

But she had. Now it was time to move forward. "Anyway, apology accepted."

Surprise flashed in his eyes. "Really?" He cocked his head at her. "Does that mean we could maybe start over?"

She considered it, surprised it mattered to him. And just as surprised at how much she wanted to erase her memory of him before and replace it with the man sitting in front of her now. "Sure."

One side of his mouth kicked up, and he reached a hand across the table. "I'm Nico. Nice to meet you."

She stretched out her own hand, met him halfway. "Bristol. Hi." She shook with him.

The last of her inner tension melted away. She felt lighter instantly, the weight in her stomach miraculously gone.

TJ squeezed her again, leaned down to kiss the top of her head. "Thank you," he murmured, too low for the others to hear. She leaned into him in answer.

The server came and took Liana's and Nico's orders. Bristol and TJ each ordered another latte. It was all suddenly so normal, the conversation resuming as though the previous exchange between her and Nico had never happened.

Over fruit and pastries, Liana told them about the treatments she had been receiving at the private medical center here—Bristol presumed under a fake ID.

She had so many questions. If the DEA or FBI knew where Liana and Nico were, they hadn't done anything about it. TJ didn't know the details either. He'd told her Nico might have worked out some kind of immunity deal with them. But there was also a chance he and Liana had entered WITSEC, and were now living here under new identities.

"So it's working?" Bristol asked, fascinated by what Liana had told them. She was receiving cutting-edge stem cell technology aided by AI, along with various immunotherapies and brand-new pharmaceuticals as part of the clinical trial.

"Seems to be." Liana's teeth flashed when she smiled. "I'm in remission."

Bristol smiled back. "That's fan*tastic*."

"Yeah. The difference is already like night and day," Nico said, watching his wife with such pride and love it put a lump in Bristol's throat. He'd risked everything to give Liana this chance. "She's getting stronger every day. Her appetite is back, her coordination is improving, her energy level is up, and she's sleeping better too."

"Speaking of appetite…" Liana peered at the napkin-strewn basket in the middle of the table. "Got any more of the chocolate ones left?"

"I'll order you a basket of your own," Nico said, grinning.

Bristol had a feeling that if Liana had asked for the rarest, most obscure delicacy in Switzerland, he would have tracked it down for her.

They visited for almost an hour. The conversation shifted from Liana's medical situation to TJ and Nico reminiscing about their time at the DEA academy together.

Fascinated, Bristol ate up every detail about what TJ had been like back then, and found herself laughing along with them at times. Meanwhile, Liana ate three *pains au chocolat*, a large tropical fruit smoothie, and some strawberries.

"This mountain air is really doing you good," Nico told her, then winced as he checked his watch. "Damn, we have to start heading back."

"Here, take these with you." Bristol hurriedly wrapped up the remaining pastries from the basket in a clean napkin and handed them to Liana. "You can snack on them later instead of having to eat hospital food."

"I won't say no, but you should see the meals I get there. A five-star chef makes us gourmet meals three times a day, and snacks if we want them."

"One more perk of private, experimental holistic care," Nico said, rising.

Bristol was dying to know how he was funding all this. She was half-convinced that he'd done all this under the radar somehow, because surely the government would have seized his assets, including investments or whatever money he had in his accounts.

He and TJ embraced and back-slapped each other.

Bristol stood and leaned down to hug Liana gently. She felt frail under the thick knit of her sweater, but her healthy coloring and sparkle told Bristol the treatment was going very well indeed. "You take care of yourself, and keep kicking ass in there."

"Oh, I plan to kick it into total submission. I've got plenty of lost time to make up for and lots to live for." She smiled up at Nico.

"Where will you go after the treatment's done?" Bristol asked them.

They looked at each other. "Not sure," Nico said. "But it doesn't matter, as long as we're together. Home is wherever she is."

Bristol put a hand to her chest. Awww, come on. What kind of hitman said things like that?

His gaze shifted to her. "I'm glad I got the chance to see you again."

Now that she'd gotten to see and meet the real him, it was impossible for her to reconcile him with the man who'd taken her captive. "Same." Without overthinking it, on instinct she reached up to hug him.

He stiffened in surprise, then returned the embrace. Gently, but held on for several seconds before letting her go and stepping back. And she could tell by the relief in his smile that he'd needed that as much as she had.

TJ stepped up beside her and set a hand on her waist, the heat of his hand sinking through her sweater. It felt like he was claiming her in front of the others, and she liked it way too much. "You guys take care," he said.

"You too. Keep in touch." Nico turned Liana's chair around and wheeled her away.

She and TJ watched them until they disappeared inside the main dining room.

"Thank you," he murmured, his hand squeezing her waist.

"I'm glad I did it. I needed that. And you're right, he is a good guy after all. I liked him. And her, of course. What a warrior." When he didn't respond, she glanced up and found him staring down at her with a mixture of pride and something else. Something more intense. "What?" she asked.

"Nothing. Just you."

"What about me?"

"Your bravery. And your huge, caring heart." He shook his head. A slow smile curved his sexy mouth, the pride in his dark eyes warming her more than the bright morning sunshine. "Do you know how much I love you?"

She suppressed a gasp. He'd never said the words before. "How much?" she whispered.

"So much that I want to rebuild my life with you at the center of it."

Ohhhh, man…

Her knees went a little weak, a sappy smile spreading across her face. He was the most complicated man, with depths she was only beginning to discover. And, apparently, he was a stealth romantic too.

She drew in a breath, blinked fast as tears gathered in her eyes. "Are you trying to make me cry in public? Because that's how you do it. And by the way, I love you too." She threw her arms around him, hugged him tight and buried her face in his chest. It mashed her glasses against the bridge of her nose, but she didn't care. She'd never been this happy.

She couldn't wait to tell Cassie about this.

He nuzzled the top of her head, his hold turning possessive. "What do you say we skip the hike and head back to the room for a while instead?" His low, intimate tone sent spirals of heat curling through her.

Her pulse quickened, her body already tingling in anticipation. "I actually hate hiking. And anyway, the only thing I'm interested in climbing right now is you."

A laugh burst out of him, the carefree, happy sound ringing in the clear morning air. He tipped her chin up to plant a kiss on her lips, smiled down at her. "Slugger, you can climb me anytime you want."

—**The End**—

Dear reader,

Thank you for reading ***Guarding Bristol***. If you'd like to stay in touch with me and be the first to learn about new releases you can:

- Join my newsletter at: http://kayleacross.com/v2/newsletter/
- Find me on Facebook: https://www.facebook.com/KayleaCrossAuthor/
- Follow me on Instagram: https://www.instagram.com/kaylea_cross_author/

Also, please consider leaving a review at your favorite online book retailer. It helps other readers discover new books.

Happy reading,
Kaylea

Excerpt from

Guarding Cassie
Crimson Point Security Series
By Kaylea Cross
Copyright © 2025 Kaylea Cross

"What a great day," Cassie said from behind the wheel as she emerged from the underground parking garage and turned onto the street in downtown Portland. By a miracle of nature, it wasn't raining, and the mellow October afternoon sunshine painted the sides of the skyscrapers a deep gold. The concert had been amazing, and she loved getting to spend time with her stepsister. "I'm really glad you came with me."

"Me too. And hey, day's not over yet," Bristol said next to her in the passenger seat.

"I guess not, if you include the two-hour drive back to Crimson Point. Unless you want to stop anywhere before we leave the city? Another homeless camp you'd like to visit maybe?" she teased.

Bristol shot her a dirty look. "Ha-ha. I had my reasons for doing that, and everything turned out in the end, didn't it."

Cassie made a non-committal sound. Bristol was too nice, always saw the good in people. What she'd gone through might have changed her world view slightly, but at her core she was still an eternal optimist. As a realist, and maybe a jaded one, Cassie worried about her.

Bristol shifted slightly in her seat to face her with an incredulous expression. "Oh, come on. You can't seriously still be holding a grudge against TJ at this point."

Couldn't she? She still couldn't believe her big-hearted,

untrained stepsister had gone on a crusade to track TJ down across this city all by herself while he'd been living on the streets.

It gave her hives just thinking about it.

Bristol had gone way above and beyond the call of duty to get him a job offer in Crimson Point, which he'd taken. Not long after that, she had inadvertently blown his cover as an undercover DEA agent and had a cartel hitman hunting them. Bristol had been taken hostage and only been plucked from a burning boat by the Coast Guard in the nick of time.

"What's he got to do to make you forgive him? He literally risked his life to try and save me."

"I know." That was his one redeeming quality in Cassie's books. "He's growing on me, okay?" She was doing her best to be supportive, had reluctantly accepted that TJ was part of her life now—but only because Bristol was the happiest Cassie had ever seen her. She held a grudge when someone she loved was wronged.

"Like a fungus or something."

"Hey, you're the only sister I've ever had, and it's gonna take me some time to trust him after everything that went down." Things had moved so fast between them. Chronologically, Cassie might only be older by a few years, but she was a lifetime older in terms of life experience. Bristol was too sweet and trusting for her own good, and Cassie didn't want to see her get her heart broken if TJ turned out to be an asshole. So she would reserve judgment for a little while longer.

Bristol gave a reluctant grin. "I actually kinda love that you're so hard-core about having my back."

She shrugged. "Can't help it. Just the way I'm wired." Because she knew all too well what it was like when no one had your back. Or worse, when someone you trusted drove a knife into it.

"Anyway, how's the whole roommate situation going?" TJ had moved into Bristol's place recently, soon after they'd returned from their trip to Europe. Given everything that had happened, it smacked of love-bombing, but Cassie was keeping that red flag concern to herself. For now, anyway.

"Good. He's been hanging out with Warwick lately. They're watching a soccer game at our place right now that he recorded."

"Newcastle, I'm guessing?" Where Warwick was from.

"I think so. Anyway, enough about me. What's going on with you and Tristan? Any news?"

"No. Well, we've got that new job coming up next week, so we'll be working together again." In a purely professional capacity. Being assigned as bodyguards for the boss's besties was a big deal, and meant a lot to her.

"Ooh, yeah. Becca Sandoza and her stuntman husband, right?"

"Yep."

"I guess it would be kinda tacky to ask you to get an autograph for me?"

"Kinda tacky, yeah," she said dryly.

Bristol poked her in the shoulder. "Fine, but that's not the kind of news I meant, and you know it."

"We work together. That's it." With the exception of the terrifying situation with Bristol, he didn't know anything about her personal life, and she'd made a point of not asking anything about his. His identical twin Gavin and older brother Decker also both worked for Crimson Point Security, and their sister Marley lived in the area too. All were former Marines. The only really personal thing she'd noticed with

Tristan was that he seemed to have a bit of a hangup about food sometimes.

"I'm well aware you work together, but I'm not blind. I saw the sparks between you two even without my glasses on when I stepped off that Coast Guard cutter."

"Sparks?" She could play dumb with the best of them.

"Big ones."

"We're just friends." She had zero time or emotional bandwidth for a relationship. She had the world's worst taste in men and didn't trust herself not to pick another toxic one. Her life in Crimson Point had allowed her the chance to start over, reinvent herself. Be the best version of herself and leave all that ugliness and pain behind her.

"If you say so."

"I do say so." She was enjoying her single era. Might never date again.

"It was nice of him to get you these tickets."

"Yeah." She still couldn't believe he'd remembered her mentioning it, let alone going to the trouble of getting her two. He'd told her a friend had comped them, but she didn't believe him. "He's a nice guy."

Bristol laughed. "You say that with such suspicion."

"Well, no one's perfect, are they? There has to be something wrong with him." Some fatal flaw she hadn't seen yet. What she knew of him so far was too good to be true. That made her wary.

"Oh my god, you're such a cynic."

"Yeah. Being a cop will do that to you."

Bristol sighed and leaned her head back. "Understandable. But not everybody's going to let you down."

"I know you wouldn't."

"And neither would your mom or my dad."

"Them too."

Bristol shot her a sideways glance. "What happened in Vegas, anyway? You've never really told me."

Tension coiled inside her like an invisible rope. She didn't talk about it. Didn't even like remembering any of it. Her former self embarrassed her. She didn't want anyone to know what had happened. What she'd willingly put up with for way too damn long. Not Bristol. Not even her own mother. "I was burned out, and finally decided to leave a bad situation."

Bristol reached over and squeezed Cassie's shoulder. "I'm glad you did."

"Me too. Turn up the tunes, will you? This is my favorite part of the drive," she said as she merged onto the highway heading west toward the coast.

"Okay, super personal conversation over. Got it." Bristol turned up the music.

"What if we stopped at that pie place on the way back?"

Bristol laughed. "You read my mind."

"That's because you've turned me into an addict."

"Well, I didn't want to be the only one. Let's do it."

The manic pace of city life disappeared behind them and gave way to rolling hills covered in farmland and vineyards dotted in rich autumn colors of gold, crimson and orange. All the lingering tension eased from her muscles within minutes.

She *loved* this. Cruising along a winding, pretty road with her favorite person riding shotgun.

Driving had always been one of the greatest pleasures in her life, both personally and professionally with all the advanced tactical courses she had excelled in. She'd obtained her license as soon as humanly possible once she'd turned sixteen, then bought a little beater with the money she'd saved up from babysitting and part-time jobs over the years. It had given her freedom and allowed her to escape her house and the toxic environment there with her mom's endless succession of disastrous boyfriends.

It still seemed hard to believe that her mother had met and fallen in love with Bristol's dad seven years ago. Absolutely incredible that she had settled in a happy, stable relationship, with the added bonus that Cassie had wound up with Bristol out of the deal. If for some reason their parents ever broke up, she was keeping Bristol.

"Wanna come in for a bit?" Bristol asked her.

"Nah, I'm gonna head home."

"Come on, we barely ever do anything social together."

"Excuse me? Did we or did we not just spend over two hours with five-thousand strangers at the concert? And did I or did I not go to that book club event with you?"

"You *loved* that," Bristol accused. "You said Beckett and Sierra's house is—and I quote—'magical.'"

"It is magical." The stunning heritage Victorian was perched high on a cliff overlooking the water and the town of Crimson Point, with lush gardens right out of a magazine spread. "I was merely shooting holes in your argument about me not being social."

"All right, point conceded. But how is TJ going to keep growing on you if you never spend time together?"

Yeah, fair. "You're right. I'll make more of an effort." He so obviously adored Bristol. That was a major point in his favor, so she was willing to try harder.

"Maybe you could bring someone to dinner with us or something?"

Cassie frowned. "What, like a double date?"

"Yeah, why not?"

She snorted. "Not likely."

"Okay, then, just a friend. You said Tristan's just a friend. Bring him."

Nopity nope. "I don't like mixing work and personal. Too messy." Boundaries got blurred way too easily. And she didn't want Tristan to get the wrong idea.

"You're so stubborn. But you're coming in for a bit when we get home, right?"

She'd planned to go straight home and jump into her pajamas to make an early night of it, but since there was pretty much nothing she wouldn't do for Bristol… "I'll say hi, stay for half an hour max, then I'm leaving."

Bristol beamed at her. "Deal."

Half an hour later they stopped for pie at the family-owned shop on the side of the highway, sitting at a window booth with a red Formica table straight out of the 1950s. Bristol had a slice of French silk pie topped with a big dollop of fresh, sweetened whipped cream, and Cassie got her usual order of their decadent lemon sour cream, also topped with a layer of whipped cream and grated lemon zest.

But later, when they finally arrived in Crimson Point at Bristol's townhouse just as the sun was going down over the water, Cassie's insides tightened a little at the sight of Tristan's white pickup parked at the curb.

Bristol shot her an innocent look, shaking her head. "I didn't know he was coming over, I swear. Warwick must have invited him."

Made sense, since Warwick was married to Tristan's sister, Marley. And she knew Bristol would never set this up to try and play matchmaker. "It's fine."

This was just another example to add to the long list of reasons why she needed to snuff out the attraction she felt to Tristan. Her life was complicated enough, and small-town living meant pretty much everyone here knew each other. There were a million little connections linking people within her little circle, a big issue for someone like her who had made it her mission to keep her personal life private and maintain clear separation between the areas of her life.

"You're still coming in, right?"

"Yeah, why wouldn't I?" She wasn't going to bail and make the Tristan issue seem like a big deal, even if she'd made it a point not to spend time with him or any of her work colleagues socially. As the only female personal security specialist at Crimson Point Security, she constantly felt pressured to prove her capability and maintain her professional image.

Also, there was the hard lesson she'd learned from working with her ex, that had ended in epic, catastrophic failure. Never again.

"Okay, good." Bristol started up the walkway, dark brown waves bouncing with each step.

Cassie's phone buzzed in her hand. She glanced at it, stopped short when she saw the message from her former captain.

How are things? Just wanted to let you know IA has officially closed the file as of this morning. Hope all is well out west.

She swallowed. Drew a steadying breath to calm the sudden spike in anxiety. It was officially over, but she'd put it behind her over a year ago, before moving here. Or she'd told herself she had.

Moving to Crimson Point had allowed her to put a physical barrier between it and her new life, make a fresh start. She was doing well here. Liked the town, loved being close to Bristol and their parents, and loved her job. She was good at it. Was determined not to let anything fuck it up.

"Everything okay?" Bristol had stopped on the doorstep and turned toward her, key in hand.

"Yep." She typed back a quick response.

All good. Thanks for letting me know. Take care.

She continued toward Bristol, pushing the ugly memories aside and steeling her nervous system against seeing Tristan outside of work.

Inside, an English-accented voice rang out loud and clear from the living room. "Haddaway an' shite! Ye daft twat, that's bollocks!"

"That was brutal! Come on, ref!" She was pretty sure that was TJ.

Bristol rolled her eyes and slipped her shoes off. "Sounds super fun."

"No one's harder on their team than a true fan," Cassie said with a smirk, following her into the living room. Warwick and TJ both looked up from the smaller of the two sofas, wearing identical scowls, bottles of beer clutched tightly in hand. Warwick wore a jersey with black and white vertical stripes.

"Game not going well, I take it?" Bristol asked, leaning over the back of the couch to kiss TJ.

"Match," he and Warwick said at the same time. The TV showed the score was 2-0 for the other guys.

Cassie looked across from them, a rush of heightened awareness hitting her when her gaze collided with Tristan's. Seated next to Marley, a warm, slow smile spread across his face in welcome.

Her pulse quickened, an unwelcome wave of heat sweeping through her.

Well, shit.

So much for just being coworkers.

End Excerpt

ABOUT THE AUTHOR

NY Times and USA Today Bestselling author Kaylea Cross writes edge-of-your-seat military romantic suspense. Her work has won many awards, including the Daphne du Maurier Award of Excellence, and has been nominated multiple times for the National Readers' Choice Awards. A Registered Massage Therapist by trade, Kaylea is also an avid gardener, artist, Civil War buff, Special Ops aficionado, belly dance enthusiast and former nationally-carded softball pitcher. She lives in Vancouver, BC with her husband and family.

You can visit Kaylea at www.kayleacross.com. If you would like to be notified of future releases, please join her newsletter.

http://kayleacross.com/v2/newsletter/

COMPLETE BOOKLIST

ROMANTIC SUSPENSE

Crimson Point Security Series
GUARDING TEAGAN (Decker and Teagan)
GUARDING BELLA (Creed and Bella)
GUARDING AUTUMN (Gavin and Autumn)
GUARDING BRISTOL (TJ and Bristol)
GUARDING CASSIE (Tristan and Cassie)

Crimson Point Protectors Series
FALLING HARD (Travis and Kerrigan)
CORNERED (Brandon and Jaia)
SUDDEN IMPACT (Asher and Mia)
UNSANCTIONED (Callum and Nadia)
PROTECTIVE IMPULSE (Donovan and Anaya)
FINAL SHOT (Grady and Everleigh)
FATAL FALLOUT (Walker and Ivy)
LETHAL REPRISAL (Warwick and Marley)

Crimson Point Series
FRACTURED HONOR (Beckett and Sierra)
BURIED LIES (Noah and Poppy)
SHATTERED VOWS (Jase and Molly)
ROCKY GROUND (Aidan and Tiana)

BROKEN BONDS (ensemble)
DEADLY VALOR (Ryder and Danae)
DANGEROUS SURVIVOR (Boyd and Ember)

Kill Devil Hills Series
UNDERCURRENT (Bowie and Aspen)
SUBMERGED (Jared and Harper)
ADRIFT (Chase and Becca)

Rifle Creek Series
LETHAL EDGE (Tate and Nina)
LETHAL TEMPTATION (Mason and Avery)
LETHAL PROTECTOR (Braxton and Tala)

Vengeance Series
STEALING VENGEANCE (Tyler and Megan)
COVERT VENGEANCE (Jesse and Amber)
EXPLOSIVE VENGEANCE (Heath and Chloe)
TOXIC VENGEANCE (Zack and Eden)
BEAUTIFUL VENGEANCE (Marcus and Kiyomi)
TAKING VENGEANCE (ensemble)

DEA FAST Series
FALLING FAST (Jamie and Charlie)
FAST KILL (Logan and Taylor)
STAND FAST (Zaid and Jaliya)
STRIKE FAST (Reid and Tess)
FAST FURY (Kai and Abby)

FAST JUSTICE (Malcolm and Rowan)
FAST VENGEANCE (Brock and Victoria)

Colebrook Siblings Trilogy
BRODY'S VOW (Brody and Trinity)
WYATT'S STAND (Wyatt and Austen)
EASTON'S CLAIM (Easton and Piper)

Hostage Rescue Team Series
MARKED (Jake and Rachel)
TARGETED (Tucker and Celida)
HUNTED (Bauer and Zoe)
DISAVOWED (DeLuca and Briar)
AVENGED (Schroder and Taya)
EXPOSED (Ethan and Marisol)
SEIZED (Sawyer and Carmela)
WANTED (Bauer and Zoe)
BETRAYED (Bautista and Georgia)
RECLAIMED (Adam and Summer)
SHATTERED (Schroder and Taya)
GUARDED (DeLuca and Briar)

Titanium Security Series
IGNITED (Hunter and Khalia)
SINGED (Gage and Claire)
BURNED (Sean and Zahra)
EXTINGUISHED (Blake and Jordyn)
REKINDLED (Alex and Grace)

BLINDSIDED: A TITANIUM CHRISTMAST NOVELLA
(ensemble)

Bagram Special Ops Series

DEADLY DESCENT (Cam and Devon)

TACTICAL STRIKE (Ryan and Candace)

LETHAL PURSUIT (Jackson and Maya)

DANGER CLOSE (Wade and Erin)

COLLATERAL DAMAGE (Liam and Honor)

NEVER SURRENDER (A MACKENZIE FAMILY NOVELLA)
(ensemble)

Suspense Series

OUT OF HER LEAGUE (Rayne and Christa)

COVER OF DARKNESS (Dec and Bryn)

NO TURNING BACK (Ben and Samarra)

RELENTLESS (Rhys and Neveah)

ABSOLUTION (Luke and Emily)

SILENT NIGHT, DEADLY NIGHT (ensemble)

PARANORMAL ROMANCE

Empowered Series

DARKEST CARESS (Daegan and Olivia)

HISTORICAL ROMANCE

THE VACANT CHAIR (Justin and Brianna)

EROTIC ROMANCE (writing as *Callie Croix*)

DEACON'S TOUCH

DILLON'S CLAIM
NO HOLDS BARRED
TOUCH ME
LET ME IN
COVERT SEDUCTION

Made in United States
North Haven, CT
09 June 2025